UNHOLY WAR

The DCI Tom Tallis stories

UNHOLY WAR

JOHN MALYON

First published 2022 by John Waldram
Copyright © John Ryder Waldram 2022
Cover photo © Ronen Zvulun/Reuters
The author's moral rights have been asserted
All rights reserved
ISBN 978-1-7399165-2-7
Computer typeset in Palatino
Printed and distributed by KDP

The cover photo shows
bombardment of
the northern Gaza Strip
in July 2014

Limit of Stability

Afternoon sun slopes onto the polished floor out of a diluted blue January sky. From another room women's voices filter through, and the faint chinking of crockery—but Mustafa Haniff, upright in his upholstered chair, has fallen fitfully asleep; the pages of a well-thumbed notebook lie splayed on the floor below his dangling right arm. A reading lamp illuminates the planes and ridges of his face, olive with heavy brows. Trimmed black moustache. Roll-neck sweater from Los Angeles, sandals from an East Jerusalem market.

Behind him, in shadow, glows an ochre bowl of Venetian glass, central on its polished shelf. Heavy books repose in glazed cabinets: a commentary on the Qu'ran, bound volumes of *Proceedings of the Royal Society*, Sufi mysticism, and early texts in Arab science. The flat is spotless, but the night's gunfire has left a thick film of dust on the outside of the window. Directly opposite are the fifth-floor balconies of the opposite side of the street, and to the left, beyond a derelict but sun-drenched empty lot, stands a small mosque with a green dome, its face in deep shadow. The faint clangs echo of someone rolling a butane cylinder between two doorways.

The nearby voices pause, and a few moments later Mustafa's wife opens the door cautiously and stands stocky and impassive for a moment. She smiles and withdraws quietly. The click of the door had its effect, however: he stirs, stretches, stands up and moves to the window.

The hulking Israeli tank is still there below. Scarcely surprising, he reflects gloomily, that his reconciling instincts have been so much in retreat over the four months since 9/11. He cranes his head to peer to his right at the remains of the police station at the end of the street. At four in the morning helicopters and armour came and bombed it out—retaliation for a Hamas assault on the Ma'ale Adumim checkpoint, and so quick there'd still been young policemen in there, clearing out weapons in the night. He'd been with others to search as the sun came up. Three bodies. They carried the remains of a young man into the flat downstairs, and Leila and their daughter Fatima helped clean the body up, Leila silent, Fatima's eyes flashing. The assault had been pointless, too: the local police had no Hamas links, they had just been trying to keep order in their demoralised way.

Now, the tank commander below is observing the police station through binoculars. Curious, Mustafa fetches his own pair and turns them downward. The young man's face is calm, partly hidden by the helmet and headphones. It is also sensitive. What does he think of what he's been ordered to do?

Discomposed, Mustafa drops back into his chair, picks up his notebook, and fretfully tries to comfort himself by reviewing its closely written equations.

For there, still, it all is: at age forty-eight, he, Mustafa Haniff, has spawned this marvellous thing. One day, he wryly fantasises with an irresistible lift of the heart, colleagues may come to applaud him as a true successor to Pierre de Fermat. As all mathematicians know, after the Frenchman's death the statement of his 'last theorem' was found written neatly beside a page of printed text, with the comment 'I have a truly wonderful proof, which this margin is too narrow to hold'. But it had taken them over three hundred years to find a proof—and what they had now was a gigantic effort, far from intuitive, that would never have fitted onto a page or two. They doubted whether Fermat's 'wonderful proof' could have been valid. Well, he reflects, they would, wouldn't they?

And now he has this thing of his own to cap it. He smiles to himself, and after a few minutes drops off to sleep again.

*

Twenty minutes later, however, distant shouts jerk him awake. He strides to the window. An Israeli foot patrol in body armour is working its way into the shattered police station. Local boys have crept up on them and are starting to throw stones. The tank commander is watching. Mustafa focusses his own binoculars, and as he does so three small figures hurry into the disc of his view, two brown and one swathed in green, close to the right-hand side of the street, school satchels on their backs. His stomach clenches.

A bang, and a cloud of white smoke sweeping over his view: someone, somewhere, has thrown a grenade. Slowly clearing. Olive-green uniforms flat on the ground, spitting automatic fire. The three small figures static, crouching against the wall. He lowers his binoculars. Another figure, high up, crouching on the roofline above them, out of sight of the foot patrol: Mustafa sees the grenade this time, looping through the air; another puff of smoke sweeping over the scene.

The whole flat shudders, and something inside the room falls with a crash, echoing the bigger crash outside: the tank below has fired its main armament.

The building by the police station crumples and a cloud of dust spurts across his view. The tank turret swivels a little to the right. He watches as the dust clears, his neck muscles rigid. The tank shakes on its haunches with another roar. The whole of the building to the right totters and slumps into the street in slow motion. A distracting racketing clatter of machine gun fire from the tank. Smoke clearing. The three small figures in a heap, partly covered in rubble, immobile, as the soldiers sweep the street with small-arms fire. Stone-throwing boys melting away. A few scattered shots. Silence, a too-long silence. Then one of the small brown figures moving, both of them. Dragging the green figure along the wall.

He leaps for the door, shouts for Leila, finds a white towel to wave, tears down the stairs, clatters down the street towards them. He gets near, gasping. Her gentle nine-year-old face untouched, eyes closed. But a great hole in the green covering, in her belly itself, young blood running everywhere, parts of her, offal, warm: cover, cover them, quick. The two boys with their satchels peering questioningly up at him. Men and women creeping out of the flats, uncertain. Someone with a broken shutter from the collapsed building, they lever the small body onto it. The crowd increasing, shouting, moving towards the tank. Warning machine-gun fire over their heads. Screaming, everyone lying down. Mustafa weeping, shouting for one man alone to help him, waving his towel at the tank, waving it again. They inch forward with the green lump on the shutter, and the two boys edge along too, hiding behind them and pressing against the wall. The rest hold back. There's Leila, her short and shrouded figure creeping towards him by the wall; Fatima too, slight and capable. Leila's eyes blank, Fatima's face pale and eyes hard, much too hard for Mustafa. The tank turns its machine gun back towards the police station. Perhaps its young commander has understood.

They struggle at last into the same downstairs flat they used in the morning. Sun bright on the sandstone wall, but the flat cool and dark inside. The dead girl's mother works in the university library. Leila and Fatima will attract least suspicion on the streets. Fatima looks penetratingly into Mustafa's face, and allows him the grim ghost of a smile. She and Leila veil themselves hastily and plunge out into the bright sunlight.

*

At last, the wailing, fury and shouting die down, and Mustafa is able to get back upstairs and wash off the worst of the blood and dust. He trembles, bows himself down, tries to pray, and finds he can't. That young policeman, this girl. The dead girl's father—his own student—dead already himself, by an Israeli rocket. The horrible task his wife and daughter have undertaken.

He turns again, hesitatingly, to his notebook. So far, for reasons he has long cogitated with anxiety, he has thought it wiser to keep his discovery secret. But now he thinks again, as he has so often done before, about Ariel Sharon and his bloody history, about Leila and Fatima. He thinks clearly and deliberately for a considerable time. And gradually he becomes aware that an anonymous finger has found its way into his head, is angling itself to reset a switch there. He shrugs his broad shoulders deeply and sighs. He draws his right hand over his moustache and chin.

11

His telephone, he remembers, is still working.

After a little further thought he sighs again and calls his ex-student Hasan in Amman. Taking a deep breath, he sets out to expound carefully what he has achieved. Hasan, once he has fully understood, is warm with courteous congratulations. However, as Mustafa has expected, he has also understood immediately the reason for the call, and before ringing off agrees, with a hint of suppressed excitement in his voice, to come down discreetly next day for further discussion.

Mustafa turns and sees it was the Venetian bowl bought for Leila in a Cambridge antique shop that fell when the tank fired. He finds a brush. He sweeps up the ochre shards and wraps them neatly in newspaper for the dustcart.

Home Base

Miranda, in Plymouth, was thinking about marriage and slicing aubergines for Hamish. Or rather, slicing them as *practice* for Hamish—since he was now living and working in Oban, it had to be admitted that he nowadays got to enjoy fewer of her new recipes than Dad did. But delightful memories were playing themselves over. The Moray House going-down, for instance: sporting his kilt and skean-dhu, light-footed as the ceilidh band jerked out the rhythm. How she'd laughed! And how his laughter, rich and deep, had come rippling back at her. She smiled to herself, couldn't suppress the smile.

She bent to slide an iron casserole from under the worktop, stood up—and caught sight of herself in the mirror. The casserole's orange enamel, splashed with August evening sunlight, clashed fantastically with the scarlet and maroon of her long skirt, and on the shadowy dresser behind her willow-pattern blues and whites made a muted backdrop. She scooped the pot into the crook of one arm and smoothed the skirt with her free hand, head on one side, smiling at the composition.

More career-minded now, Hamish was... She worked at the potatoes. Onions. Garlic. Heated the oil... Consulted her recipe, calculated; peered pouting at the clock; frowned, and ran to the sitting room.

'Won't be ready till nine, Dad! *Sorry!*'

Tom didn't reply. She saw the compressed lines round his mouth, and, without thinking about it, observed also how graphically his tousled fair hair and blue eyes set off his dark compact outline on the sofa. Sunday gardening had relaxed him a little, but now he seemed to be stressed out again.

Back in the kitchen, work folders on the worktop awaited her attention, but her heart ached a little for him. A *plod*, he called himself, just as he always said he'd no green fingers. Why, wondered Miranda, did he keep insisting that she and Jack had turned out so much cleverer than him and Mum? For, as far as she could see, he always did manage to sort out his cases, just as his flowers always came into generous bloom. She got her casserole into the oven, and turned briskly, but with a little sigh, to her lesson plans.

At last she had to break off and switch her mind to whisking the meringue topping. She shouted to Tom she'd be ready in ten minutes, and heard him move to fetch a bottle from the drinks cupboard. Glasses chinked. Last lap: smiling broadly, she bore in her moussaka. He moved slowly to the supper table and poured the wine.

She caught his eye, served him, slid the salad bowl across. 'Help yourself.'

He did as he was told, and Miranda filled her own plate. Still he said nothing. She decided not to push, but when the silence persisted took a different tack and remarked: 'Something on my mind, Dad.'

He seemed to shrink into himself a little and his eyes stayed down.

She wondered, and waited a moment. 'My year-ten project.'

He took a slow breath and wiped his mouth on his napkin. 'There's a problem?' he asked at last.

'I'm wondering whether the kids will find my theme too disturbing.'

'And it is?'

'Hiroshima.'

For a moment he seemed not to have heard. But then he set down his knife and fork, sat up straight, swallowed and raised his eyes to hers. '*Mass carnage*?' he said quietly. He picked the fork up again and went on eating.

'Aged fifteen.'

'Yes,' he said. 'Year ten… Why d'you want to get them into all *that*?'

'Dad!' she said. 'You think I shouldn't?'

Tom shrugged. 'Depends what you're trying to achieve.'

'Make them think about the morality. Drama in the painting too, of course.'

Tom pursed his lips, but offered no more comment.

A little hurt, and wanting to settle her anxiety, she poured more wine, but he continued slowly with his moussaka, and something made her hold back. When he'd finished she took away the plates and fetched her apple snow. He said nothing during the second course, either. But when she came back with a tray of coffee things he said slowly:

'Can I ask *you* something?'

She smiled. 'Yes.'

'Those 9/11 terrorists…' He opened his eyes very wide. '*How* can a man be single-minded enough to fly himself and more than a hundred innocents into a tower full of thousands more? Bang, crunch, like that, instant oblivion—just to make a religious point.'

'Dad!' she exclaimed.

He seemed more angry than anything. 'What's your answer?' he pressed.

She thought it over. 'I suppose they *weren't* just making a point,' she said at last.

'What d'you mean?'

'For them, it was *war*.'

'Which makes the rules different?'

'For a lot of people it does.'

'Like the Americans deciding it was OK to nuke the Japanese?'

'For those terrorists it was *Jihad*.'

'Holy war… *Un*holy war, more like.'

He lapsed into silence again; but Miranda still hesitated to press. They munched on. When they'd finished he thanked her for the meal and cleared away the plates. The daylight was fading, and he drew the curtains; the heavy cotton was rosy in the lamplight. Then he turned to the kitchen to wash up. In putting the question to her his voice had been restrained, but his temples had glistened in the lamplight.

It reminded her of the way he'd looked the day that Beth died. After the shock, of course, she'd ached and wept as he had, but strangely it had been less devastating to her than to Tom, and in some inarticulate place, she knew why. It wasn't that she'd lacked a bond. The opposite, in fact: the bond with her mother had never been broken: Beth, inside her, wouldn't *let* her grieve, had passed on to her a mantle, a role. Tom needed her. Miranda suffered for him, read the sensitive lines of the face he considered plain.

She poured herself a second cup, carried it over to her favourite easy chair, and turned distractedly to her folder. But she couldn't concentrate. At the back of her mind, as she worked, she heard him finish the washing up and climb slowly to the bedroom he used as an office. She heard him moving about upstairs.

An hour and a half later, he came down again to

lock up. He seemed unready to talk any more and told her he was going to bed. Soon, she could hear him turning restlessly on the divan in his spartan bedroom. A little after midnight, she went up too. He'd left the reading lamp alight in his office, and she went in to turn it off. Lying in the pool of light was an exercise book, on the cover of which he'd written in block capitals *LOCAL RESPONSE*; it looked already well used. She was sorely tempted to open it. But she forced herself to leave it where it was and switched off the lamp.

He'd left the window open. Looking out, she became aware how chillingly the cloudless and moonless summer sky had deepened to a true indigo, and how fiercely, amidst the pin-prickle of lights, Altair was sparkling to the south.

Threat

DI Iain Gemmill, whose office was on the back ground floor corridor at Police Headquarters, was waiting when Tom arrived. Monday had dawned as scorching as the day before and the big fan beside the computer screen was whirring. Tom removed his cycle helmet and clips, found himself a chair and settled himself astride it, facing the backrest.

Iain inspected him thoughtfully. At last he said, 'Well?'

'Impossible,' said Tom.

Iain sighed, opened a file and extracted a handwritten page of notes. 'This all came from the Friday intelligence briefing?' Iain, in his imperturbable, Kilmarnock, son-of-the-manse way, liked to be sure of his facts.

Tom nodded.

'No hint before?'

'Nope.'

'But not Special Branch this time?'

'Manfield was there, but he didn't do the talking… Young chap, stocky. Calling himself John Smith.' Tom smiled distantly.

Iain raised his eyebrows. 'MI5?'

'I guess. Not revealed.'

Iain screwed up his face. 'And it really all hung on just this one piece of evidence?'

'Yup.'

'Intercepted satellite call from the mountains east of

Kandahar—like some cheap spy thriller?'

'Yes.'

'On the 25th July?'

'Just over a week ago.'

Iain frowned. 'And the link, again?'

Tom leant back and smoothed his hair with both hands from forehead to neck. 'The caller said to implement, quote, *the Plymouth Plan.*'

'And that was *all* he said?'

'Short and sweet.'

'And no other relevant intelligence whatsoever?'

'None divulged... As I told you, this John Smith did say to take it seriously. Time for something big, they seem to be thinking.'

'Nearly a year since 9/11?'

'That's what he meant. Al-Qaida may have got their hands onto nuclear material.' An imagined image had jumped back into Tom's mind: the city scraped bare, the road and rail bridges over the Tamar blackened and twisted into the river. It had been plaguing him over the weekend, but in a peculiar way—uncertainly, speculatively. He wasn't quite able to take it seriously. Not yet.

'But he didn't specifically predict an attack on Plymouth?'

'Not as such, no.'

'And that was it?'

'Yes.'

'OK.' Iain turned over his sheet of paper. 'Say again what the analysts made of it.'

Tom clasped his hands on the chair back and hauled himself back to reality. 'Both satellite phones previously used by al-Qaida.'

'Mm.'

'Receiving instrument in Cairo.'

'Yes… And the conversation?'

'Brief. Cultured Arabic. No names used, neither voice recognised.'

'But the words *Plymouth Plan* were in English, you said?'

'And the Cairo speaker repeated them in a standard UK accent.'

'So the guy could've lived in Britain?'

'That's what they thought.'

'But no information on who he might be?'

'No.'

Iain sighed. 'And the Super's put you and me onto it half-time, no extra help?'

'Bless him!'

'And we're to say nothing to *anyone*—not colleagues, not customs, not the Navy?'

'Apart from the Super and Special Branch. So the guy said.'

'This is madness, Tom! … Why so secret?'

'Don't want al-Qaida to realise their calls are being intercepted.'

'And activity by us might give it away?'

Tom shrugged. 'That's what he said. I got the feeling he wasn't telling us everything.'

'Isn't there another Plymouth in Massachusetts? How do they know it's our one?'

Tom smiled. 'My atlas lists nine Plymouths, six in the US.'

'But the guy had an English accent?'

'That's the point.'

*

Tom was usually a non-smoker, but he now illicitly lit and dragged at an Embassy, a rite reserved for difficult investigations. Iain, frowning, produced a tin for an ashtray, and assembled a new ring binder, an A4 pad with punched holes, and a sharpened pencil. They settled down on opposite sides of Iain's desk, fenced in by filing cabinets.

'How the hell are we supposed to go about this?' said Iain.

'Stick to our brief?' said Tom. '*Search for signs of a terrorist cell somewhere in the city.*'

'*Here already, or arriving soon...* What'll they look like, Tom? That's not a stupid question, you know.'

Tom nodded. 'The 9/11 cells were all Arabs who had lived in the West.'

'Three teams of five and one of four, all willing to smash themselves to bits... How the hell can religion do that to a man, Tom?'

'God knows... So *probably* middle-eastern—no reports of westerners recruited so far. But you never know.'

Iain frowned. 'So how will they try to be inconspicuous?'

Tom gave his head a shake to clear it. 'Try to behave like locals. Attend Friday prayers, and so on.'

'So we need to be talking to Muslims on the ground?'

'But how can we, without giving away what we're up to? Pity we can't use Aliza...'

'Agreed.'

'... Don't think she attends prayers, but her parents do.'

'So what *can* we do?'

'Best review the official guidance.'

Each of them had been studying copies of the Terrorism Manual over the weekend, and now they worked through them again, as Iain's fan churned its way through Tom's cigarette smoke.

'This,' said Iain when they'd finished, 'is ridiculous! It would take fifty of us to tackle all this.'

'Yes,' said Tom, 'and it's written with the IRA in mind, not al-Qaida... And most of it they aren't allowing us to do anyway.'

'If there *is* a cell here,' said Iain, ruffling sandy hair, 'the one thing we really need is to check out the hotels and B&Bs... But as our brief stands, we can't.'

'Exactly.'

'And then,' went on Iain, unfazed by Tom's exaggerated frown, 'Plymouth's a ferry port. Natural place to bring in lethal material... City airport, too.'

'So we need to review tactics with Customs and Immigration. But we can't.'

'*And* we need to know more about what's going on at higher level,' said Iain. 'MI5 and SIS and GCHQ won't be sitting on their hands. What are they up to?'

'Hell,' said Tom. 'We're hamstrung in every direction. *Surely*, finding the cell if it's here is what matters. If some observant terrorist notices our activity, that's a risk that's got to be taken, isn't it? ... We need to get back to Manfield.' He made as if to stand up.

'Hold on,' said Iain. 'Before we go running upstairs, shouldn't we get a bit clearer what we reckon this cell might be planning to do?'

Tom sniffed, but sat down again and thought for a while. 'That's a tough question,' he said. 'I suppose what upsets al-Qaida, basically, is the West polluting their culture—they get furious at liquor stores and shameless American women anywhere near Mecca. And they want to do something really huge to stop it.'

'But even 9/11 didn't get the Americans out of Saudi Arabia, did it?'

'Which suggests they'll want something even bigger

now,' said Tom. 'But what the hell could that possibly mean in Plymouth, of all places?'

'Those nuclear subs?'

'Not global enough,' said Tom doubtfully. 'Still, yes, I suppose so... And the easiest way to attack the dockyard is by bringing in a bomb on a merchant ship—a nuclear bomb, even. Instead of stopping at the commercial docks, she just carries on a mile up the Hamoaze, and *bang!* Nothing to stop her.'

'They could attack the civilian population in the same way, with a dirty bomb.'

'And, apart from the Navy, that's the only other thing I can see al-Qaida wanting to do in a place like Plymouth: kill a very large number of people.'

'But Tom, it'd be easy for the Navy to stop all shipping. Search them outside the breakwater.'

'Yes... So we need to go over all this down at Devonport.'

'They could attack the dockyard with hijacked planes, like 9/11.'

'Airline security's been tightened a lot since then. If I were an al-Qaida planner, I'd be trying something different this time.'

'They could *charter* a plane? Flight plan showing them landing at the City airport, and then come crashing onto the dockyard at the last minute?'

'Other vulnerable targets too—reservoirs, oil depots, public buildings. What else?'

'What about...?' A conflicted mixture of doubt and assertion had flitted across Iain's face.

'What?'

'Just an idea I had.'

'Out with it.'

'That John Smith. Knew something he wasn't saying, you thought?'

'Yes, I did.'

'Well.' Iain tilted his head a little to one side. 'Probably quite wrong.'

'Come on!'

'Could it possibly be, d'you think, Mr Blair's organising a meeting which just happens to be somewhere near here?'

Tom sat up sharply. 'And they've chosen not to tell us because it's secret and high-level?'

'That was my idea.'

'And al-Qaida have got to hear about it, and are going after the delegates?'

'Exactly.'

Tom nodded. 'Someone like George Bush, even? … *That* could explain why MI5 are so ready to assume it's our Plymouth.'

'It just came to me,' said Iain complacently.

'But if al-Qaida were after someone that big, the target wouldn't be arriving on the Santander ferry or at the City Airport. He'd fly in to an airbase, and helicopter in Marine One to some secluded estate.'

'In that case security would be concerned about an attack on his plane.'

'During the 9/11 attacks the Americans worried big-time about mid-air attacks on the President… If it's him, he might not arrive by air at all, but on some US Navy ship.'

'There's another thing,' said Iain. 'We've been told to look for the cell in Plymouth. But it might actually never be on our patch at all, attack from elsewhere using a plane or a missile.'

'Quite right,' said Tom. 'And equally, *Plymouth Plan* might mean a cell based here, with the blow falling somewhere else in the UK. Or overseas… Or, the plan might involve Plymouth in some way we haven't thought of yet—the Navy, perhaps, or something involving the ferries or the airport, or Muslim students at the University. There's far too many possibilities, Iain… OK, let's go see the boss.'

*

Two days later, on 7th August, a middle-aged man was driving a big motorhome through Dubrovnik, alone, on his way from Kosovo to Paris.

Had western intelligence been alert to his significance, they would no doubt have quickly discovered that he was Egyptian, and unearthed his early links with Algeria: he still carried scars on his arms from a French army snatch squad. More recently, however, he had been living in Marseilles — so long, in fact, that he'd taken to Gallic ways: he liked to hide his commitment behind a relaxed sense of the ridiculous, helped by his lanky figure.

He had been enjoying the mountain scenery and the flowery verges of the winding roads, smiling to himself. But now the ungainly vehicle looked out of place in the narrow and crowded old streets. Its modifications were as complete as the Kosovo Liberation Army workshop in Niksic could make them. They were shortly to be tested, and, in spite of his smiles, the man was chain-smoking Gauloises. He had a gruelling drive ahead.

Western intelligence were aware that the KLA had recently broken into a store of plastic explosive in Niksic, but didn't know where the heist had gone. By August 14th they had passed this information to MI5, but since there was nothing to link it with Plymouth, nobody told Tom and Iain.

Developments

The Super, relatively young and still new to his job, seemed relieved when Tom rang, and told him and Iain to take the lift up to his airy office. In his bluff way, he settled them into the tubular visitors' chairs but himself remained standing by the big window, his eyes a little narrowed.

Tom explained their concerns.

His boss looked out over the old spires and the fifties redevelopment, and at last turned back. 'But,' he said, 'what you were asked to do was clear enough. Your job is to look for signs of a cell. That and no more... We haven't been told what the other agencies are up to—all the things you want may have been covered already... They seem so damned determined to force us into these ridiculous chinese boxes. *Need to know only...*'

'But that policy is dangerous,' said Tom. 'If we don't know what else is in train, we can't see the gaps in our own approach... And we just can't afford that: the whole city's at risk.'

The Super sighed. 'I'm only too well aware of what's at stake,' he said. 'So you want me to go chasing back to higher authority?'

Tom and Iain both nodded.

The Super smiled wanly. 'Which means Manfield in the first instance... Well... Just supposing I did feel willing to do it, what's your *minimum* request? We won't get anywhere asking for too much.'

Tom glanced at Iain. 'The top priority,' he said slowly, 'is more information. We've *got* to know what bases are already covered. At least within Plymouth itself.'

'I do see that.'

'Second, permission to collaborate... With customs, with the navy and the other services, and at least some of the security services.'

Iain nodded.

The Super raised his eyebrows, but said nothing.

'Then *surely* we must be allowed to make some sort of direct checks on hotels and B&Bs, and on the local Muslim community. Put at least some specific questions.'

'They won't like either of those.'

'We can make sure it's done discreetly.'

The Super looked doubtful.

Tom pressed on. 'And more manpower.'

The Super sighed again, but nodded. 'Like what?'

'Secretarial help, and full-time for us two, for starters.'

Another resigned nod.

'And Sergeant Aliza Akinci to be cleared to work with the local Muslim community.'

The Super looked up sharply. 'Ah,' he said.

'She'd be extremely useful.'

'That had occurred to me too... I had her security dossier sent up.'

Iain glanced at Tom. 'And?' he asked.

'OK, as far as it goes.' The Super walked over to his desk, picked up a red folder, and passed it to Iain, who set about leafing through it.

'Personally,' said the Super, 'I don't have any doubts. Promising young officer... But what about her family?'

'Some of it's in here,' said Iain.

'Just so,' said the Super. 'Turkish... Father emigrated to Germany in 1962, mother in 1976 when they married... And they all moved on again from Dusseldorf to Plymouth in 1989.'

'When Aliza would have been thirteen,' said Tom. 'Locally educated, I suppose?'

Iain turned a page. 'John Kitto College.'

'Followed by Police College,' said the Super. 'But it says nothing about what her parents were doing. Do you know?'

'Her father emigrated to Germany to get work,' said Tom. 'Not sure what he did there originally, but later he became a butcher. Still is... That's all according to her, of course.'

'Sounds harmless enough... With his own business?'

'In George Place, near the ferry dock.'

'Funny choice of place... Is he exporting?'

'No idea.'

The Super looked at Iain, who shook his head. 'The security people would certainly want to check out his trading contacts... And Aliza's still living at home with them?'

'Yes.'

'Is she religious?'

'Not conspicuously.'

'And you've never seen any hint of extremism in her?'

Tom opened his eyes very wide. 'Nope!'

'Nor in her parents, I suppose?'

'I've only met them once... But no.'

The Super looked out over the city panorama again and seemed to be thinking. After a while he again smiled faintly and looked down at Tom.

'All right,' he said. 'I'll talk to Manfield... But before

that, I'd like you to put a few questions of my own to Aliza. You don't have to tell her why you're asking.'

Iain nodded and gave a pleased grin. Tom too was relieved, but not in the mood for grinning.

*

Aliza, summoned by Tom, knocked at his office door and slipped quietly in, self-possessed and serious. Dark hair in a neat pony tail, tidy uniform, navy tights, black regulation shoes. Twenty-six. A bony face, large dark eyes.

'Sit down, Sergeant,' said Tom, his eyes on his papers. 'The Super's asked me to put some questions to you.' He looked up; she was frowning intently. 'Security issues.'

She said nothing. The door opened again and Iain entered, carrying three mugs of coffee. He passed them around.

'Background again is it, Sir?'

'Purely precautionary,' said Tom. 'You're *not*, repeat not, under any sort of suspicion.'

'Some of my colleagues,' said Aliza, 'seem to think I'd be massacring Christian babies in my spare time if I took Islam seriously.'

Tom looked up.

'Muslims are *peace-loving*, you know?'

'I do understand that, Sergeant.' He paused. 'However, I have to put these questions to you.'

'Yes, Sir.'

'Right... First, why did your father emigrate from Turkey to Germany? Do you know?'

'For a better life.'

'Doing what?'

'Scaffolding. He was a *gast-arbeiter*.'

'The overseas-worker programme?'

She nodded. 'But then he found there was a shortage of halal meat. And because he'd done some slaughtering in Turkey, he was able set up as a butcher.'

'OK. And your mum?'

'Dad met her when he went back to Ankara for a visit. They got married, and he brought her back to Dusseldorf.'

Tom wrote down her answer. 'Where you were born, I believe... Do you have brothers and sisters?'

'No, Sir.'

'Right... Do you know what your father's politics were in Turkey?'

'CHP.'

'Which means?'

'*Cumhuriyet Halk Partisi.*'

'Could you spell that, please?'

Aliza gave a little smile and obliged. 'The Republican People's Party. It means Dad wanted to keep the republic secular.'

'Even though he was religious?'

'Yes.'

'So he never supported the Islamists?'

'Never!'

'And your mother?'

Aliza smiled. 'She has no politics of her own.'

'She backs your father, then?' asked Iain.

'Always... My parents are good Muslims. They hate violence.'

Iain nodded.

'What was the reason for the move to England?' asked Tom.

'A Turkish sailor told my father there was an opening for a halal butcher here in Plymouth. So he came over to look around, got started, and then we all came.'

'When you would have been thirteen?'

She nodded. 'I had to learn English in a hurry.'

'And he's still a butcher, I think?'

'Yes.'

'But his place is down by the docks... Does that mean he exports?'

'Since three years ago. He calls himself Akinci Halal Exports Ltd now.'

Tom wrote again. 'Butchered meat?'

'No, live lambs to French halal butchers. He'd prefer to export meat, because the animal rights protesters want to stop the live trade. But our slaughterhouse isn't big enough, and we don't have a refrigerated lorry.'

'And they go over to Brittany on the ferry?'

'Yes.'

'You live with your parents?'

'Yes, Sir.'

'You told me once you're not as religious as them?'

'When I was a little girl they wanted me to be a good German, so in spite of how much it means to them, they allowed me not to be so very Islamic.'

'But they're still serious? They attend Friday prayers?'

'Oh yes.'

'But you don't?'

'Not usually.'

'There's no proper mosque in Plymouth, is there?'

'They meet in an old stationers, in George Street, near Mount Wise. There isn't a regular imam—a man comes down from Exeter sometimes.'

'Is it well attended?'

'Twenty or thirty, perhaps. Just quiet, ordinary people.'

Tom smiled. 'Not a hotbed of extremists?'

She smiled back. 'Certainly not.'

'Don't let your coffee get cold, Sergeant.' He scribbled some more. 'Now, finally, just for the record: Do you, or do your parents, or any of your close relatives, have any sort of sympathy for, or any sort of contact with, Islamist extremists?'

Her jaw set for a moment. 'No, Sir,' she said. 'Of course not!'

Tom looked enquiringly at Iain, who nodded.

'Thank you, Sergeant,' said Tom.

*

A few days earlier, on 4th August, a senior member of the Muslim Brotherhood had been in Cairo. His safe house was well appointed, but concealed in a filthy and crowded souk; he'd been there for four days. But he was used to moving at short notice: it was only three weeks since his return to Egypt. He was a man who, disgusted by the filthy irruption, as he saw it, of western licence into Islamic culture, had come to believe, without compromise, in the efficacy of Sharia law and Muslim statehood. So far, the al-Qaida leadership had treated him as too valuable to lead a suicide mission: he took a grim pride in that.

But preparations for discreet disappearance had been in train for some time, and his departure, when it came, was simple enough. A few minor changes to his appearance. Then, with the street market at its busiest, the son of the family rode up to the house on his motor-scooter. The man ran up the greasy basement steps to meet him, threw a leg over the pillion, and was driven off with a roar.

This manoeuvre had, however, been observed by a small boy, who ran into a narrow boutique that displayed Scottish knitwear amidst the clay lamps and local cottons. Within a few hours SIS had informed MI5.

*

The Super's efforts with Manfield must have been cogent, because it was quickly agreed that Tom could press his points with the security authorities. But a higher level of security clearance was required first, and an impassive man with scuffed black shoes, who seemed to know already the names of all his school friends, appeared and interviewed him in a Plymouth café. Over tea and scones he warned that Tom's personal contacts would be checked out.

Jane Allison rang him that evening to report, quietly but a little distressed, that she'd been cross-questioned vigorously for more than an hour. Tom knew it had been inevitable, but still felt violated.

Briefing

The duty sergeant at the Special Branch Exeter Establishment directed Tom to the first floor. He climbed the polished stairs and found the conference room door open. Inside David Manfield was sitting at a modern elm table, talking to the 'John Smith' who had delivered the briefing in the Citadel. An elegant standard lamp was set on the gleaming oak floor alongside two cheerful rugs. Laid out on the table were a pewter ashtray, and a large cafetière of coffee with three porcelain cups and a jug of cream.

Manfield looked up, and pulled at his sandy moustache, 'Come in, come in,' he said, and immediately poured the coffee, a little unpractised. 'You met Mr Smith,' he added.

John Smith shook hands, helped himself to sugar, and sat down at the table. 'Glad you got your clearance, Chief Inspector,' he said with an apparently friendly grin, as Tom and Manfield sat down too. 'Your Superintendent's arguments were mostly judged convincing at divisional level, I'm pleased to say.' He extracted a paper from a file.

Tom nodded hopefully and got out his Filofax.

'First, direct liaison with all three services approved; and also with customs, the airport, the post office and BT. But *only* with designated officers in each, who have the appropriate clearance… Here's a list.'

'Thanks,' said Tom. He took the paper and studied it.

'Second, agreement that *limited* enquiries at hotels and B&Bs are on balance necessary. But this was agreed only reluctantly, and if you intend to circulate an enquiry, it *must* be very discreetly worded, and I'd like David here to check it out.'

Tom nodded.

'Third. Your Turkish sergeant making enquiries in the Muslim community. This was considered distinctly dodgy; but was eventually agreed to, *provided* she meets certain security checks of our own.'

'Understood,' said Tom.

'But for God's sake insist she keeps it as low-key as possible. I'll let you know this evening whether she's in the clear. Happy?'

'Yes,' said Tom, and nodded.

'OK, right. Now, some briefing. It was agreed you should be made aware of the following items. But they are all top secret, and you *must* keep them strictly to yourself.'

Tom nodded.

'First, we've recently received some new information.' John Smith extracted a yellow fax from his file and handed it to Tom. It read:

ex CAIRO STATION. Target observed 4/8 hurriedly leaving suspected safe house al-Gamaliyya with travel bag, almost certainly Uthman al-Azmeh.

JIC GLOSS: Uthman al-Azmeh is a Muslim Brother and second-tier figure in al-Qaida, suspected of having been in England June/July, location unknown. Egyptian but speaks good English. Trained as an orthopaedic surgeon in Chicago, practised two years in

Detroit hospital. About 40, heavy, 5´8˝, brown eyes,
black curly hair and beard. No photo available.

Tom looked up uncertainly. 'The speaker on the Cairo satellite phone?' he asked.

John Smith gave a tiny nod.

'How sure are you?'

'Our analysts think it's almost certain. You can pass the *description* on to your police colleagues—but don't let them use it in questioning the public. And keep the background info to yourself.'

'Understood… Would this al-Azmeh be the leader of the cell?'

'At the right level, certainly.'

'Pity there's no photo.'

'Yes…' John Smith pursed his lips for a moment. 'Now, three extreme top-secret items.' He looked hard at Tom. 'We avoid putting things at this level down on paper. Manage that?'

Tom nodded again.

'The first, and most important, is this.' Another pause. 'Back in February the Prime Minister persuaded President Bush there should be a conference, a Heads of State conference.'

Tom composed his face as best he could to appear mildly interested.

'In Britain. On the Palestine question.'

'Ah.'

'Monday 26th to Friday 30th August. But only the final two days will involve the Heads of State, and it's to be kept secret to give it more chance of success. The Norwegians involved in the Oslo Accord are helping…'

'Where?' asked Tom cautiously.

John Smith hesitated. 'Blenheim Palace,' he admitted

at last. 'Closed to the public, of course… Bush, Sharon and Arafat all fly in to RAF Brize Norton on the Wednesday 28th in the evening. After the conference ends they have private discussions on the Saturday, and fly out again from Brize Norton early on Sunday 1st September. Got all that?'

'Starts the 26th… Sharon, Arafat and Bush arrive the 28th, out again on the 1st… Brize Norton.'

'Correct… The Palestinians have been told the dates, but nothing at all about the destination, or movements, or security. The CIA and the Israelis, however, wanted, and were given, full details.'

'But I'm not to tell even my closest colleagues?'

'I thought I'd made that clear, Inspector… Major headache for us, of course. Hamas will have learnt the dates through Arafat's office, and al-Qaida will certainly have heard through Hamas. So we've had to consider whether al-Qaida might make some attempt on Bush or Sharon at the meeting—or on Blair, for that matter.

'On 25th July, as you know, we picked up that satellite call referring to a *Plymouth plan*. We couldn't see much in Plymouth that provided a serious target for al-Qaida—but the *timing* suggested al-Qaida had got wind of Blair's proposal, and that the Plymouth plan might well be part of some scheme to attack the Heads of State. And Plymouth looked well chosen as a base: far enough from Blenheim and Brize Norton to be outside any immediate security sweep, and a convenient point to bring in hardware by ferry.

'But *that* was a big worry in itself.' John Smith frowned. 'It only made sense if al-Qaida knew not only the dates but also the places and probably the movement details well before 25th July… And how could they have known them?'

Tom looked up sharply, but said nothing.

John Smith looked at him quizzically.

Tom nodded. 'Disturbing,' he said. '… These timings make everything rather urgent, don't they? It's the 9th August today, and the conference starts on the 26th, so your scenario implies the terrorist cell arriving on my patch very soon now.'

'Correct! Now, that satellite call didn't *prove* they intended to attack the heads of state. We intercept a lot of traffic, but none of it seemed to refer to anything imminent in the UK. And we weren't then aware of any suspects moving in… But now, the second extreme top-secret item. A week ago, the 3rd, we picked up a *further* satellite call. Same voices, same two places: one east of Kandahar, and a place we've pinpointed in the suburbs of Cairo. The Cairo voice said, in Arabic, "The plan advocated last month is to proceed, if Allah is willing" That, combined with al-Azmeh having left Cairo almost immediately afterwards, suggested we were on the right lines.'

Tom nodded thoughtfully.

'Got all that? Now, the *third* thing you need to know may come as a surprise: it appears that three Israeli intelligence officers have turned up on your patch.'

'*Mossad*?' said Tom.

'They're in the Alfred Hotel. Small place near the Barbican—expect you know it? Going by English names: John Gage, Adam Gopel and Heather Stone. They arrived in Plymouth two days ago. We haven't asked them why they're there, and they don't appear to realise we've noticed their arrival.'

'You've told Mossad about the phone calls and al-Azmeh leaving Cairo?'

'Certainly.'

'So why haven't you asked them what these agents

are up to?'

John Smith looked down, then up again. He sniffed pointedly. 'Relations with Mossad a trifle strained just now,' he admitted.

Tom raised his eyebrows.

'We'll be watching them—leave that to us,' said John Smith. He turned his gaze sharply at Tom. 'I assume this Heads of State conference *was* news to you?'

'Oh yes,' said Tom.

John Smith continued to gaze, but at last blinked, shifted the papers in front of him and remarked, 'Now, I believe you had some questions for us…?'

David Manfield came to life and poured second cups of coffee.

'Several,' said Tom. 'First, what you think of our moves so far.' He explained.

They seemed to approve.

'And still no suspects of your own in Plymouth?' asked Tom.

'That's correct,' said John Smith.

'About incoming communications,' continued Tom. 'Are you running checks on emails and telephone calls? What about the post? What about banks?'

John Smith frowned, and counted out his replies on his fingers. 'Emails: nationwide automated checks by GCHQ—you'll hear soon enough of anything relevant to Plymouth. Telephone: harder—in practice you need to give us a suspect telephone number. Post: harder still, needs an address and a warrant.'

'But couldn't we make deductions,' asked Tom, 'simply from knowing that mail was coming to a given address from a particular country, or even parts of Britain with a large Muslim community?'

John Smith looked at Manfield.

'Perhaps the sorting office could help us?' persisted

Tom.

'Don't see why not,' said Manfield slowly. 'They should be able to tell you anything they can see just by just looking at the outsides of envelopes.'

'So should I let you know what we'd like them to do?'

'Perhaps you'd better,' said Manfield, and John Smith nodded.

'And the banks?' prompted Tom.

'All banks have instructions to report suspicious money movements,' said John Smith.

'And physical surveillance? At customs for instance?'

'Plymouth customs have been equipped with the latest detectors. Should pick out a nuclear warhead or dirty bomb material even if shielded. Twenty metres away, they say. The chemical sniffers should detect conventional explosive, too, if it's loosely packed. For explosive inside a bomb casing or a rocket, it depends how thorough al-Qaida are at cleaning the outside before they leave home. For biological materials the detectors are greatly improved, but if your terrorists use something new it might be missed.'

'And you've got no information about where or when this al-Qaida cell might have been formed?'

John Smith hesitated and drummed his fingers on the table twice. 'We're fairly sure...' he said at last, 'that a new cell was formed earlier this year.'

'At the level of a significant international attack?'

'Affirmative.'

'Based where?'

'Definitely in Egypt,' said John Smith reluctantly. 'Probably Ismailia.'

'But you don't know its target?'

'No.'

'Descriptions of likely operatives?'

John Smith smiled. 'Many hundreds *might* be involved. No point giving you details until we know more. And any new cell's sure to contain some cleanskins.'

'Right,' said Tom. His exasperation was rising. 'Next, what about the threat? We know about this conference, but we can't rule out other possibilities, can we?'

'Correct.'

'Have you picked up any intelligence about targets in Plymouth, or the sort of target they might go for in the UK generally?'

'No specific Plymouth targets. Our guesses are much the same as yours. The Navy's arranged there'll be no nuclear submarines in the dockyard for the time being, and some nuclear material has been moved away by road. We have arrangements for scrambling RAF fighter patrols at short notice, though there are no recent reports of suspects learning to fly, for instance. We know al-Qaida have been trying to get hold of fissile material as well as stuff for a dirty bomb, and they've been having intense discussions for months about the best targets and how to attack them.'

'But nothing *specific*?'

'No.'

'By and large, then,' said Tom, rather grimly, 'there isn't much useful to us coming from general intelligence, is there?'

John Smith scowled. 'A great deal of work is going on, Chief Inspector, and intelligence is certain to come in. Be assured you'll hear when it does.'

That covered Tom's questions. But he had a request to make.

'I'm working closely,' he said, 'with DI Iain Gemmill, and we talk over most things. To me, it would make a lot of sense if I was allowed to tell him two things.'

'Which?'

'First, the Israelis. He may come across them.'

John Smith frowned.

'Second, the *existence* and *dates* of the conference. No more. If we have deadlines, he needs to be aware. I wouldn't need to pass on any of the intelligence or the security arrangements.'

'Not security cleared, is he?' said Manfield.

'No.'

John Smith was still frowning, and clasped his hands together. 'Tricky,' he said at last. 'Need to consult. Get back to you.'

With that, Tom had to be satisfied. He checked that he'd remembered correctly the movement dates and the names and address of the Mossad agents, refused a now tepid cup of coffee, donned his issue raincoat, and shook hands. With his fists thrust down into his pockets he walked thoughtfully back to his car.

The engine sprang dutifully to life. He drove a quarter of a mile, grimaced into the driver's mirror, and stopped. Finding a loose scrap of paper, he wrote:

In 28th Aug, out 1st Sept, Brize Norton
John Gage/Adam Gopel/Heather Stone
Alfred Hotel

He folded the paper and placed it carefully inside his official notebook. So far, so good, he thought. 'John Smith' had been efficient and hadn't stood on dignity. Young puppy, though. Tom wasn't sure he liked him much. He didn't like it that the intelligence allocated to him was so obviously rationed. And he'd hoped for more help, much more.

*

When Tom reached home that evening, Miranda knew where he'd been, but not why. She refrained from asking questions, so he said:

'Can't tell you. Wish I could.'

She nodded, and smiled to reassure him, then became serious.

'Jane rang,' she said.

Tom looked up.

'She wanted to know if she could call round.'

For the whole of their complicated past two years, Jane had avoided visiting his home. 'She wanted to call round *here*?'

'That's what she said.'

'When?'

'Sunday evening. I didn't want to seem discouraging, so I said "of course", and she's coming about 9.30. Hope I did right?'

'Yes,' said Tom. He was taken aback, but his heart had lifted.

Leg Work

John Smith rang Tom back first thing on the Saturday and, to Tom's considerable surprise, acceded to his requests about what he might tell Iain. He also said that Aliza was in the clear.

Iain called her in to Tom's office. 'Take a seat, Sergeant,' he remarked when she arrived. 'This is a bit urgent. New job for you.'

Tom explained what it was about, facing her over his desk, as Iain listened. 'We're under pressure,' he said, 'and your knowledge of the Muslim community should give us a bit of an edge. But if we ask you to sniff around looking for terrorists, how difficult would that be for you, personally?'

'It *will* be difficult, Sir... But I can see why you need it. I can do it.'

'You know what you'd be looking for?'

'Dangerous extremists.'

'Could be *very* dangerous. Think you can cope?'

'Yes, Sir.'

Tom smiled cautiously at her. 'Good. Thank you, Sergeant. If they're like the al-Qaida Hamburg cell, they'll be well-educated youngish Arabs with good jobs. But, of course, this lot might be different... How big d'you think the Muslim community in Plymouth is?'

'I don't know, Sir, not exactly.'

'You said only twenty or thirty attend prayers?'

'But there are plenty of others. Foreign sailors on the ferries... Young guys who did electronics in Bradford or Glasgow. Lawyers and doctors. Teachers, too... Some schoolchildren and university students. A hundred? Hundred and fifty? I don't know really.'

'Any suspicious recent arrivals you know about?'

'If there had been, Sir, I'd have told you. But there are always comings and goings—my dad's shipping clerks, for instance... The most recent came from Bradford.' She smiled and tilted her head a little to one side. 'And, guess what, my mum reckoned him a suitable boy, you know?'

'Suitable for *you*?' said Iain.

Aliza nodded. 'But I didn't agree, and he only stayed two months.'

'If it's really only a hundred people, Sergeant,' said Tom, 'you ought to be able to find out something about most of them in a couple of days or so.'

She raised her eyebrows.

'Why don't you work out a strategy for covering the whole Muslim community within a twenty-mile radius? Then decide what you should and shouldn't ask them. Call me back with a plan after lunch. I'll go over it with you, and you can make a start over the week-end. Preliminary report by, say, Wednesday.'

She looked thoughtfully at Tom, then nodded.

Iain said quietly, 'Quite a tall order, Sergeant.'

'It is,' said Tom, 'but we don't have much time... OK?'

She nodded again, tidied her notes, then marched off with a half-smile.

'Sure of herself, now, isn't she?' Iain added with some satisfaction, once the door was closed.

*

When she appeared at Tom's on Sunday evening, Jane exchanged a quick kiss with him, but then sat herself down in his sitting room some distance from his chair. She was rather crisply dressed: skirt just-below-the-knee, mid-grey linen with a matching cutaway jacket. He waited and she smiled at him, narrow face tilted a little to one side. Miranda said she'd make some coffee.

The outfit suited her, he thought distractedly, but why the formality? If she was taking in what his house was like, she gave no sign of it. She asked how Jack was finding life in London.

'Well,' said Tom, and smiled. 'Merchant banking's quite a change for him. But we think he's enjoying it; he doesn't get down here to see us so often now.'

Miranda brought the coffee and asked how Jane's new placement was going.

She laughed. 'It's a funny old practice,' she said. 'Right out on the moor.'

'You're liking it, then?' asked Tom.

'Well, my problems haven't vanished away, of course. But I'm loving the *place*. Why not? Genuine people... And I think they like me, too.'

'Country patients?'

'Farm hands, snotty kids, retired sheep farmers and their wives.'

'Weather-beaten types?' asked Miranda, always the artist. 'Cider-apple cheeks?'

Jane smiled. 'I guess that's true, some of them... They don't expect much—treat doctors like honorary vets.'

Tom felt pleased and started to relax.

'I'm here to ask a favour,' Jane went on after a while.

He looked up.

'You know I've been in touch with Laurel?'

Laurel was a sailing friend from Brittany; Tom had last seen her in hospital two years earlier, after a sailing accident, just before his traumatic transatlantic crossing with Jane. After these events Jane had lost confidence and her boat *Ariel* had been laid up. But during the last three months Tom had been helping her with relaunching and setting up rigging. Since then she had made two short single-handed trips.

'Laurel's fully recovered?'

'Oh yes... The thing is, she wants me to sail over to meet her.'

'How d'you feel about that?' he asked, cautiously.

'It's not that Roscoff's too far, as such,' she said. 'But she's assuming I'll be crossing solo...'

'And you'd prefer to have a crew?'

She laughed. 'Will you, Tom? Laurel would love to see you again.'

'That's not asking a favour! Of *course* I will. When do we start?'

'She wants the weekend of 31st August. It would mean a night crossing, starting on the Friday evening.'

Tom was pulling out his diary before he remembered.

'Oh *no*!' he said. He glanced at Miranda, who was watching him thoughtfully over her coffee. 'I can't... Damn and blast! For any other weekend there'd have been some way of fixing it, but for this one I just can't.'

Jane's face had fallen. 'Oh,' she said. 'What a shame... Well, I suppose I'll have to tell her the date's no good.' But she was frowning.

'She can't do another date?'

'Well, really she can't.'

Tom felt there was something here that shouldn't be let slip. 'Hamish sails, doesn't he?' he said quickly to Miranda. 'Why don't the two of you give Jane a hand?'

Miranda glanced at Tom to be sure how he meant this, and then at Jane. '*Could* we?' she said. 'I'd *love* to—and it wouldn't be hard to bully Hamish!'

'I'd like that too,' Jane said, with a little nod. But then she hesitated. 'I need to think... How much sailing have you done?'

'I've done a reasonable amount, and Hamish a lot more—he's been sailing a Westerly Storm in Scottish waters with a syndicate.'

'That sounds good,' Jane said, and smiled quite positively. 'Can I get back to you tomorrow?' And as soon as they'd finished coffee, she made her excuses. But at the front door, before driving herself home, she smiled gently and with both hands pulled Tom's head down and kissed him on the lips.

*

At 10 am on 10th August, an arresting young woman was passing through immigration at Charles de Gaulle Airport, about to rendezvous in the long-stay car park. She had been living with her mission long enough not to be over-excited—indeed, had been relaxed enough almost to miss her flight from London in the rush of getting off. But she was a little concerned about her clothes. Her role was to be that of a young Frenchwoman setting off for a walking holiday in Scotland with her husband—not an easy part for a strict unmarried Muslim. But she was a close observer of her western sisters and had planned her wardrobe with care. No one else would have doubted that her tailored trousers, flowered silk top with a dipping neckline, solid but stylish

48

sandals, and designer shades, struck the right note. To these might complacently be added the scent and lip gloss, the long walking jacket draped over one arm, and the pristine copy of Elle. *Her French was less idiomatic than her English, but with luck she wouldn't have to say much.*

*

Aliza had registered with some satisfaction how heavily Tom and Iain were relying on her. They had agreed that it might prove productive for her to explain at home what she was doing, in general terms at least, and she tackled this first. After some initial anxiety, her parents entered into her enquiry extremely seriously. Mr Akinci, his white-flecked beard wagging earnestly and his hands waving, laid down, in carefully turned English, weighty principles concerning the threats posed by Islamic extremism, and the foolishness of certain younger imams, while her mother listened respectfully, hands folded. Then, after a proper pause, her mother offered, on a rising pitch and in Turkish, an undeflectable stream of shrewd—and rather more useful—observations on all her Muslim acquaintances, which her father confirmed from time to time by nodding magisterially.

The following three days were extremely busy, but less difficult than Aliza had feared, and she encountered no obvious dangers. On the Tuesday evening, ankles still aching, she typed up her preliminary report:

```
To:  DCI Tallis and DI Gemill
Subject: MUSLIM COMMUNITY IN PLYMOUTH —
PRELIMINARY REPORT

I contacted 76 people so far. Summary of con-
clusions:
```

I   Attenders at Friday prayers. This group is positive for exposing any terrorist threat. But no one thinks there is any sort of extremist group active in or near Plymouth.

II   Overseas travel. No one admits to recently visiting Saudi Arabia, Palestine, Yemen, Indonesia or Afghanistan. But there were recent visits to Egypt and Pakistan — see below.

III Suspects. None obvious, but the following need further checks:

Dr Raja Said.   Egyptian doctor who has worked in the City for 17 years as a GP, aged 64.   He is liked by everyone.   However, when a student at Cairo University he had friends in the Brotherhood, and when interviewed he volunteered hearsay information about Islamists on the run from Egyptian Police.   He visited his daughter in Cairo this year for 3 weeks from 16th Apr.   He is knowledgeable about Islam and gives talks to local schools. His Jordanian receptionist moved from a practice in Lambeth 4 months ago.

Students at the University of Plymouth:

Ibrahim al-Khalif. First-year Iraqi studying electronics. Had flying magazines on the bookcase in his bed-sit.
Muna Qurashi.   Third-year student from Libya studying accountancy.   She may have family links to members of Col Gadaffi's defence establishment.
Deborah Ishmail. Third-year from Lebanon studying marine biology.   Smart and westernised, but had very strong feelings about the Israeli massacre at Shatila in 1982.

These three know each other slightly, but do not form a group.   None of them responded strongly to religious questions, and I concluded they were not sufficiently engaged to be terrorists.

```
Teachers:
2 recently appointed secondary school teachers
who discuss Islam together. Jaffa Alfredi
trained in Glasgow, teaches biology, emigrated
from Syria in 1996 and to Plymouth this year.
Sherifa Mernissi trained in Pakistan, she vis-
ited her family in Peshawar last summer, and
came on to teach maths here last year. They
work at different schools, but know each other
quite well. Intelligent. They both wish to
expel Americans from Saudi Arabia.

Casual workers who arrived within the last 18
months:
The following seem unlikely as terrorists, but
need to be checked further because they are
recent arrivals:
    At Akinci Halal Exports Ltd. 2 butcher's
assistants from the Mile End Road in London,
and shipping clerk from Bradford (recently
departed).
    At Kaffe Antioch in Dock Street. 5 restau-
rant workers.  3 grew up in the UK, one Turk-
ish Cypriot and his friend from Turkey
(Ephesus).
    At the massage parlour behind Union
Street. Young Sumatran woman.  Not been able
to confirm she is Muslim.

I shall cover the remaining 30 names by tomor-
row evening. I have uploaded a database of
names, addresses and evidence obtained onto
the group server.

Signed: A. Akinci
Dated: 13/8/02
```

Tom was pleased with this report and began to feel
they were making progress. Iain and Sgt Howe had
activated the routine precautions. Detailed discussions
with Customs, the City Chief Executive, Brittany
Ferries, the Airport Manager, the Naval Dockyard, the
Royal Mail sorting office and the barracks were under
way. The Super had put him and Iain on the job full-

time and was allowing his efficient Miss Baines to help Tom for two hours a day. But the dozens of enquiries she'd posted to hotel proprietors and landladies had so far elicited only two responses:

From Mrs W. Errol-Smyth. 'Booking made in mid-June by Mr and Mrs Omah of Bradford for my self-catering holiday home at Elfordleigh for 10th–31st August.'

From the Belsize Hotel. 'Booking just made for 6 adults by Mrs Hanna Saddiqi of London for weekend of 24th–25th August. She keeps a yacht in the Queen Anne Battery Marina and often books in with her husband.'

Skimming through the various reports, Tom paused over Dr Said and his new receptionist, the flying Iraqi student, and Mr and Mrs Omah. But, he lectured himself, it was far too early to be giving weight to uninformed instinct. Systematic, plodding police work was what was needed.

Pursuit

By the late evening of Saturday 10th August, the man and the woman had completed their drive to Roscoff. They tidied themselves, rehearsed their personalities, pocketed their forged passports, and timed their arrival at the ferry terminal so that the big motorhome was near the back of the queue. There were no problems at French customs. She went straight to the lounge deck to read Elle. He first studied how the cars, vans, buses and trucks were arranged on the vehicle deck, then came up to join her.

Shortly after departure, a loudspeaker announced augmented security checks on arrival in Plymouth, which might mean a delay of up to two hours. They exchanged glances and found their double cabin. He bolted the door from the inside and after reading his evening prayers aloud settled to sleep on the floor; she took the bed. She read no prayers, but before closing her eyes rehearsed a private litany of the fates of her school friends, as she often did.

The ferry docked at 6.30 am, while the air was still crisp; and since theirs had been almost the last vehicle to board the night before, it was now almost the last off. At the passport control office they had to leave their van and join a queue inside. The man managed a joke with the immigration officer, and their documents passed muster.

They returned to the motorhome. Ahead of them sniffer equipment was being used by many figures in orange vests, startling in the brilliant sunshine. His hands began to shake, and again he lit up. But when their turn came at last, the *inspectors tramped over the raised floor without comment, and the sniffer machine found nothing. As they drove out beneath the exit gantry, he was having trouble steering steadily and her chic new underwear was drenched with sweat.*

*

Tom and Iain had been struggling with an illicit desire to discover a little more about the Israelis at the Alfred Hotel.

'I could drop round there with a few choral parts,' said Iain.

'Choral parts?'

Iain grinned. 'Annie's the manageress there.'

'Really?' Tom grinned in his turn. Annie was choir mistress at the United Reformed Church. 'A friendly call in working hours?'

'What I had in mind.'

So Iain walked round in plain clothes with his music case, and was welcomed into Annie's kitchen in his shirtsleeves, where the fan was buzzing in the heat. She smiled, and gave him a cup of coffee. He mentioned the three names.

She shook her head. 'They left,' she said.

'Oh… When?'

'A week ago… But I know where they went.'

Iain put down his coffee and found his notebook.

'The Providence.'

He scribbled. 'Small hotel in Emma Place? Down by the ferry terminal?'

'That's the one.'

'Know anything about it?'

'Not really. Newly set up. The man's from out of town—I suppose they're hoping the area will develop.'

'And did these three tell you why they wanted to move, Annie?'

'No. And I can't imagine—we're much more central here.'

'And what were they like?'

She pursed her lips and considered. 'Executive types... Uptight.'

'Anything odd?'

'Not really... They had some very heavy suitcases.'

'Ah,' said Iain. 'Thanks... And, Annie, mum's the word!'

'Teach your grandmother!'

He stepped out into the sunlight, took a deep breath of summery air, and called Tom on his mobile. The move to the Providence, he pointed out, had taken place only two days before Tom's Exeter briefing, so Special Branch's failure to detect the switch could perhaps be excused. After some further discussion, Iain marched down to Emma Place. The hotel was near one end of a row of Georgian houses, and newly painted, with parking spaces reserved for guests on a garage site opposite, and he could see no obvious sign of Special Branch surveillance. So he walked in and asked at reception to see the manager. He was shown into a back office and produced his warrant card.

'Here's trouble!' muttered the manager.

'Oh, no!' said Iain. 'As little trouble as may be... You have three persons staying here, I believe, sur-names Gage, Gopel and Stone.'

The manager consulted his computer. 'Yes,' he said, 'we've got 'em.'

'How long for?'

'Last night the 29th.'

Iain nodded slowly. 'Right!' he said. 'Now... I'm not in a position to explain why we're interested, but it's particularly important, you understand, that you forget completely I was here and what I asked you. Say nothing to *anyone*. Understood? Not even your wife!'

'Not married.'

Iain sniffed. 'So much the easier for you,' he said.

The phone on the manager's desk rang, and he broke off with an apology to answer it. Then he looked up sharply at Iain.

'Yes, she is,' he murmured into it, 'can I give her a message?' The other voice said something and rang off.

The manager put the phone down and paused. 'Well!' he said. 'How's that for coincidence?'

'What?'

'Some man asking whether your Heather Stone was here.'

'What did he want?'

'Wouldn't leave a message... Said he was speaking from the Alfred.'

'From the *Alfred?*'

'Yes.'

Thinking quickly, Iain snapped: 'Dial 1471!'

'Front desk for that.'

This worked, to Iain's surprise. He called HQ on his mobile, and they traced the calling number—not to the Alfred but to a public telephone box in Union Street, two hundred yards away. Iain rushed out of the hotel, tore down Stonehouse Street, but slowed to a walk as the pair of call boxes on the far side of Union Street came into view.

Almost at once, a man emerged from one of the boxes, only twenty yards away, and looked towards Iain. He was heavy, clean-shaven, perhaps early forties, swarthy, with dark curly hair, and wearing a green walking jacket. Had he stayed on in the box to make another call? At this moment, a bus came eastwards along Union Street and stopped at the bus shelter, hiding him. Iain took the opportunity to run forward, but the bus drove off almost at once, and the man had disappeared.

But Iain had observed that the man wasn't wearing gloves. He hurried forward to guard the phone box, called in again on his mobile, and settled down to wait for Sgt Howe and the finger-print team.

Once they were on the scene he returned to the Alfred.

'No,' said Annie. 'I didn't tell any of my staff where they were going. And if they made friends with anyone here, I didn't see it. Like I told you, they were uptight.'

'Interesting!' said Tom, when Iain got back to the office. 'You and I think, don't we, that he wasn't anyone from the Alfred, and he can't have been a Special Branch watcher, who would have blocked 1471, would have worn gloves, and wouldn't have stayed hanging around in the box. So who could he have been? Must've felt very secure. Or perhaps he was in a hurry.'

'He didn't seem at all hurried,' said Iain.

'Howe says the dabs are excellent… And you say he looked middle-eastern?'

'For what it's worth, yes,' said Iain. He'd rather enjoyed the chase.

Acceleration

Two days earlier, on the 12th August, a man in his late twenties had been humming down the M4 towards Bristol in a small Peugeot he'd hired that day at Heathrow. His face was olive and his brown hair slightly receding; he wore slacks and a roll-necked dark nylon top. He had dumped onto the back seat a small holdall, a sleeping bag, and a new but already battered laptop. His motives were complex: amongst other things, his family had suffered and he wanted justice. Like his colleagues, he was experienced enough not to be nervous, but on this operation, as it was developing, he had a particular sense of elation, and had to discipline himself not to attract attention by speeding. His long hands caressed the steering wheel lightly.

*

At five Iain came and sat on Tom's desk.

'These Israelis,' he said, frowning. 'What are they here for?'

'Not to locate the terror cell,' said Tom, leaning back in his chair.

'Why?'

'If that was it, they'd have cooperated.'

Iain clasped his hands together and cracked his knuckles. 'To *attack* it, then?'

Tom narrowed his eyes. 'Mossad's not afraid of extra-territorial executions.'

'And they know we'd never go along with that?'

58

'Just so,' said Tom. He nodded and was silent for a while. 'But you know,' he said at last, 'if the guy you saw was a member of the cell, we now have a further intelligence question about the Israelis, rather more puzzling.'

Iain looked up, questioningly.

'He asked for Heather Stone by name, and he knew exactly where to look for her... If he *is* part of the cell, how come he was so well informed about Mossad?'

*

The following day Tom's secretarial assistant opened a neatly typed letter:

From Mrs W. Errol-Smyth

Dear Miss Baines,
I wrote last week, as requested, to let you know of the booking by Mr and Mrs Omah of my self-catering holiday home for 10th-31st August. On Saturday, I drove up to Elfordleigh to hand over the keys, and am writing again now to let you know my first impressions.
Both of them were very civil and friendly. They looked Pakistani or Middle Eastern, but were wearing good quality western-style clothes. Mr Omah told me he was a solicitor, and knows the Conservative candidate in Bradford East. He sounded educated, a little colonial perhaps. Mrs Omah said she grew up in Bradford, but she speaks well too, not northern at all. She told me they go to Wimbledon every year and are National Trust Life Members.
The are driving a VW camper van, and Mrs Eldon (next door) tells me they've been out in it to go hiking every day.
They seemed quite harmless to me, I must say, so hopefully we can all sleep soundly in our beds!
Yours truly,
Emma Errol-Smyth

When he read this Tom smiled, but paused for some time over Mrs Errol-Smyth's descriptions of the accents. He also recalled the match he'd noted earlier between the Omahs' departure date and the ending of the conference. He and Iain decided to investigate a little further.

When questioned by phone, Mrs Errol-Smyth and Mrs Eldon gave fuller descriptions of Mr Omah, which sounded not unlike the man in the phone box. So Iain went to look for himself, peering through binoculars from a nearby upstairs window.

It was indeed the same man.

Tom called Manfield, who confirmed at once that Mr Omah was not a security service agent. He seemed inclined to take Tom's report seriously, but insisted they should keep away from the Omahs until further instructed.

*

The next day Manfield called back. 'I'm to pass on appreciation of your good work,' he said gruffly.

Tom smiled. 'Nice to hear it,' he said. He pulled a pad towards himself and found a biro.

'The agreed strategy is not to arrest the Omahs. A team will be watching them.'

'OK.'

'Consequently, you and your colleagues are to remain well clear—understood?'

'Sure.'

'In the meantime, though, there's something else. We need to find out whether the Omahs have made any contacts in Plymouth.'

'Good point,' said Tom.

'GCHQ are checking the phone records and tapping the phones of the suspects listed by Sergeant Akinci.'

'What, all of them?'

'Yes… In addition, we'd like your team to set up a search of CCTV footage for any recent traces of the Omahs and their van in Plymouth public places. Done that sort of job before?'

'Yes… It'll take us some time.'

'Understood. But you have the local business contacts.'

'Sure,' said Tom.

Manfield grunted. 'Next, these Mossad agents.'

'Yes?'

Manfield sniffed. 'They're being tailed, and it's been decided you should be informed about progress.'

Tom opened his eyes wide at his desk but didn't reply.

'They've moved from the Alfred to the Providence Hotel, in Emma Place. On Thursday 15th, they all three drove to Oxford.'

Tom waited.

'In a dark blue Citroen… And separated there…' said Manfield. He gave a little cough. 'Unfortunately, the watchers then lost track of them.'

'*All* of them?' said Tom.

'Apparently.'

'Hm…' Tom hesitated. 'Blenheim Palace is near Oxford, isn't it?' he said.

'Exactly,' agreed Manfield tartly. 'And so is Brize Norton… We do know, though, that they drove back together to Plymouth the same evening.'

Tom scribbled.

'Then on the Friday,' went on Manfield, 'the woman caught the 3 pm ferry to Roscoff.'

'She took the *ferry*?'

'And returned by it, early on the Saturday morning.'

'Very odd… Anything else?'

'Apart from that, they've remained indoors, and MI5 have detected no communication with the outside world… We've got photos, you'll be receiving copies.'

*

Tom and Iain set up the CCTV search and talked through the new revelations.

Then Manfield called back with further news. On the 20th, he said, the surveillance team had spotted the Omahs setting off in the camper van and had tailed them. Mr Omah had dropped his wife off at Plymouth railway station, and one of the MI5 men had been left behind to follow her. She had bought no ticket at the time, so her exact destination was unclear, but she'd caught a London train. The agent followed at a distance, mounted the next-door carriage—and then was unable to locate her again.

'Pity,' remarked Tom.

Manfield let the comment pass. The other agent, he explained, had remained in his car and followed Mr Omah's VW up the M5. At Junction 18, however, he lost it: Mr Omah had turned off as if for the east-bound A4 into Bristol, but at the last moment switched lanes while screened by a removal van.

Tom and Iain were not impressed.

Next day, Manfield called yet again. Neither of the Omahs had returned to their let in Elfordleigh, nor to the correspondence address in Bradford. Local enquiries had shown that Mr Omah had rented a flat there from 3rd June for three months, but had lived in it only in June and early July, and then again for a few days in early August. At none of these times had any woman accompanied him, and he was certainly not a solicitor in practice locally. The camper van had been hired for a month from 6th August from Avis in Shipley.

*

On 19th August there was news that was rather more helpful: the CCTV search had paid off. The Omahs' VW camper van had been recorded in Plymouth on 13th August, arriving at the Sainsbury's car park under the A38 roundabout. The camera showed them returning to it from the store at 12.46, when they remained seated without driving away. At 1.02 pm a small Peugeot had arrived and parked nearby. Two men got out of it, walked over to the VW, got in, and were driven off. In the evening, at 7.37, the VW had reappeared; the same two men emerged, got into the Peugeot, and drove off, as did the VW. The registration number of the Peugeot was readable. Aliza discovered it had been hired at Heathrow on 12th August in the name of Ismail. But no-one of that name had arrived by air at the airport that day.

The CCTV pictures were image-enhanced, and the technicians prepared freeze-frame versions of the best of them. The team added their own annotations:

> A. Man who arrived as passenger in the Peugeot. Tall, mid-thirties, about 6′1″, wearing sunglasses, darkish complexion.
>
> B. The Peugeot driver, presumably the 'Mr Ismail' who hired it at Heathrow. Slim, twenties, about 5′8″, dark complexion.
>
> C. 'Mrs Omah'. Twenties, about 5′7″, dark complexion.

D. 'Mr Omah', the man in the phone box. Heavy broad-shouldered, early forties, about 5´10˝, curly black hair, clean shaven. Fingerprints on file.

*

Aliza's list of local suspects had now all been checked out by MI5, but to no useful effect. Dr Said, for example, was evidently exactly what he'd said he was, and there was no sign of contact with extremists since his student days. On Friday 23rd August, however, Aliza was surprised to receive a call from him.

'Sgt Akinci?'

'Speaking.'

'I have some information… information that I think you should hear.'

'Thank you.'

'Yesterday I was in Bristol, for a meeting.'

'Yes?'

'And I happened to see a man there.' Dr Said hesitated.

'A man…' Aliza prompted.

'In a restaurant… His father is a relative of mine, you see.' He hesitated again. '… I was extremely surprised to see him in Bristol, because I had heard quite recently that he was back in Cairo.'

Aliza waited.

'I believe, you see… that this man has links with Islamists. Or so I have heard, at least.'

'Ah… What is his name?'

'In normal times, I would not wish to be passing on the names of relatives to the police of a foreign country.'

Aliza made a sympathetic noise.

'But now… His name is al-Azmeh.'

Aliza felt herself smiling. 'And his first name?'

'Uthman… Uthman al-Azmeh.'

'Thank you very much, Dr Said.'

'I must beg you not to use this information lazily or carelessly.'

'We shall be extremely careful… How certain are you that it was Mr al-Azmeh?'

'Perfectly. I last saw him three years ago. And I used to know him really quite well, many years ago when he was a student… Fortunately, he did not catch my eye in the restaurant, and I left as unobtrusively as I could.'

'Was he alone?'

'He was lunching with a younger man. I fear I cannot remember the young man at all clearly. He might have been a Lebanese. He wore a dark sweater, with a rolled neck.'

'You didn't hear them speak?'

'They were too far away.'

'Exactly when was this, and which restaurant?'

He told her.

When Tom heard all this, he decided to visit Dr Said in his surgery. He found a broad-shouldered and ample man in his sixties, with a fleshy olive face, and dark eyes that were liquid, kind, and anxious. Shown the photos of the suspects, he immediately identified Mr Omah as the al-Azmeh he had seen in Bristol, and, with a slight hesitation, Suspect B as al-Azmeh's lunch partner. He did not ask Tom where he had obtained the photos, but his concern seemed to deepen. He was unable to identify Suspects A or C. Tom pressed him hard for more detail, but nothing further emerged, except that he himself was long-since widowed, with three daughters and two sons all living prosperously in Egypt.

Dr Said, it appeared, was on the side of the angels.

*

Later that day Aliza, reviewing her notes, was idly turning over the CCTV photos when the picture of Suspect B caught her attention. She took it to the window and spent some time studying it. Then she picked up her files, went to find Tom and laid the photo on his desk.

'What about it?' he said.

'I'm not *sure*,' she said, 'because of the sunglasses… but I think I know who that is.'

'You do? Who?'

'Kali,' she said, quietly.

'Kali?'

'My father's shipping clerk. The one who left.'

Tom looked down and thought for a while. 'But you're not sure?'

'Not completely.'

'Mm.'

'But, all along, I felt this one was ringing a bell.'

'Say again when he arrived in your father's firm, and when he departed.'

'He came on May 28th and left on July 16th.'

'And what exactly was his job?'

'Everything to do with the shipments. Planned deliveries, worked out the weights, made the ferry bookings, organised extra drivers and hired trucks if my father needed them.'

Tom nodded slowly. 'Did he leave suddenly?'

'No, he gave proper notice. He said he would prob-ably leave the UK, but wasn't sure where he would end up.'

'What else can you remember about him?'

'He said he'd grown up in Bradford. But his accent wasn't northern.'

'Educated?'

'I suppose.'

'And you noticed nothing odd about him?'

'No. He was friendly and good fun—I told you my mother thought him a suitable boy for me. *I* didn't…. And he wasn't interested anyway.'

Disaster

It was now 24th August and the conference was due to open in two days' time, so the Super called in Tom and Iain for a review. It had been agreed that the figures in the CCTV pictures must constitute the terror cell. But they had all disappeared: MI5 and the local police had tried and failed to find Mr Omah and suspect B with the VW van in Bristol, Mrs Omah had vanished in the general direction of London, and suspect A could be anywhere. Security in Plymouth generally had been stepped up. The Super cancelled all leave for the police and Tom and Iain camped out in the HQ control room.

On Monday 26th, however, Exeter called Tom to report that the delegates had flown in and the conference was under way. On Wednesday evening they called again to say that the Heads of State, too, had arrived safely. There remained the possibility of an attack during the remainder of the conference, or one on the Sunday when Bush, Sharon, and Arafat would all be flying out of Brize Norton. Or, of course, of some totally unconnected horror in Plymouth.

*

Jane's plans for the crossing to Roscoff in *Ariel* had matured: she intended to leave about 8 pm on Friday 30th and sail overnight. With luck, they would then be in Roscoff by about 2 pm the following day, when it would be high water and possible to get into the inner yacht harbour. At Friday lunchtime she went over the forecast with Tom. It was ideal: good visibility, and a steady easterly, force 4–5.

Hamish arrived at Crownhill with his kit at six. Miranda was relaxed and enjoying seeing him, but Hamish a little edgy—he hadn't met Jane before, and had been wondering how much sailing responsibility might fall be about to fall on him if she proved to be short of confidence. Tom drove the two of them down to the marina as soon as they'd eaten.

Shortly afterwards, Jane arrived, smiled calmly at Tom, and drove down the slipway to the pontoon gate to unload her final items of kit. They all helped carry everything down to *Ariel*. Tom left his best wishes for the trip, gave Jane an encouraging hug, and drove off hurriedly.

Time and daylight were slipping away.

'Throw all that in the cabin... Warm gear and oil-skins, please.'

Hamish looked quickly at Jane, decided he had no need to worry, and made a point of changing briskly. Miranda wasn't far behind.

'Safety harnesses on.' Jane started the Volvo, left it ticking over, and switched on the navigation lights: the pontoon to their left glowed red and the boat to their right green. 'Bow and stern lines, please.'

Miranda and Hamish brought in the mooring lines and coiled them.

'Stern spring to the end of the pontoon.' The engine was in reverse now, and *Ariel* was edging backwards out of her berth, pivoting to the right.

'Let go bow, slacken stern spring.' Jane eased the engine into forward gear. 'Let go stern.' *Ariel* moved forward. The water, oily black in the gloaming, showed mottled reflections from the street lamps below the Citadel.

'Take the wheel, Hamish… Swing her round to the left, then due south once we're into the channel.'

Hamish wasn't used to wheel steering, and *Ariel* was a good deal bigger than his syndicate's Westerly Storm. He looked anxiously around for other craft on the move, but there were none. He kept *Ariel* moving south, out into the left side of the main channel. The wind began to ruffle hair.

As they moved down the sound to the east end of the breakwater, Jane and Miranda hoisted the un-reefed mainsail and the big genoa. *Ariel* swayed strongly to the wind and her wake lengthened astern, and once she had settled to the course, Jane cut the engine. They passed the breakwater and moved out into the dark sea ahead.

Miranda jotted down the latest forecast from the VHF, and Jane modified her sketch weather chart. 'Not so good,' she said. 'That easterly we were relying on, it's easing and going round to the south. That'll slow us down a lot…' She found and studied the tidal stream atlas at the cabin table, and Miranda watched over her shoulder.

'Running east at around one knot.' Jane plotted the tidal offset on the chart, stuck her head into the open air to look around for the lighthouse, and then came down again to mark up the course. 'Will you tell Hamish to keep her close-hauled for the moment? See how near that will take us to the Eddystone.'

Miranda clambered up to deliver the message and things on deck quietened down.

At last, as they were approaching the lighthouse, Jane climbed back on deck and looked around again. 'Miranda, can you make us all some cocoa and ham rolls?' she said. 'Then you'd better get some sleep. Hamish can steer till about one, and I'll potter around till we're through the coastal shipping. Then you can get up and steer for a bit.'

They ate the rolls and felt the hot cocoa warming them from inside. In the fore cabin, Miranda kicked off her sea boots and wriggled into her sleeping bag, with most of the rest of her clothes on. She was soon asleep.

*

During the night, as predicted, the wind went round to the south and fell light, and they were forced to begin a series of long tacks against a choppy head sea. Jane soon decided there was no hope of getting into the inner harbour at Roscoff on the 2 pm high tide and as Hamish watched she studied the pilot book and kept recalculating her tidal corrections. Spirits wilted, and Miranda felt queasy when she came on deck to relieve Hamish at 1 am

Eventually it grew light and the sun warmed their faces. About mid-morning the wind began to swing round to the west and to strengthen. Gradually, clouds rolled up and they plunged into a band of rain. When they emerged, however, the wind was warm and westerly, Force 4 and still increasing, and they began to make a brisker pace southward. Hamish opened tins of Irish stew for a hot lunch. They had seen no other boats for some hours.

*

Just after 2 pm on the Saturday, A was in Plymouth, parked in the big motorhome a little way down the hill from

Emma Place, and smoking. His mobile phone rang; he took the call and listened. He stubbed out the Gauloise.

He started his engine, drove forward, and turned left. Looking carefully in his mirror, he saw a blue Citroen towing a small pale-blue caravan coming down the hill behind him. He smiled, and dawdled as if uncertain of his way. By the time he reached the mini-roundabout at the turning for the ferry terminal, the Citroen had caught him up.

He turned slowly right and entered the terminal queuing space. An official directed him to enter the right-hand queue. A minute later, the Citroen, which had been given the same instruction, drew up behind him. As it approached, he could see in his wing mirror that its driver was a man, with a woman in the passenger seat. He remained seated, and unfolded a copy of the Times so that his face could be seen neither in the mirror nor from the road.

*

By six *Ariel* was ten miles from Roscoff, and the wind was going round to the north-west, driving them along. The seas had become quite steep, but Hamish and Jane were enjoying the sail. She had decided they would have to anchor south of the ferry terminal at Bloscon, half a mile or so east of Roscoff proper, and radioed the harbour master there to get permission. She also raised Plougasnou Coast Radio and put through a call to Laurel's home phone. Hamish, who was steering, watched as she climbed back on deck.

'How have you been keeping?' he asked. He felt slightly man-of-the-worldish and also a little curious.

Jane paused for a moment. 'A lot better,' she said. 'Tom keeps me cheerful, and this boat does me good. And you?' she asked with a smile. 'How's your fisheries research working out?'

'I love the work,' he said. 'And I like the people I'm working with.'

'And how d'you think Miranda's enjoying teaching?'

'She really loves it. Driving herself getting all those lesson plans spot-on.'

'Pity you're so far apart.'

'But this looks like being a good weekend.'

Jane glanced down at the binnacle. 'What course are you averaging now, do you think?'

Hamish concentrated for a few moments. 'About one-seven-five.'

She went down to write in the log and adjust the chart, and returned. After a while she asked, 'And how do you think Tom is?'

'Tired... Miranda reckons there's something going on about terrorists.'

'But it's not just tiredness—it bothers me. I don't think I've ever seen him so stressed... Whatever can they be so afraid of?'

*

About 7 o'clock, as it was getting dark, B and D had driven the VW camper van up the lane to Haw Wood, near Avonmouth. They parked it facing downhill, and trudged quietly into the wood, each carrying a large and heavy package. They halted just over the skyline where they could see westward down to the Bristol Channel, and hear the traffic roaring in the M5 cutting below them. At 7.15, D's mobile rang and he took a brief call. B and D then separated by twenty yards. At 7.26, the phone rang again. D listened carefully and signalled to B. Two minutes later there was a roar from the east, and after a few moments a big jet flew low over their heads, climbing huge into the night sky, the strobe light on its tail flashing steadily, up into the western dusk clouds touched with pink at their top edges.

Shortly afterwards, two scarlet threads climbed lazily up from the wood, and then accelerated, chasing, chasing the strobe light as it winked ahead of them. The threads closed with the strobe, and for a moment there was nothing to be seen but the steady flashes and the bat-like spread of the wings. Then a great orange flower blossomed, and another, bursting up into the night, and the dusk clouds were for four or five seconds brilliantly lit from below. Almost at once, the left wing parted from the fuselage and began to spiral down into the sea, a huge, slow, flaming sycamore seed. The fuselage and right wing, free of flame and dark against the western sky, continued forward for a moment, then curved downwards. Down and down they plummeted, but it was too dark to tell when they struck the surface of the sea. Finally the spiralling left wing crashed into the water, and a fiery sheet of kerosene shot outwards, some three miles from the shore, and continued to flicker on the sea surface.

*

By 8 o'clock, after some anxious business over anchoring, *Ariel* was safely settled in Bloscon, and her crew were wondering how to get ashore. Hamish had managed to find the Radio 1 news bulletin. At the end, the announcer said:

'News has just come in that at 7.30 this evening a large aircraft taking off from the British Aerospace airfield at Filton, caught fire and crashed into the Bristol Channel. We'll bring you any further information as soon as we have it.'

'God!' said Hamish. 'Terrorists?'

'Thank heaven it wasn't Plymouth,' said Miranda

doubtfully.

Jane bit her lower lip. 'Don't switch it off,' she said.

But though the news flash was repeated twice, no further information was added. It became darker. The wind had risen to Force 6, but they were well protected and not rolling too badly.

About 9.45 they first saw the lights of the evening ferry coming in from Plymouth. As it got nearer they realised by how much it dwarfed the harbour, rows of bright windows and portholes, a tower block in gliding motion. It slowed, and made a broad turn, swinging majestically away from them. At last it stopped and began to reverse towards the jetty, where minuscule figures awaited it, silhouetted by the harbour lights.

But then, as they watched, its gentle glide was interrupted by an uncanny jerk and shiver. Almost at once a great scarlet flame burst out of the hull, and their ears were shattered by a detonation, a sharp and painful assault on the eardrums, followed by a roar that seemed to go on and on. They were jerked forward and at once pushed back by a great pulse in the air. A huge cloud of smoke shot out and up. Immediately, the ferry began to squat down into the water and cant towards them. As it sank, its keel grated onto the rocks below, and, with its reverse momentum, it very slowly rolled over, like a great whale. It took about two minutes to reach this state. On its now visible deck there were people, hundreds of people, sliding towards the water in heaps.

Jane had leaped up. Miranda looked questioningly at her: there were a mere half dozen yachts in the anchorage, *Ariel* the only one showing lights—faint cries were already reaching them on the wind. There were no boats near the ferry in a position to help. At first Jane's face remained completely rigid, her eyes on the doomed ferry; but then, after what felt an eternity, she made a sharp movement of one hand, and turned. 'Anchor winch,' she rapped out. She shook the hair out of her eyes, bent down and started the Volvo; the engine roared into life.

Hamish and Miranda rushed forward, but it seemed to take for ever to get the winch set up, and for ever again to get the anchor off the bottom. As soon as it was free of the ground, Jane had the engine at full throttle, oblivious to the danger of snagging, and their breaths were coming in gasps before they had the anchor up to the bows. 'Don't try to bring it in,' shouted Jane. 'Make sure the pawl is holding the chain.' *Ariel* surged towards the ferry, leaving them a few minutes to get their breath, and to think what they would have to do.

However, when they had covered about half the distance to the ferry, Jane suddenly closed her eyes for four or five seconds. Then she glanced distractedly at Miranda and sank down onto the cockpit seat, one hand still on the wheel but the other covering her forehead.

'*Jane!*' shouted Miranda.

Jane bent down. Then she raised her face to look again at the ferry. She slowly shook her head. 'I'm sorry,' she said at last, raising her voice to be heard over the engine noise. 'I'm not going to be able to handle this…'

At first Miranda simply stared. 'Are you ill?' she shouted at last.

Jane seemed almost annoyed. 'No.' she yelled. 'Not ill… Just forget about me. *You two* will have to cope between you, that's all. Take the wheel, Hamish.'

Hamish moved back to do so and Jane got to her

feet, turned and climbed quickly down into the cabin.

Hamish stared after her. 'Bloody hell!' he said quietly, and looked around.

'Is it OK? Can we?' asked Miranda.

'I don't know,' said Hamish.

The rocks were preventing the ferry from sinking deeper, but there were scores of limp bodies at the water's edge, hundreds of white faces at the inky margin. As they drew nearer, an increasing babble of angry, desperate shouting reached them, punctuated from time to time by screams. The lifeboats on the side facing them had been crushed as the ferry rolled over, all but one that had broken away from its cradle and was afloat, held by the falls from one of its davits.

'What are we going to do?' asked Miranda.

'Go alongside, I suppose... Starboard side to...'

'God... Are you sure?'

'Yes...' He was watching the echo-sounder. 'But we need to get the rail unshipped.'

'You do that, I'll take the wheel.'

Hamish slashed at the wet lashings holding the rail to the stanchions with his pocket knife. As soon as the wire and spray-dodger were rolled out of the way he gave Miranda a thumbs up, and ran to prepare the bow and stern lines. He then returned to the wheel, throttled back and brought *Ariel* gently alongside one of the crushed lifeboats and threw the engine out of gear in case there were people in the water near the screw. *Ariel* came to rest. Miranda made fast the bow to the lifeboat and Hamish secured the stern. The sea of faces confronting them was by now for the most part silenced and stoical, but a few were still bellowing and there was a stench of burnt flesh.

Other hands had already managed to haul from the water two half-drowned elderly couples, and Hamish and Miranda hoisted them moaning aboard. 'Casualties on deck?' suggested Miranda, and the couples were disposed around the fore hatch.

'Most serious next,' Hamish shouted so that everyone could hear. Flames were gushing from the exploded section of the ferry, and three flash burn cases were pushed forward, one a screaming teenage girl who had lost half of her long blond hair. They were arranged on the side decks, and Miranda scrambled below to find dressings. She found Jane sitting upright at the chart table, her eyes closed.

'I'm sorry,' Miranda said, 'but we need the first aid box.'

Jane looked up.

'Burns,' said Miranda. 'They smell disgusting.' She leant past Jane to get at the box on the shelf behind.

'Third degree,' Jane muttered, as if to herself.

Miranda made a face.

Jane was still frowning. 'Know how to treat them?'

'No.'

Jane closed her eyes again and swallowed. She took a deep breath, then opened her eyes and held out her hand for the box.

Miranda hesitated.

'Give it me.'

'Will you be OK?'

'Yes.'

Miranda handed over the box and climbed back on deck; Jane followed and silently began work on the screaming girl's roasted and bloody scalp.

Hamish was trying to work out who should be taken next and had provisionally selected two elderly people apparently with leg fractures, when there was an interruption: a compact group of three able-bodied men and an athletic-looking woman appeared suddenly from behind the lifeboat and looked down at them all. The woman gave a signal, and all four jumped down onto *Ariel's* deck.

'*No!*' yelled Hamish.

But the woman pushed past Jane and jumped down into *Ariel's* well. The three men followed, and climbed rapidly down the companion way into the main cabin. The fore cabin door slammed.

Jane stood up. The woman turned to her and yelled: '*Now,* you take us to the shore.'

Jane stared at her.

'*Immediately!*' insisted the woman. She pulled something from inside her coat and jabbed it at Jane. '*Take us!*'

It was a compact sub-machine gun.

'*Like hell we will!*' yelled Jane back at her. 'I'm a doctor. My job is here.'

The woman glared. Then she looked hastily around, seemed to think better of her demand, and moved to join her companions in the cabin.

Jane glared back silently, shrugged, and continued with her work.

Hamish and Miranda settled the elderly fractures as gently as they could onto the cabin top. 'Now the youngest kids,' yelled Hamish. Several white-faced youngsters were pushed forward and guided down into the cabin, plus a mother clutching an infant. After another fifteen minutes *Ariel* had twenty-three casualties on board and could take no more. Hamish put her engine back in gear and took the wheel as Jane and Miranda continued their work on the burns, and they all rolled over the waves to the ferry jetty.

By now there were blue lights flashing on the road. An inshore lifeboat had arrived beside the ferry, with a cluster of yachts. The ferry crew had begun to manoeuvre the one detached lifeboat and to launch life rafts. They had deployed a scramble net, which was now covered with human ants working their way down towards the sea. Hamish brought *Ariel* alongside the jetty.

As he did so, the athletic woman reappeared on deck, stepped briskly over the casualties on the side-deck, sprang ashore and ran up the ramp towards the queue of cars that had been waiting to board the stricken ferry. *Ariel*'s crew paid her no attention, and many hands helped the injured ashore. It was half an hour before the last stretcher was lifted away into the night. Miranda looked around: there were now several lifeboats by the ferry, a fleet of ambulances and paramedics. They could do no more.

Jane climbed awkwardly down into the well and slumped onto the seat; she covered her face with her hands. Miranda sat alongside and put one arm round Jane's shoulders. Then she looked at Hamish, and nodded towards the cabin.

Hamish frowned, and took a deep breath. He got to his feet, opened the hatch and climbed down.

Two of the invaders were still in the main cabin, perched alertly on the settee berths, both holding guns like the woman's.

Hamish looked at the weapons, and then at the men.

With his spare hand one of them was warning him to come no nearer. Hamish's exhausted brain was racing. He examined the man's face.

'We understand you will be angry,' the man remarked quietly. 'But you must wait.'

Hamish looked towards the fore cabin.

The man shook his head slowly and expressively.

Hamish decided it was wiser to retreat. 'I can go back on deck?' he suggested.

The man looked enquiringly at his companion, who nodded.

Hamish climbed back into the well. 'Not good,' he reported. 'They've got guns too. They say we must wait.'

So the three of them, exhausted, stayed put. After a few minutes, the woman reappeared on the quayside accompanied by two further men, her gun again at the ready, and without a word jumped aboard and climbed down into the cabin, leaving her companions on the quay. After waiting a short time, Hamish decided to follow her. She peered round at him, held up her hand and continued speaking quietly to the two men in a slightly guttural language that he could not place, though it seemed oddly familiar. At last she turned to face him. 'We are sorry for this intrusion,' she said. 'You will understand in a minute why we have been obliged to behave in this way. It is now safe for us to leave.'

She nodded, and one of the men opened the door of the fore cabin. A third man emerged: in his seventies but stocky and vigorous, wearing an open-necked checked shirt. He seemed angry, alert, and then a little shamefaced. He shook Hamish's hand warmly, though without saying a word.

It was Ariel Sharon.

The four Israelis climbed on deck and stepped ashore, joining their newly arrived colleagues to form a tight body with Sharon at its centre. They strode up the ramp, Uzis at the ready, and disappeared into the night.

Reaction

Tom first learned about the plane downed in the Bristol Channel on the control room TV, which was tuned to a news channel. Then at 8.20 pm a heavily capitalised fax buzzed off the printer. He snatched it up: the threat status had been raised to critical. He rang Exeter, but Manfield was extremely tight-lipped. He referred in very vague terms to the aircraft, but said there was nothing to link it with Plymouth. Tom called Iain in and they continued to watch the news, without, surprisingly, learning any more about what plane it was, though there was much speculation about a possible terrorist attack.

Then at 10.30 the Brittany Ferries manager rang to report there'd been a massive explosion on his 3 pm sailing as it arrived in Roscoff, with many dead. Tom's mind leaped at once to *Ariel* and her crew. But first he called Exeter a second time; the news had reached them already, however.

He quickly tried Jane's mobile, but got no reply and left a message. He had no more luck with the other two. Half an hour later he tried again, unsuccessfully; but about midnight Miranda reached him from Laurel's apartment in St. Pol.

'How near were you?' he demanded at once.

'Right in the thick of it, Dad! … But we're all OK.'

'Thank God for that! What happened?'

Miranda described the explosion, and how they'd

moved *Ariel* to the stricken ferry and taken what casualties they could on board.

'How did Jane cope with all that?' he interrupted.

'Dad, there's something I need to tell you first.'

'What?'

She described how the Israelis, and Sharon, had invaded *Ariel*'s cabin.

'*Sharon?* My God,' said Tom, and paused for so long that Miranda asked him whether he was still on the line.

'All right,' he said at last, 'And Jane?'

'She was OK. But she had a bad moment.'

'What sort of bad moment?'

'It *was* pretty traumatic, you know. For all of us.'

'OK, but what happened?'

'Well, straight after the explosion she was getting us all going. But then suddenly, she sort of froze, and I was afraid she was going to crash out completely. But when the wounded started coming on board she got it together and started treating them.'

'Mm… How is she now?'

'Quite bad.

'Would she come to the phone, d'you think?'

'I'm not sure that's a good idea, Dad,'

'Try her.'

'Mm… All right. Hold on.' There was a very considerable pause. At last Miranda's voice came again. 'She says she's not up for it.'

'You're can't persuade her?'

'I did try. But she just said, no talking, tell him I'm sorry.'

'Oh,' said Tom again, and screwed his face up. There was another very long pause. 'Have you told the French police?' he asked at last, with a sigh.

'About Sharon? Not yet. The gendarmes just took

83

our details and told us to come back tomorrow.'

'I think it might be better if you said nothing till the morning… From what you said, the blast was low down on the starboard side, near the stern. On the vehicle deck?'

'I think so.'

'I guess they had Sharon hidden in a truck or something—and that he insisted on getting some fresh air. If he'd remained where he was, I don't suppose he'd have survived.'

'It looked like the Israelis were on the top forward deck when the bomb went off,' said Miranda. 'Or in the observation lounge behind it. If they'd been anywhere else, they couldn't have reached that lifeboat housing in the time they had.'

'Good places for keeping his face concealed in the dark,' said Tom. 'I don't suppose you saw anyone else behaving suspiciously? Bombers trying to get ashore unobserved?'

'Well, no. It was just chaos everywhere.'

'I didn't imagine you would. You said it was two men and one woman with Sharon?'

'Yes… There were two more Israelis they met when they landed.'

'That fits. Did they comment at all on what happened?'

'No,' said Miranda. 'They said almost nothing. They were calm, but determined and very tense. Sharon himself shook Hamish's hand, but the others were just intent on getting him away safely.'

'Nothing else you can think of?'

'No…'

'Mm… And how are you and Hamish now?'

Miranda took a moment to reply. 'Well,' she said. 'Pretty shattered… I've thrown up a couple of times, and Hamish has gone totally silent… But we did OK while it was happening.'

'Sounds like you did a good job. Must have been tough.'

'But we were thinking, Dad,' she said after a moment. 'This is a strange sort of terrorism, isn't it?'

'How d'you mean?'

'Blowing up a ferry that'll sink quickly and drown a lot of people, that's like 9/11. But the target doesn't seem global and symbolic enough for al-Qaida, and why do it in shallow water? On the other hand, if Sharon was the target, it looks more like angry Palestinians. Who are these people, and what were they trying to do?'

'Good question,' said Tom. He paused. 'Truth is,' he said at last, 'we were expecting something bad, as you may have guessed… It's going to be chaos from here on in, I'm going to have to ring off… Just tell me again: you're all OK?'

'Basically, yes.'

'Including Jane?'

'I'm sure she'll be all right by tomorrow.'

'Let's hope so… Lots of love, to all three. Tell the others.'

*

Iain had been listening. 'The Israeli Prime Minister was on that ferry?' he said.

'Yes.'

'Good grief, man! But he escaped?'

'That's right.'

'What the hell was he doing there? He was supposed to be flying out from Brize Norton tomorrow… today, that is.'

'Who knows?' said Tom, and turned to ring Manfield, who showed distinct signs of panic when he heard about Sharon.

Iain called in Aliza and Sgt Howe, who rushed into the office about 12.30 am. Aliza had discovered that one of her father's shipments of lambs had been on the ferry.

About 1.30 Manfield called back.

'Contact for you,' he said.

It was John Smith. He first asked Tom to describe in detail what he knew of the Sharon episode. Then he said, 'Can you get yourself over there?'

'To Roscoff? I suppose so... Why?'

'To investigate. Chaos here, resources over-stretched.'

'What chaos? D'you mean the plane down in the Bristol Channel?'

'You don't know?'

'Know what?'

'You haven't been told what it was?'

'No.'

'It was Air Force One.'

'*What*? ... Christ!'

'The president wasn't on board, however. But it was brought down by a pair of shoulder-launched missiles, fired from UK soil.'

'Jesus!' said Tom.

'The Americans have lost their president's plane and its twelve crew. So, as you might guess, we have the CIA round our ears like a ton of hot bricks.'

'I bet,' said Tom. 'Right... I'll get myself over to Brittany.'

'But listen! We think Sharon was travelling in a small pale-blue caravan towed by a blue Citroen.'

'OK, thanks… Any other details?'

'Later,' said John Smith. 'Absolutely right, you need to know. But there's a heck of a lot of ground to cover.'

*

Tom reached Roscoff late on Sunday afternoon, expecting to have to spend time in encouraging and reviving *Ariel*'s skipper and crew. But he soon discovered they were no longer in Bloscon, and when he called Laurel's apartment, she told him *Ariel* had departed.

'*Departed*? For England, you mean?'

'Yes, Tom.'

'But weren't they exhausted?'

'Certainly… It was not wise to go so soon.'

'Did you tell Jane that?'

'Yes.'

'What did she say?'

'That she would sleep during the crossing.'

'You mean Hamish and Miranda were going to do the sailing between them?'

'Yes.'

'Weren't they exhausted too?'

'Hamish needed to be back for a conference.'

Tom thanked her, rang off and decided to put through a marine link call to *Ariel*. But when the Plougasnou operator tried to make the connection, either *Ariel*'s VHF set was switched off or no-one was keeping listening watch.

With that Tom had to make do. Disturbed, he went to find and liaise with the French police, who, as previously arranged, were happy to have a native English speaker question the ferry crew in a preliminary way.

The survivors were housed in a hostel attached to the ferry terminal. The Captain told Tom that the number of dead was about sixty, mainly passengers who had moved down to the vehicle deck in preparation for arrival. Some had been blown apart by the explosion; others had drowned in their vehicles. A number, mostly elderly, had reached the open air, but drowned through slithering down the steeply sloping decks into the sea. It was very lucky that the ship had been in such shallow water. The explosion had blown out the bottom of the hull, and it was not surprising that she had lost stability and turned over so quickly. Most of the engine room crew and part of the vehicle deck crew were dead.

The Second Mate was in the hostel cafeteria; he asked Tom if it was OK to smoke and lit up at once. He had been in charge of vehicle marshalling and had survived because he'd gone up to the bridge ready to oversee the unloading, which he did through CCTV cameras. Tom asked him how the vehicles had been arranged, and whether he could tell which one had carried the bomb.

'We load through the bow ramp in Plymouth, so they were facing the stern, ready to unload.' He flicked a little ash from his dark trousers. 'We got inside the overturned hull this morning. There's a staggering great hole in it: I reckon the bomb must have been in one of the two left-hand rows.'

'Left-hand from the driver's point of view? Facing the stern?'

'Yes. Three or four vehicles back from the stern doors. You can't tell for sure now. The front vehicles were blown all over the place, and everything slid sideways when she turned over.'

'Can you *remember* what was there?'

'Lorries in the left-hand row. Vans and caravans next to them. Buses in the middle, and cars to the right. One lorry none of us will forget: cattle truck with a trailer towards the front. Carrying lambs.' His hand was shaking, though almost imperceptibly. 'Must have been near the bomb—bits of those lambs went everywhere.'

'Akinci Halal Ltd?'

'Could be. Regulars, they are.'

'Could the bomb have been on that trailer?'

'Possibly. Its bodywork went completely.'

'Mm… We think the target was in a blue caravan.'

'*Target*?'

'Yes. They were after one man in particular.'

'Bloody hell! What man?'

'Can't tell you that… If you were a terrorist, how sure could you be of parking your bomb close to such a thing?'

'Near a caravan? Not easy at all if you're in an ordinary car, we spread them out as we load. So you're sure to be separated from the caravans by at least one row, probably more. Easier for a lorry or bus, because we load 'em in lines next to the vans. But easiest by far for cars towing caravans or trailers, or mobile homes, because we load 'em in a line, and you'd just need to get yourself into the queue immediately behind your target. Or immediately ahead.'

'It was probably a smallish pale blue van towed by a blue Citroen. Recall anything of that sort? Near the explosion?'

The Second Mate frowned. 'There *was* something to the right of the cattle truck.'

'Notice the people in it?'

'Saw a group leaving that caravan long after loading. I noticed, because they came from the van door, not the car, and because they were so late. Passengers should have been up from the vehicle deck long before. Couldn't see what they looked like.'

'That figures: late decision by the target not to stay cooped up. Let's suppose that was them. To their left was the truck with the lambs. What was in front, behind and to the right?'

'To the right would be one of the coaches. Can't remember which. In front, can't remember, except it was quite big. A motorhome, I suppose. Behind, a white van with a trailer. Toby Shailer & Sons. French vegetables for the Plymouth market. I know the driver by sight.'

'And he's not a Saudi or anything?'

'No, no. Regular son of Devon.'

'We'll need to trace all the vehicle bookings, and the passengers too. Names and addresses from your Plymouth office?'

'That's right. We get just the registration numbers, not the names.'

'You don't remember any other passengers from vehicles near the explosion?'

'Sorry, no. Too many people moving about at loading to remember.'

Tom paused. 'And you lost some of your vehicle deck crew?'

'Three.' Long drag on the cigarette, and the tiny oscillation of the Mate's hand eased for a moment. 'We had to fit together the bits of two of them. For the body bags… You going to get the guys who did this?'

'We certainly are,' said Tom. He always did say that.

'Good.' Long exhalation.

*

Hamish and Miranda made Plymouth station with ten minutes to spare. It was still raining, as it had been during most of their crossing. They slumped onto a seat and watched the puddles growing on the edge of the platform. 'We finally made it,' Hamish said with relief and some pleasure. 'But I'm *completely* knackered… How about you?'

Miranda merely nodded. A mustiness left over from the steam age mingled with smells of wet earth and diesel.

After a while Hamish turned to look at her and remarked: 'Jane lost it completely on the way home, didn't she?'

'Yes.'

'You've never told me what's behind it all.'

Miranda didn't reply.

'What happened when she first met your dad? D'you know?'

'Some of it.'

'And?'

'Look… It's *her* story. I only know by accident.'

'I thought we didn't have secrets from each other.'

'Not our own. This one's hers.'

'But I need to understand.'

A crow was pecking at a chocolate wrapper stuck under one of the rails. The wind rolled an empty polystyrene mug along the platform. Miranda pondered.

'I'll tell you the bare bones,' she said suddenly. 'That's fair… something happened during a transatlantic single-handed race.'

'When?'

'Two years ago. A man got onto *Ariel* and attacked her…'

'What man?'

'A terrible man, a psychopath.'

'And?'

'She shot him.'

'*Shot* him? What with?'

'A rifle. Shot him dead.'

Hamish's head jerked round. 'Did they take her to court?'

'No.'

'Why not?'

'She claimed self-defence. The CPS decided there was no case to answer.'

'Bloody hell, Miranda! It's not real.'

'It doesn't feel real to me, either.'

'Mm... But I don't understand. Why does she still have problems now?'

'Don't be stupid.'

Hamish frowned.

'How quickly would *you* expect to get over something like that?'

'Well, yes... But two years ago...'

'It doesn't feel surprising to *me*... And it's been affecting her professionally.'

'Professionally?'

'Yes... Shooting the man seems to have stuck her with some crazy idea that she's *wicked*, some sort of universal bringer of death. She's even got scared she might be a sort of Harold Shipman...'

'*Harold Shipman*?'

'Yes. If a patient dies, or even just gets ill, she's scared that *she* must have brought it on... She gets to feel guilty. Even though she knows she's done everything right.'

'Hm... Does she see a shrink? She's a medic, must have the right contacts.'

'I'm not sure. I think she tried, and it didn't work...
She even lived in a religious community for a few
weeks.'

'Really? I wouldn't have thought she was religious.'

'She isn't. It was through some contact she had.'

'Ah...'

A long and distant squeaking, of trucks being shunt-
ed. More rain in spatters, not so very heavy, but
swirled by the gusty wind. Another crow arriving; a
crow-squabble.

'But how did she get mixed up with your dad?'
asked Hamish at last.

'He was involved in her case.'

'In America?'

'That's right.'

Hamish's train was announced.

'He went to the US to investigate it?'

'Yes. And, somehow, they came back together on
Ariel.'

'Hm! And got to like each other?'

'Yes.'

Hamish nodded. 'Seems to me she's a very good
thing.'

'Me too.'

'And they've been close ever since?'

'*Most* of the time, very much so. He's helped her a
lot.'

'Over all the legal stuff?'

'And other things... But it's odd—quite often, she
seems to be trying to keep space between them.'

'Hm... Do they sleep together?'

Miranda made a face. 'I wouldn't know, would I?
But my guess is not.'

Hamish considered. 'She's quite a lot younger.'

'Yes, she is, and I think it bothers Dad a lot. But it

93

doesn't bother *me*... He needs someone.'

Hamish nodded. 'Yes,' he said firmly. 'I'm sure you're right... Here it comes.'

The roar of the approaching train grew louder. At last the carriages squealed to a stop in front of them; they scrambled to their feet and stepped forward. Miranda felt suddenly pleased with Hamish, and he got a lengthy and rather enveloping farewell embrace.

Disclosure

On Monday morning the news about Air Force One was finally made public. Then came the Downing Street press conference, and an announcement that the Prime Minister would address the nation at 10 pm. By mid-morning the media had invaded Plymouth. Teams of investigative reporters saturated the city, turning over the police and security organisation, the ferry crews, the hotels, the whole of the local Muslim community and the general public. Staff leaving police headquarters to interview a witness had first to think how to keep the cameras away, and when Tom returned exhausted from Brittany at noon, he was grabbed to brief the press officer.

At three, he was at last brought properly up to date by John Smith. He went immediately to Iain's office.

'You OK?' Iain asked.

Tom slumped into an office chair. 'Bloody security services!'

'What?'

'*Now* they tell us! … You can take notes.'

Iain pulled a pad towards himself.

'First what you're supposed to keep to yourself… How's this for starters? According to this John Smith, in mid-March the CIA was questioning a young Pashtun, personal servant to some war-lord in the east of Afghanistan. And the lad heard a visiting Saudi negotiating with his boss to buy Stingers.'

'Anti-aircraft missiles?'

'Shoulder-launched—the Americans used to hand them out to the Mujahadin when the Russians were there. The Saudi was probably al-Qaida, and didn't realise the boy knew Arabic.'

'And the boss didn't bother to warn him?'

'Apparently not… Two Stingers changed hands, at a pretty exorbitant price. And they were needed *for the end of August.*'

Iain's eyebrows shot up.

'Naturally, this threw the conference security into panic mode. At first, they were going to cancel the whole thing. Or they were going to bring everyone in by sea… But then in mid-April GCHQ deciphered some encrypted e-mails between a cyber-café in Islamabad and a public workstation facility in Cairo University. The messages weren't explicit, but Cairo seemed to be saying that he'd recruited a team of four for, quote, "BN". Islamabad had evidently forgotten what "BN" meant, so Cairo respectfully typed "air-base" to remind him.'

'Oh man,' murmured Iain.

'Exactly. The *date* of the conference would've been known to al-Qaida all along. But the location and travel arrangements should *not* have been known: the Palestinians hadn't been given those details, and "BN" seemed too close to "Brize Norton" for comfort. For various reasons, GCHQ and the CIA believed the leak must have come from Israel, and confidence in the Israelis dropped to rock bottom…'

'But they went ahead nevertheless?'

'In the end, because it seemed al-Qaida was planning something definitely at Brize Norton, they hatched a new plan. The delegates would be flown in to RAF Benson instead. It's a helicopter station, but it's got an adequate runway. No-one was to know this in advance apart from the Station Commander, and the planes would be diverted from Brize Norton only in the last half hour of their flights. Helicopters would patrol the countryside around Brize Norton in the hope of catching the terrorists...'

'When did they decide all this?'

'Late May.'

'Long before we knew anything!'

'Of course... If nothing happened on arrival, the heads of state would shorten their private discussion and would be flown out a day early, on the Saturday. And not from Brize Norton or Benson, but from the British Aerospace airfield at Filton near Bristol. This was chosen as a place that the terrorists were unlikely to guess, and only one senior manager at Filton was told and agreed the plan in advance. Within the UK security apparatus, only four senior people knew the details. After hot debate in London and Washington, the Israelis were given them, too, but told to limit their circulation.'

'But in the event, the terrorists were ready and waiting near Filton?'

'I'm coming to that... In late July, as we know, GCHQ picked up the satellite call which referred to the "Plymouth plan" and didn't know what to make of it. Al-Qaida likes spectaculars, and the first thought was that this was something separate, timed to coincide with the conference attack. On the other hand, it might have been an ancillary part of the conference plan—perhaps the conference attack cell was to be based in Plymouth. MI5 originally decided that you and I should be told about the threat to Plymouth, but *nothing* about the conference plans, for fear of something getting back to the cell through us. Then I asked for fuller briefing, and they *did* tell me something about the conference—but they gave me the original, not the revised travel plans, understandably I suppose.

'Back in mid-May, however, when they heard about the Stingers and the "BN" call, Mossad had been convinced the security leak had been a *British* one, and under these circumstances they weren't happy to leave Sharon's security to the UK authorities. So they cooked up a private arrangement that, at the last minute, a Mossad team would collect Sharon from Blenheim to take him home.'

'The three in the Providence Hotel?' said Iain.

'Just so. Their plan was to choose an unlikely route: in a specially prepared caravan to Plymouth, by ferry to Brittany, then in a car with bullet-proof glass to Paris, and home by El Al jet with extra armed guards. Although this plan was laid in mid-May, it was only revealed to British security on the last day of the conference, and reluctantly accepted.'

'So although the Israelis had this ferry plan in mind from mid-May, our lot didn't know about it until the last day of the conference?'

'Exactly. The Americans were told at the same time. It was decided not to tell the French at all. So, when I called them on Saturday morning, Exeter knew already that Sharon had been on that ferry. They were just thankful to know he'd survived—they hadn't had any news from the Israelis.'

'But that means…'

Tom nodded wearily. 'Somewhat similarly, about three weeks ago the Americans concluded that flying Bush out by jet from any British airfield was too risky. So they proposed flying him in their own armoured helicopter direct from Blenheim Palace to a US war-ship in the Bristol Channel, which is what they did—so he's safe, too. However, the arrangements for flying Air Force One out of Filton were allowed to stand, so that the terrorists shouldn't be alerted to the change of plan. As we now know, this proved only too effective: it was shot down soon after taking off.'

Tom paused wearily, and Iain scribbled more notes.

'So now,' went on Tom at last, 'as you would imagine, the security authorities in all three countries are in total meltdown, because it has become evident that *al-Qaida must have known almost all the details of the revised plans, in spite of the really extreme measures taken to keep them secret.* It was a matter of luck that Sharon survived, and if the Americans hadn't varied the plan at the last moment, very likely Bush would have been dead by now.'

Iain frowned. 'You said the American change of plan was laid *about three weeks ago*?'

'Yes,' said Tom. 'But it looks as though the terrorists didn't get to know about that.'

'No,' said Iain thoughtfully.

'That's about it,' said Tom. 'Now, better get Aliza and Howe in for a quick review.'

*

When Sergeant Howe and Aliza appeared, Aliza looked a little flushed, and Iain grinned. The Daily Mail had heard about Mr Akinci's cattle truck, and someone must have told them what his daughter did for a living. Several newspapers had pressed the Super very hard for an interview with her, and in the end he had been forced to give them ten minutes, which in the event extended to twenty.

'Enjoy yourself?' Tom asked.

'Not a lot,' she said, with a grin.

'The boss said you did well… Can we all have some coffee?'

Sergeant Howe went to organise it, and there was a general shifting of chairs.

'Now,' said Tom at last. 'We know by now that that the plane brought down in the Bristol Channel was Air Force One. And it was downed by a pair of Stinger missiles fired from British soil.'

Aliza and Howe nodded. 'But George Bush wasn't on board,' Howe added.

'Fortunately. We also know that Ariel Sharon was on the Santander ferry, in a caravan, and was lucky to escape being blown up.'

'But this all means,' said Howe, 'there must have been a huge security breach.'

'Yes indeed,' said Tom. 'I've been briefed a bit on that, but I can't give you the details.'

'Arafat got home safely?' asked Aliza.

'As you'd expect… Now, we've been told to put these national issues out of our heads and concentrate on our own patch. What I can tell you is that the three agents in the Providence Hotel were in fact the Israeli team whose job it was to get Sharon safely home; and also that intelligence think the four characters in our Sainsbury's CCTV pics are definitely the terrorists responsible for the two atrocities. But our job's not over. Very soon, we're going to be asked two hard questions. Number one: exactly how were the terror-ists working while they were on our patch? Number two, and harder: who were they, and where are they now?'

'Well,' said Iain, 'on how their plan worked, we know they must have been hiding somewhere a very large bomb, and also a couple of Stingers.'

'What about vehicles?' asked Howe. 'Was the bomb

on the camper van?'

'I doubt it,' said Tom. 'Not big enough. The ordnance people are saying there was probably between a quarter-ton and a half-ton of explosive.'

Aliza looked up. 'I can't see how something as big as that could have been smuggled onto my dad's cattle truck,' she said.

'And they'd have had to bribe the driver,' said Tom. 'I don't think so, too chancy. The second mate told me there was something like a big motorhome immediately ahead of Sharon's caravan... We'll have to go over the vehicle list with a toothcomb.'

'How do we reckon the four were deployed on the day of the disaster?' asked Iain thoughtfully.

'We know Mr Omah was watching the Israelis in Plymouth beforehand,' said Aliza.

'One of them would be needed to manoeuvre the bomb near to Sharon's caravan on the ferry before it sailed at 3 pm' said Iain, 'and presumably the same person travelled on the ferry to set it off at the right moment.'

'And firing the Stingers would have required two people,' said Tom. 'But not before 7 pm. The same two could have been helping in Plymouth earlier: plenty of time to drive to Avonmouth between 3 and 7.'

'Where d'you think the woman was?' asked Aliza.

'If it *was* a motorhome,' said Iain, 'maybe the woman was in it with one of the men? To appear as man and wife, you know. Returning from holiday.'

'Yes,' said Tom thoughtfully. 'But if that was the plan, why did she split up from the others and travel off by train after their Plymouth meeting? You'd think they'd have stuck together.'

'As to who they are,' said Iain, 'we think Mr Omah is this Uthman al-Azmeh. But not a thing on the other three.'

'And as to *where* they are now, we've nothing,' said Tom. 'Alerts have gone out, of course, for the camper van and the small Peugeot, but no joy.'

'Can MI5 do anything more with our CCTV pics?' asked Howe.

'They've tried,' said Tom, 'but except for Omar they don't fit anyone. In fact, they don't have a single woman in the frame to be fitted. There have been a few women Palestinian suicide bombers, but no one at the international plot level.'

*

By the time of the 8 pm news bulletins a bunch of satellite dishes had sprung up like giant mushrooms on the Hoe, and world-weary commentators beside them were busily mouthing to camera. Tom, released at last from work and having twice failed to get through to Jane's mobile, drove round to her flat, but no one answered the bell. As a last resort he carried on through wet streets down to the marina, and parked. When he reached *Ariel*'s berth he could dimly see the top of her curly head lying flat on the cabin table below him. He called down gently.

She looked up. 'Oh Tom!' She made a face.

'Come aboard?'

She nodded.

He stepped into the cockpit, took off his wet raincoat and shook it and folded it inside out, then clambered down into the cabin and worked his way along the side of the table opposite to where she was sitting. She had the cabin lights off and it was hard to see her properly. A half-eaten sandwich lay on a plate in the gloom.

'I heard you had a bad time... How was the trip back?'

'Shitty.'

'You must have been totally exhausted, all three of you.'

'What about you? Aren't you worn out, too?'

'Well, yes,' said Tom, 'I've been over in Roscoff on my own account... What a terrible thing. It's really not surprising it got to you.'

She didn't reply.

'OK to switch the light on?' he asked.

She nodded.

He worked the switch, and her demoralisation was obvious. 'Super wants me to go to Bristol with him for a security conference tomorrow,' he said. 'He'll drive... Give me a chance to cat-nap.'

Her face fell.

'What?'

'Don't you *ever* crack, Tom?'

He said nothing.

'When I saw that ferry rolling over, I was just *useless*, totally paralysed.'

'Not quite what I heard.'

'I *was*... And I'm still doing my locums in a panic...'

Tom moved his hand towards hers across the table.

'Don't touch me! ... Oh Tom!'

'What?'

'There was something *new*...'

'New?'

'Something horrible.'

He waited.

'When we were half-way over to that ferry I suddenly felt... the *terrorists*.'

'The terrorists?'

'I must be going mad!'

'*What* did you feel?'

'That I was *on their side*.' She gave a little sob.

'On their side?'

'Don't get upset Tom, I'm coming out of it now.'

'Look here,' said Tom. 'I can understand why you still feel guilty about having shot Carl, of course I can—how it might make you *feel* you're a wicked person. I can even understand how that might make you *afraid* that you've become some sort of danger to your patients. But you've absolutely nothing in common with these bloody people. What *they've* done is top-of-the-scale appalling.'

'It's all right, Tom, I do understand that now.'

'And you don't need to attack yourself for having frozen. From what I heard, you only froze for a moment—you got out there and treated those injuries.'

'Yes I did. But all the same, can't you understand? Look—there are two sorts of people in this world. People who've killed someone, like me, and people who haven't, like you. I did a terrible act, I shot Carl in cold blood. But although it was a terrible act I did it *for a reason*, and I desperately need the world to understand my reason. Well, these terrorists have killed scores of innocent people. But *they* did it for a reason too. Half way over to that ferry I suddenly felt that if I wanted the world to understand *my* reason, then it was up to me to get in there and understand *their* reasons. It was suddenly something I *shared* with them. Somewhere on that ferry there was a terrorist, but however horrible he might be, he was on my side of the divide, and I *owed* it to him to understand.

'I can't go along with that,' said Tom. 'Think about it. These people are *vile*. They just killed the best part of a hundred people who were completely innocent, for no comprehensible reason whatever. But you, you shot Carl, who wasn't innocent at all, because he was trying to murder you.'

'I know,' she said. 'I can see there's a difference. I kept telling myself that as we were sailing home. But all the same, I couldn't help it, I was still on their side of the divide.'

Turn of the Screw

By next day Iain and Aliza had made good progress on the vehicle list. Of the five whose owners and origins were not yet confirmed, only two would have been in the caravan queue. One was a Transit camper van. Its ticket had been bought for cash at the Plymouth terminal two days before sailing in the name of Mr and Mrs N. M. Brown, and the address given was in Adelaide; the ticket clerk couldn't remember the purchaser. The other was a Hymer Prestige motorhome carrying a single Frenchman, a M. Concarneau; this vehicle had travelled in the opposite direction on 10th August carrying both M. Concarneau and his wife. The two-way ticket had been booked on the web from a public library in Marseilles. None of the occupants of these two vehicles had been listed as survivors by the Gendarmerie.

Tracing the bus and foot passengers had hardly started, however.

There was also news from the Bristol police. Eye-witnesses had reported that the two Stingers had risen together from behind Air Force One as it climbed, and the launcher tubes had been found abandoned on the west side of a wood a mile down the west-bound flight path from Filton. There were no finger prints, but wheel tracks corresponding to a VW camper van had been found at the scene. Exit 17 of the M5 was nearby: the firers would have had no difficulty in escaping unnoticed in the dark.

There was one further intriguing piece of information. The Bristol police had realised that the firers of
the Stingers would have been unable to watch the
runway at Filton directly, because the wood and the
fall of the ground blocked their view. The investigators
wondered therefore whether the firers might have had
an observer to tell them when Air Force One was
taking off, and went to some trouble to analyse all
mobile calls in phone cells near Filton in the hour
before take off. Most of them turned out to involve
phone accounts that were easily traced, but there were
two between a pair of pay-as-you-go phones that
could not be identified. When the histories of these
phones were examined, they positively bristled with
suspicion.

Tom had worked slowly and carefully through the
details.

They had been bought for cash three months earlier,
in Leeds and the East End of London, and, remarkably,
had *never* been involved in a call that could be traced
to an identifiable person.

On the day of the disasters, phone I had been
switched on *in Plymouth* at 1.47 pm, and made a very
brief call from near the ferry terminal at 2.06, when it
was switched off. It was then switched on again at
7.02 pm, now near Filton, and at 7.15 it had received a
call from phone II, which lasted about forty seconds.
However, phone II was not near Filton as anticipated,
but in Harmondsworth in West London; it had been
switched on only just before the call. At 7.26 there was
a second call from phone II, still in Harmondsworth, to
phone I, which again lasted about forty seconds. Both
phones were then switched off.

The call from phone I in Plymouth had been to a

third mobile, phone III, also near the ferry terminal and also switched on at 1.47. Phone III had remained switched on and had moved out of the cell at about 3.10.

Phone I had been involved in occasional earlier calls with phones II and III, and also with a *fourth* phone, phone IV, in Bristol. All were on untraceable Orange pay-as-you-go accounts, and phones III and IV had been bought for cash at different stores near Bradford. The Orange network had detected none of these four phones subsequently.

Apart from the Harmondsworth location, none of this was hard to interpret. Tom was sure that all four phones were now in waste bins or lying at the bottoms of harbours.

*

Tom missed the Prime Minister's broadcast, but watched the late news on Tuesday night: emergency cabinet committee, beefed up security services, amended Terrorism Acts, tighter links with the CIA. Wednesday's newspaper headlines were huge and black, but he did manage to cat-nap during the drive to Bristol.

The security review was understandably edgy. There were about thirty people present: police, senior MI5 and Special Branch officers, a civil servant representing the emergency cabinet committee, and six Americans, two of them Air Force officers.

A Special Branch officer from Scotland Yard summarised progress. He began by referring to the threat posed by the apparent high-level breach of security—but this crucial issue was to be off-limits for the present meeting.

He described the search for the terrorists. Tom already knew much of what the Bristol police had been doing, but now learnt more of the hunt for a possible base in their area. There were new details from Yorkshire, too. The VW camper van hadn't been returned to Avis in Shipley. Finger prints found in Mr Omah's flat in Bradford matched those in the Plymouth phone box and the Elfordleigh let; others had been found in Bradford, too—though not Mrs Omah's. Mr Omah had opened a bank account with Barclays in Bradford, but closed it on 29th August. It had received payments from a trading account in Hamburg belonging to an Egyptian, but this man had disappeared, also on 29th August; further investigations were under way in Germany. Payments made from the Barclays account were being investigated. One oddity was a substantial payment to a wholesale grocer.

At the end of the meeting, the civil servant from the cabinet committee stood up and said:

'There is an important further matter, a little delicate, which I must explain to the police officers present. Our American allies have, of course, lost Air Force One with her crew of twelve and came near to losing their president; and, as you might suppose, the CIA has in any case been closely involved in this investigation from the outset. It was yesterday agreed, at cabinet level, that it is now imperative, for reasons of liaison, to attach two US officials to each police force involved. The new colleagues allocated will join you today. They will work closely with you, but will maintain their own links with Whitehall, and with Washington. I need hardly add how important it is that this liaison should work well, as I'm sure it will.'

Tom glanced at his Super, who was studying his

finger ends. Someone asked whether there would be any equivalent links with Mossad.

'Not at police force level. We are, of course, in very close touch with Mossad in other ways.'

As soon as the meeting ended the Super went off to find their new colleagues.

*

'Hi, Tom! How ya doing?' James Coghlan, short and round, sounded New England. His suit was baggy, and rimless glasses perched on his nose. The eyes behind the glasses were active.

'Hi! Fine, thanks,' said Tom, as he shook hands.

The Super gave a little smile. 'And this is Colonel Cyrus Halbrit.'

Col Halbrit was an air force officer in uniform, shorter than Tom, slight, with close-cropped straw hair, about forty. His eye-contact was brief, and he shook hands impassively.

James made a few comments on the reports from Bradford. He rattled on, and seemed anxious to be on comradely terms. Col Halbrit added a few laconic remarks in a South Carolina drawl and then lapsed into silence. The Super asked both of them how they came to be involved. Col Halbrit was a US Air Force attaché at the London embassy; James Coghlan contented himself with saying that he'd studied Middle Eastern affairs at university, and had continued to do so for some time.

The two of them were to be ferried to a hotel in Plymouth. The Super drove, Tom sat beside him, and their new colleagues settled into the back seat, spreading out files on their knees and comparing notes; they appeared to have a partnership of some standing,

110

though perhaps not an entirely easy one.

Eventually, James Coghlan said: 'I guess it might help us now, Tom, if you explained how you've been working.'

The motorway reared up over the Avonmouth Bridge ahead of them. Tom described how the team had set about its task, and James scribbled in a small notebook. The Americans seemed to know already what they'd discovered.

James cleared his throat. 'Do I have it right, then, you have just these three officers assigned? Tom here, Detective Inspector Iain Gemmill, and this Sergeant Aliza Akinci?'

'Yes,' said Tom. 'Plus some secretarial help. Another sergeant helping with interviews, other staff brought in for particular aspects; but primarily it's us three.' In the corner of his eye he was aware of an exchange of glances on the back seat.

The Super had apparently caught it too in the driving mirror. 'Remember,' he said, his eyes returned to the road ahead, 'originally the threat was very unspecific, and we were told to keep a low profile.'

There was quite a pause, and more studying of papers. At last James said, 'This Sergeant Akinci. Got herself interviewed by the Daily Mail.'

'And about a dozen other newspapers,' said Tom.

Near Gordano Services, James began again. 'We're looking here, Tom, at Sergeant Akinci's report on Muslim suspects in your city. Quite a few. But no arrests. That right?'

'Yup.'

'Why would that be, Tom?'

'Why no arrests? What grounds would we have? Being aggressive won't help. We need to keep the Muslim community on side... Aliza went around, talked to them. I've interviewed Dr Said. MI5 made checks on him and others… In the case of Mr and Mrs Omah, we were instructed keep clear.'

'Yeah. And we hear some agent followed Mrs Omah, and lost her, and some other guy followed Mr Omah's van to Bristol and lost him too?' James Coghlan accompanied this question with an engaging grin, but Col Halbrit wasn't grinning. He was peering out of the car at the traffic on the opposite carriageway.

'Seems so,' said Tom.

Col Halbrit cleared his throat. 'Those two Stinger missiles,' he said slowly and deliberately, still looking out of the window. He paused, and cleared his throat again. 'Guess they were hidden in that darn camper van. Outside this vacation property in Elfordleigh. Right under your noses.'

The Super gave a slight shrug.

'And none of you thought to search it, hey?'

'As I said, we were instructed not to approach the Omahs,' said Tom. 'And, yes,' he went on, 'the Stingers *may* have been in the camper van. But we need to remember the cell must have had another, larger, vehicle—the one that brought in the bomb. We think it more likely the Stingers were in that. Probably moved to Bristol soon after it arrived.'

'You think so?' said James, with another engaging smile.

'Only Mr and Mrs Omah were left in Plymouth after the meeting on 13th August. Mr Omah was seen in Bristol with Suspect B on 22nd August. We think they must have had another base, perhaps near Filton.'

'But why move that bomb all the way to Bristol and then bring it back?'

'You think it stayed in Plymouth?'

'Yeah,' said James. 'We do.'

'But where?'

'On that cattle truck. Where else?'

'The Akinci truck? … That's not likely, too conspic-uous, and not under their full control. It was a large and heavy bomb. And the cell had no Plymouth base after they'd given up the holiday home.'

'Don't know that for sure, do we, Tom?'

More rustling of paper. 'This Egyptian physician, Dr Said,' said James, 'our analysts figure he's al-Qaida…'

'Why? MI5 couldn't find anything wrong with him. And he identified Omah for us.'

'Sure… But then, if he's al-Qaida he likely deduced MI6 told you already al-Azmeh was in the frame. So he had nothing to lose, making that identification.' James put his fingertips together judicially and nodded slowly. 'Only his word Omah's in Bristol, Tom.'

Tom frowned.

'Could be so? Leading you a dance?' James smiled yet again.

Cheshire cat's smile humanised, thought Tom angri-ly. He said nothing. The Super looked across at him. There was a pause.

'And these other Muslims,' added James. 'We figure there's more to that Libyan woman, and the Lebanese, a heck of a lot more than you seem to think… That's what the CIA are telling us.' James rubbed his hands together.

'Remember,' said the Super carefully, looking again at Tom, 'how important it is to keep the moderate Muslims on side. Dr Said's a popular man. Widely regarded as kind and moral.'

Col Halbrit's teeth closed, audibly.

James coughed. 'This category of moderate Muslim. Includes your Sergeant Akinci, I guess?'

'*Yes,*' said Tom.

'And her father?'

Tom said nothing.

'But, Tom, Mr Akinci *employed* your Suspect B— welcomed him, took him on to his payroll… You sure you're justified keeping that sergeant of yours active on this case?'

Tom decided it was time to get a grip on his feelings. 'Look,' he said. 'We're open to all suggestions. But we didn't decide lightly to be cautious with these people. When you get to meet my team, we can talk it all through. As for Sergeant Akinci, she's a young officer but effective. She's done a difficult job with the local Muslims and done it well. Wait till you meet her.'

The Super nodded his agreement. James paused in thought for a moment, then smiled broadly at both of them in turn. 'Sure, sure!' he said, rubbing his hands again, and returned to his files for the rest of the drive.

Throughout this conversation Col Halbrit had continued to watch the green English countryside rolling past, his hands loose, palm-up beside his uniform trousers, and the corners of his mouth turned down.

*

The Super drove the Americans to their hotel, and it was four o'clock before they met the team. The visitors took quickly to Iain—perhaps his Ayrshire Scots and plain-speaking inspired confidence. But they spent a great deal of time questioning Aliza. At six a new message came in from Bristol that Tom and Iain had to attend to, so Tom suggested the Americans should continue with Aliza in her room.

The payment by Mr Omah to the wholesale grocer had turned out to be for three hundredweight of icing sugar, which had been delivered in paper sacks to a warehouse on the Crook's Marsh trading estate. This unit had been hired by Mr Omah from 8th August for six months, and proved to be empty apart from some large drums and two shovels; but there were traces on the floor, and in the drums, of the icing sugar and of another white powder, which was being analysed. There were also on the floor the tracks of a large vehicle and a small car. It looked very much as though the cell's Bristol base had been discovered, and that it had been used for mixing a large quantity of home-made explosive. Presumably, the large vehicle had come in with a primer and enough plastic explosive to be sure of detonation, and gone out again as a fully primed half-ton mobile bomb.

*

At 8.30 the Americans returned to Tom's room and announced they were off to their hotel. As soon as they'd left, Aliza marched in, her face tight.

'They roughed me up,' she said.

Tom looked up very sharply.

She gave a short laugh. 'Not physically,' she said. 'But by the end they were shouting I screwed up the enquiry.'

'In what way?'

'They're very suspicious of Dr Said. Looks like the CIA have got something on him... And they think *you* are too soft on all the suspects, Sir. They said we need to get results quicker... Then they started on my family.'

Tom opened his eyes wide.

'What part of Turkey did we come from? Were we Kurds? Where did my father get his money? How was Kali recruited? Who drove the cattle truck? Where was the bomb prepared and loaded onto it? …

'Did I attend Friday prayers? What does *jihad* mean? What did I feel when the Twin Towers fell? How could I be loyal to Islam and the British Police at the same time? …'

'*Totally* out of order, Sergeant,' said Tom.

'To start with, it was Mr Coghlan. Then Colonel Halbrit jumped up. He pushed his face right down into mine…'

'What?'

'And asked if I'd got it, quote, into my fucking pretty head twelve American airmen fucking burnt to death in the fucking Bristol Channel, unquote.'

'We must take this to the Super,' said Tom.

'I stood up, too. I shouted back.'

Tom's eyebrows shot up. 'You did? What did you say?'

'What the *hell* did he know about Islam? What did he know about my family?' She was shaking now.

'You OK, Sergeant?'

She gave him a long hard look. 'Oh, yes,' she said, but her mouth was violently screwed up in anger.

Cerebration

Next day, to Tom's surprise, the Americans failed to appear. Good news had come in of the hunt for the vehicles: the Peugeot had been found abandoned on an empty building site near Paddington, and the camper van in a Tesco car park in Dover. Both sets of number plates had been changed: the vehicles had been identified from their chassis numbers. They had evidently been thoroughly cleaned, and no useful clues were found in either. It looked very much as though Suspects B and D had left the country through Heathrow and Dover, though the passenger lists at the relevant time gave no immediate confirmation. A team had been set up to review all the bookings.

Rather more informative was the wreck of the motorhome parked immediately ahead of the Israelis on the ferry. The explosives experts were certain that it had carried the bomb. The registered address of the card account used to buy the ferry ticket was a non-existent number in a large block of apartments. The postal arrangements there were primitive: the post for the whole block was tipped into a communal box, and the concierge was supposed to sort it into pigeon holes. But she'd been sick for some months, and the residents did their own sorting. The Police Judiciare were reviewing all the residents, and now had three suspects who were being followed up. The vehicle had been bought second-hand in Marseilles in June. It was a cash sale, and since this was unusual, the salesman remembered it, and had a vague memory of the purchaser—tall and Mediterranean. He thought he'd recognise him again.

*

Late in the afternoon, Tom called a team meeting in his office.

'Manfield on the blower again,' he explained. 'Higher authority wants all staff to review the tracing problem.'

'Meaning what?' said Sgt Howe.

Tom nodded. 'Information about the suspects has been accumulating. They seem to think we might know more about them than we realise… So Iain's going to read us some summaries. Chip in if anything occurs to you.'

'Right,' said Iain, picking up a folder. He extracted a paper from it but didn't look optimistic. 'Suspect D,' he said. 'Uthman al-Azmeh.' He looked around at everyone.

'We assume he's the cell leader—he's a Moslem Brother from Cairo and a member of the al-Qaida hierarchy. In June he was in Bradford, when he bought the phones and booked the holiday home in Elfordleigh. In late July he was back in Cairo when he took two satellite calls and reported to al-Qaida higher authority that his plans were complete. He left Cairo on 4th August and must have returned to Bradford, where he hired the VW camper van. Then he turned up in Elfordleigh as Mr Omah on 10th August.

'On the 13th the terrorist cell assembled in Plymouth, and he was caught with the others on the Sainsbury's CCTV. After that I observed him watching the Israelis, but on the 20th he left Plymouth and drove the VW to Avonmouth, where he probably helped with preparing the motorhome bomb.

'On the big day, the 31st, the motorhome and the VW were driven back from Avonmouth to Plymouth, where we think D kept watch on the Israelis while they and the motorhome were boarding the ferry. He then drove the VW to Haw Wood, where he took the phone call from London and must have loosed off one of the two Stingers. Some time later he abandoned the VW in Dover, and presumably left the country by ferry.'

There was a general nodding. 'Right,' said Tom. 'Anything to add? No? Does any of that help? … Where do we think he is now?'

Aliza looked round the room and shrugged.

'Back in Cairo?' said Howe.

'If he has any sense,' said Iain, 'he's lying low somewhere.'

'And the SIS are far more likely to know where to look than we are,' said Sgt Howe.

Tom nodded. 'I agree,' he said. 'Any more thoughts?'

Nobody had any.

Tom made a face. 'Let's move on. What about B?'

Iain extracted another paper. 'B is Kali,' he said. 'He was Mr Akinci's clerk from the end of May to early July, when he got to know how the ferries worked. He flew in to Heathrow from somewhere unknown on the 12th August, hired the small Peugeot calling himself Mr Ismail, and drove down to Avonmouth in time to pick up A before the Plymouth meeting. Later he helps prepare the motorhome bomb, and on the 31st travels to Haw Wood with D and fires the other Stinger. He later abandons the Peugeot in Paddington, takes the Heathrow express and flies out—into the unknown.'

'Dr Said saw him in Bristol with D,' said Tom. 'He didn't recognise him but thought he might be Lebanese.'

'But how could he have worked that out?' said Aliza, and everyone looked doubtful.

'You told me he was in love with his computer,' said Tom. 'How much in love?'

Aliza laughed. 'A lot,' she said. 'But he didn't talk to me about it.'

'Did he seem like a professional man?'

'Could have been. He spoke quite educated English.'

'But since we've no idea where he came from' said Iain pointedly, 'he doesn't seem very easy to trace.'

'No,' agreed Tom, with a sniff.

Nobody had anything further to contribute.

'How about A?' asked Tom.

'We think he may have been living in Marseilles, where he bought the motorhome for cash at the end of May. On 10th August he meets up somewhere with C, drives to Roscoff, and they take the Plymouth ferry, travelling as M. and Mme Concarneau, and probably bringing the primary explosive charge and the Stingers with them. He drives the motorhome on to Avonmouth and probably helps with preparing the bomb. On the 31st he drives it back to Plymouth and onto the ferry, sets it off to explode at Roscoff, and disappears... We've got nothing about his background at all.'

'But he is just a bit more hopeful,' said Aliza. 'The French police ought to be able to unearth something in Marseilles.'

'You're right,' agreed Tom. 'I reckon he's our best chance of making progress.'

'He also must have some link with whoever bought the Stingers from the Afghan warlord,' said Iain.

Howe nodded.

'OK… That leaves C.'

'Well,' said Iain, 'we know she came over on the ferry with A as Mme Concarneau, and then became Mrs Omah at Elfordleigh. On 20th August she takes the London train. On 31st she calls D from London.'

'Oh, and…' said Aliza suddenly.

Tom looked up.

'Anyone else hear the lunch-time news?'

'No, what?' said Tom sharply.

'Some reporter discovered we'd been tracing calls, and announced there'd been one at the time Air Force One was taking off.'

'*Damn*,' said Tom.

Iain frowned. 'Bristol police talking out of turn?' he suggested.

'More likely some enterprising reporter rang round the phone companies,' said Tom. 'Was there any speculation about the call's significance?'

'Not a lot,' said Aliza. 'Just that it was probably some sort of coordination.'

Tom and Iain exchanged glances.

'After that date,' went on Iain at last, 'we have no information about C at all.'

'Or any background?' asked Howe.

'No… She has quite a dark complexion.'

Aliza laughed. 'That doesn't get us anywhere,' she said. 'But what puzzles me is—what was she doing in London between the 20th and the 31st, while the other three were all so busy?'

'That's an important question,' said Tom. 'But unfortunately we don't know the answer.' He made a face and shook his head. 'And where is she now?'

'Still in London?' suggested Aliza.

'We just don't know.'

'All of which means we've got precisely nowhere,' said Iain. 'What the hell are you going to tell Manfield?'

Aliza had her chin on her hands. 'When and where did D recruit the other three cell members?' she interrupted.

'Probably while he was in Cairo,' said Tom. 'But we can't be sure.'

Aliza looked thoughtfully at him.

Superior Force

Next morning Tom, concerned about Aliza, hurried in to work by 7.45. The desk sergeant scowled up at him and remarked, 'Boss wants you, Sir, ASAP,' so he took the lift to the top floor.

The Super was quartering his large office. 'Sit down,' he said sharply, but continued pacing. Tom chose the leather-and-chrome affair by the window. The Super stopped by his desk, jerked back the chair, eased down onto it and leant forward, right fist raised to his cheek.

'Soon as I got in,' he spat out. 'Bloody chaos.'

Tom waited.

'Fax, direct from the Home Office… First off, all dealing with the Muslim community out of our hands.'

Tom frowned. '*Why*? Why ever? Did they say?'

'No.'

'Who will take over?'

'Special Branch… Second, they're using the Terrorism Acts. *All* Muslims in any way suspicious to be detained indefinitely without trial.'

'They can't!'

'They *can*. Secretary of State's authority. Emergency amendments to the Act, through both Houses of Parliament today or tomorrow.'

'American pressure?'

'Obviously.'

'They've moved damn fast… Which Muslims? Do

they list them?'

'Dr Said; Dr Said's receptionist; the Iraqi student; the Libyan student; the Lebanese student … hold on! Mr Akinci and more than half his staff… Basically, all of them.'

'Yes… And third… *Aliza herself to be detained.*'

'*Aliza?*'

'For questioning, they say… There's some tin pot posse on its way. Here in half an hour.'

Tom put his head in his hands.

'Never been so humiliated, ever!' said the Super. '*Own bloody officer!*'

'Have you told her?'

'*No*! Instructed not to.'

'Hell and damnation,' said Tom.

'Precisely… Could do with a bloody stiff whisky!'

Tom did a double-take.

The Super caught his look and gave a wan smile. 'Possibly not… Black coffee?' He buzzed his PA. 'Two black coffees!'

*

Tom found Iain and together they kept an eye on the HQ car park. At 9 am a black Volvo drove slowly in and disgorged three Special Branch officers carrying brief cases. Plus Halbrit, in uniform.

Tom walked down to Aliza's office hoping at least for a brief word with her. But a Special Branch officer outside told him he couldn't go in. He returned to Iain's room and together they kept watch. After about half an hour the men reappeared with Aliza and a number of bulging black bin bags. They walked her out to the waiting car. As far as Tom could see, she was maintaining her poise. She climbed into the back seat, the other three piled in, and the car reversed out of its slot and drove smoothly away.

Iain made a grim face, and left to find out from Sergeant Howe, who shared an office with Aliza, what had happened; Tom returned to his own room feeling nauseous. After a few minutes he heard a noise and looked up.

Cyrus Halbrit was standing in the open doorway, one hand on the doorknob.

Tom became still.

Halbrit raised one eyebrow eloquently. After a moment he said quietly: 'Old Britannia better get off her butt.'

Tom didn't reply; he felt his fists clench.

'That old dame put my President at risk of death.' Halbrit slowly shook his head. 'Too *lax*, Tom. *Quite* a bit too relaxed… You *got* that?'

Tom sat, watching Halbrit's face. Then raised both fists gradually to his mouth, thumbs against his lower lip.

'Got a tongue in your head?' enquired Halbrit.

Tom narrowed his eyes. 'Expecting me to use it for your benefit?' he said at last. 'After this?'

'Oh sure!' Halbrit was smiling for once. 'Sure… You and I, Tom, we got a war to fight. Against these shit Arabs.' He turned, and stalked off.

*

Sgt Howe told Iain that the Special Branch men had taken all the files from Aliza's cabinet, and when Tom rang David Manfield about contacting her he was told very firmly to pipe down. David wouldn't even say where she was. He wouldn't say anything about the questioning of the other detainees, either.

For the next two hours Tom was so consumed by fury that he found it impossible to do anything useful. But at last he and Iain began to set damage limitation in train. Iain contacted the University to explain what had happened to their three students and called the Health Authority to regularise the situation at Dr Said's surgery. Tom went down to Akinci Halal Exports, where he found a handful of English staff and a distraught Mrs Akinci. Her English was very poor. He managed to explain what had happened and she burst into frantic tears: she'd been looking to Aliza to help her cope with her husband's disappearance. Mr Akinci's yard manager, Mr Jones, was doing his best. Tom spent time with him discussing the situation, made some suggestions about securing the finances, and gave Mrs Akinci the address of a local solicitor with London contacts.

The humiliation continued to gnaw. On Friday and Saturday they got on, as best they could, with what remained of their job. Iain made more checks with Mr Jones. The cattle truck had been a rented vehicle, hired along with its driver, who had picked up his load from a farm outside the city only an hour before boarding the ferry. The truck had at no time been parked on the Akinci premises. The firm from which it was hired was one much used by local farmers. The driver was dead.

*

On the Sunday morning, Tom managed to get an hour or two free at home. Miranda decided he needed distraction, and rang Jane to see whether she could come round.

'I'm not sure that's a good idea,' said Jane. 'He needs

126

someone soothing.'

'He needs an antidote to this horrible American.'

'Who's that?'

Miranda explained.

'Oh,' said Jane, and paused for a while. 'I'll come,' she said eventually. And half an hour later she appeared. Miranda noted with approval that she was wearing striped sailing top and deck shoes. She settled into an easy chair near Tom's and asked about Col Halbrit, while Miranda organised coffee.

He said a little, and then became silent.

She looked at him.

He tightened his lips a little.

'You're *knackered* Tom,' she said quietly.

'Yes… I am.' He looked away. 'Mad too,' he added.

'With this appalling man?'

'Mostly.'

'Why is he being allowed to ride roughshod over your work?'

'US bullying.'

'And why does he have it in so much for your poor Aliza?'

'Why? Because she's a Muslim.'

'Fight to the death of ideologies,' called Miranda from the kitchen. 'All Muslims enemy aliens now.'

'If 9/11 had happened in London we'd be feeling the same,' said Tom.

Miranda returned with a tray. 'A lot of American airmen just got blown up too,' she said.

'But undermining Tom's work isn't rational,' said Jane.

Miranda poured, and passed round the cups. When they were settled she said abruptly, 'These terrorists, Dad.'

Tom looked up.

'I've been thinking… Do you understand their *motives*?'

'Not yet.'

'Aren't they just Palestinians?' said Jane. 'Out to get Sharon?'

Tom hesitated. 'Not necessarily,' he said.

'What d'you mean?'

'I can't go into that,' said Tom.

'Mm,' said Miranda with a frown. 'Well, whatever their motives they must be pretty clear-thinking people, just to have organised and executed what they did so successfully… Possibly more political than fanatical.'

'How can you *possibly* say that?' said Tom. 'The 9/11 bombers thought coherently, too. They seemed like civilised and intelligent people, but they were fanatic all right. Just look what they did.'

'Is part of your feeling mad directed at the terrorists?' said Jane. 'Knowing what they've done?'

'Not really, no.'

'You're not burning up energy hating them?' asked Miranda. 'The way this Halbrit seems to?'

'No.'

'So what *do* you feel about them?'

'I don't,' said Tom.

'Why not?'

'Too shadowy.'

Miranda sipped her coffee for a while. 'I suppose real fanatics are pretty hard for us easy-going Brits to understand,' she said at last.

Jane looked up. 'But perhaps one of this lot *was* a Brit.'

'Why d'you say that?' said Tom sharply.

'Wasn't there a phone call from London just before the plane went down? It was on the radio.'

'Should never have been on the radio,' said Tom angrily.

'A terrorist who was Londoner?' mused Miranda. 'Isn't that even harder to understand?'

Tom frowned. 'I don't *need* to understand,' he said with some annoyance. 'And anyway, we just don't know, we've no way of telling.'

'Telling what?'

'Whether she was a Londoner.'

'*She*?'

He looked furious with himself.

'A *woman*? A woman terrorist?'

He finished his cup of coffee, and there was another pause. 'I'm sorry, Miranda,' he said at last. 'You *know* I can't go into the details. And I can't discuss this stuff about motives either. I really can't… Let's talk about something different.'

'How about a walk?' asked Jane diplomatically. 'It's nice and sunny. Do we have time?'

Rewind

Aliza marches into the team office. Sgt Howe is working quietly at his desk. She settles herself, sets about crystallising an idea that has just popped into her mind, scribbles a few notes, types out on her PC some vigorous questions along the same lines, and calls Tom.

He doesn't answer.

She hears a faint shuffling in the corridor, but pays no attention. It ceases. She strengthens her questions at a few points and saves the file onto the team server. Sgt Howe coughs and moves slowly to his filing cabinet.

A voice sounds faintly outside and a double knock reverberates. She looks up, puzzled. Framed in the doorway is an unknown inspector. He peers around, then at her.

'Sergeant Akinci?'

She jerks her head back. 'Yes?'

He smiles severely, then beckons with two fingers.

She frowns but does not move. 'Is there a problem, Sir?'

He smiles. '*You* have a problem, Sergeant.'

'Yes?' she says impatiently.

'I'm sorry to have to inform you… You're nicked.'

Howe's head swings round.

Time stands still. The inspector beckons a second time.

'You're *arresting* me?'

'Detaining.'

'Detaining?' She swallows. 'What for?'

'Terrorism Act 2000. As amended... You don't get to know what for, Sergeant.'

'The *Terrorism* Act?' An image of Halbrit's face jerks into her mind. 'On whose authority?'

'Home Secretary.'

Sgt Howe closes the cabinet drawer and clears his throat. 'Sir!' he says. 'You haven't cautioned her!'

'Not required for detention under the Act, Sergeant.' The inspector opens his briefcase. He selects a document and dangles it between thumb and finger.

She stands at last, walks towards him, takes it, struggles to read... She says, 'I need to speak to my section leader.'

He shakes his head again. 'Just what you can't do lady, I'm afraid.' He walks to the door and returns with two male sergeants, each carrying a pile of blue plastic crates. They set them down just inside the doorway.

'Notebook, please!'

She still stands, uncertain, the warrant hanging from her hand.

'Your *official notebook,* Sergeant!'

She finds it.

'This your desk? These your filing cabinets? Keys, please... Sergeant, your *keys!*'

She fumbles for them, hands them over. The inspector unlocks her cabinets. His two assistants step forward, peer inside, riffle through her file labels.

'Let's get a move on.' The sergeants begin dumping Aliza's files into the crates.

Her insides are liquefying. She shuts her eyes hard. When she opens them again the men are still there.

When they've finished crating her files, they wrap her desktop computer and box of data CDs in black bin bags and seal them.

'Handcuffs? Night stick? Gas spray?'

'In my locker.'

'They can stay there… Anything else hers?'

Sgt Howe, static by his filing cabinet, has become abnormally silent.

'Speak up, man! These box-files too? That it? Do we have the lot?'

Howe nods. Aliza says firmly, 'You've got everything.'

The inspector consults a check list. He looks up. 'Right, Sergeant… Better make use of the facilities. Bit of a drive ahead.'

She gets herself into the women's toilet. The detention warrant is still in her hand—Home Office stamps all over it.

When she's finished in the cubicle, her arms are shaking. She grips the rim of the basin, but the shaking magnifies itself. Panicky eyes peer back at her from the mirror. She dabs her cheeks, tidies her hair, adjusts her uniform cap fiercely.

Outside the loo door, the men are waiting.

As they march her out of the building the desk sergeant looks up in consternation. They pile the crates and her computer into the boot of their Volvo. The inspector holds the back door open for her, and she gets in. One of the Special Branch sergeants piles into the seat beside her.

Flight Information

On the Monday morning, soon after Tom got in to work, Jane rang him.

'Tom!'

'Oh! Yes?'

'I've been thinking... That woman terrorist.'

'I *told* you both. I can't talk about that.'

'I know... All I want is to pass on some naive amateur thoughts to you, just in case they might be useful. You don't have to respond.'

Tom said nothing.

'She made that call just before they fired the missiles... She *must* have been supplying from London something they needed to know for the launch itself.'

Still Tom said nothing.

'So, you see, I asked myself what it could have been...'

'Look,' Tom interrupted firmly. 'I said, I can't discuss this. I'm not permitted.'

He heard her intake of breath, and there was quite a pause. 'All right,' she said at last, quietly. 'Point made. I'll pipe down... But there's something else I want to say...'

'Yes?'

'I know I was in a bad state when you came down to *Ariel* last Tuesday and I want to be sure you understand... I've got over that. I'm *not* identifying with this woman, or with any of the terrorists, so please don't think I am. I know she's on a different side from me.'

'Good.'

'And I really do hope your investigation gets somewhere soon.'

'Me too!'

She made conventional ringing-off noises.

'Look,' said Tom. 'You do realise I shouldn't have been talking to you *at all* about the case? Even the little bit I did say.'

'It's OK Tom, I understand. Silent as the grave!'

*

Tom went to find Iain.

'That phone call,' he said.

'The one from Harmondsworth?'

'What were the timings again?'

Iain rummaged in his filing cabinet and produced a paper. 'Phone I switched on near Filton at 1902,' he read. 'Phone II called it from Harmondsworth at 1915, and the call lasted 40 seconds. At 1926 phone II called again and call again lasted for 40 seconds. Both phones were then switched off.'

'And do we know precisely when Air Force One took off?'

'No,' said Iain promptly.

'But the news reports gave 7.30 as the time of the disaster?'

'Yes.'

'We need to find out,' said Tom. 'But assuming the take-off was scheduled for 7.30, the second call came only a minute or two before. So what was it about?'

'We discussed that before,' said Iain. 'It *must* have been essential information about the take-off itself.'

'Yes. But what?'

'That the plane had been cleared for take-off, or had actually taken off?'

'I don't think so,' said Tom.

'Why?'

'Because they could easily have got that information more directly—someone watching the airfield through binoculars. Or listening in to the radio conversation with the control tower: radio hams can do that.'

'I suppose you're right.'

'So what *was* it about?'

'I've no idea, Tom... Who else would have information about the flight? ... Air traffic controllers?'

Tom frowned. 'Mm,' he said.

'Would Air Force One have been controlled from Filton itself?' Iain asked.

'Its take-off might be. Not after that, I should think.'

'Well then, what about the Filton control tower?'

'It was checked,' said Tom. 'There were only two people in it, both rock-solid British staff who've worked there for years. And they weren't told what was happening until 6.30. After the disaster both MI5 and the CIA went over their personal records with fine tooth combs and found nothing.'

'What about air traffic control more generally? Do we know how it works?'

'Perhaps we should be finding out.'

'Higher authority will have all that stuff already—another request to Exeter, I suppose.'

'That would take for ever,' said Tom. 'We could get a rough idea more quickly by Googling... Why don't I give it a go?'

Half an hour later he had his answer.

If Air Force One had been an ordinary commercial aircraft, it would have been handled by the Filton control tower during take-off. But long before that a flight plan would have been logged into the traffic control system, and after take-off Filton would have handed the plane over to Southern England Air Traffic Control, at Swanwick near Southampton. Filton and Swanwick had separate radar systems for tracking the planes, and Air Force One would have had a transponder that sent information back to these radars automatically. The area controller would have been monitoring its progress on an electronic display, labelled with its call-sign, height and speed.

So when would Air Force One's flight plan have been circulated, and what information would have appeared on its label?

'But Air Force One must surely have been different,' added Tom aloud to himself. It was probably controlled not by Swanwick but by the US Air Force or the RAF. And wherever it was controlled from, the US Air Force must surely have had some private system to tell them where it was at any instant. And there would be other US communications systems—the people who deal with the president's black box that transmits the nuclear codes, for instance.

He reported all this to Iain.

Then something else occurred to him. He made a call and half an hour later the cell-phone engineer who had located the calling phone rang him back: 'Perfectly possible,' he said. Suspect C, it seemed, *might* have been making her call from inside the perimeter of London Airport.

*

That evening , his head spinning, Tom felt he desperately needed time to unwind, and attempted to relax with a book on the sofa in his bedroom-office.

136

But after two chapters a further idea that had been hovering at the back of his mind for some time suddenly insisted on attention. He sighed, put down the book, booted up his PC and began a Google search.

He eventually found what he was looking for on a CNN website entitled *Air Force One: 'The Flying White House'*. He'd remembered right: on August 9th 1974, when President Nixon resigned office while in mid-air, the plane's call sign had been immediately changed from AF1 to SAM 27000.

So, if the call sign was attached to the President personally rather than to the plane, then knowing the call sign at take-off provided confirmation that the President was on board. Had the Americans retained the usual call sign as a deception, or had they transferred it to the armoured helicopter, which seemed to be the usual routine? Was *that* what the phone call had been about?

Tom sighed, but not despondently.

Detention

Her brain won't turn over. Where are they taking her? HMP Exeter? Rough place for a serving police officer. But she's learned from street-wise Turkish cousins, she's fought Dusseldorf racism, survived police-college misogyny. She can cope with the inside of a British prison if she has to…

'Where are we going?'

The sergeant beside her shakes his head and gives her a sidelong glance.

'Wait and see,' says the inspector from the front.

'What's the basis for this, Sir?'

'You know the Terrorism Acts, Sergeant. Working assumption is, you're a danger to the state. You don't get told the basis.' He still seems faintly amused.

The car is tearing up the A38 in the outside lane, exceeding the speed limit. The sergeant driving seems loose-limbed, relaxed. The whole squad is perfectly at ease.

A new panic: the CIA has judged her dad suspicious… They could detain him too… or deport him. She swallows. She remembers Halbrit's closely-shaven face jutting towards hers two days earlier, and snaps her head higher so suddenly that the sergeant beside her looks round in astonishment.

*

Before the junction with the A30, to Aliza's surprise, the Volvo slows, turns right and sets off gently in the direction of the River Exe and Starcross. They meander through sunlit country roads for a while, then turn in at a pair of handsome wrought-iron gates beside a royal blue board bearing the legend in gold 'Holy Sepulchre School for Girls'. They crunch gently along a gravelled avenue flanked with chestnut trees. Buildings appear, solid red brick.

The car draws to a halt, and they all scramble out. The inspector leads the way into an entrance lobby. On a chair beside the door is a burly moustached man in prison officer uniform, drinking a mug of tea and thumbing through the *Sun*, and behind a desk an impassive woman in her thirties, also in uniform. High on a pointed arch a CCTV camera surveys the scene, its neon winking slowly in the shadow.

The inspector marches Aliza over to the desk. Papers are exchanged and signed. The blue crates and her computer are brought in and carried away. The detention squad file heavily out, leaving her standing by the desk. The crunch of the Volvo on the drive fades to a buzz, and then gradually to nothing.

After a while the female officer looks up and examines her, an unsmiling twitch to her lip. 'Policewoman, hey!' she remarks tonelessly, and turns to make a brief call on a house phone. She opens a locker, and silently issues Aliza with pyjamas, a set of underclothes, and a pair of luminous green dungarees. She reaches into a drawer, removes from it a box of surgical plastic gloves, extracts a pair, and pulls them on. Then they wait; and the lobby becomes very still, except for occasional rustles of the newspaper.

After a long time a larger and older woman pushes through the entrance door, her hair covered in a scarf tied with a large knot on top of her head, a bunch of keys jangling at her belt. The prison officer steps out from behind her desk and jerks her head at a different door.

All three troop along an echoing corridor and into a women's loo.

Leakage

On the morning of Tuesday 10th September, just before Tom and Iain set off for coffee, the Super came and sat on the edge of Tom's desk. 'Intolerable situation,' he remarked.

'Bloody Americans,' said Tom.

The Super nodded. 'I've been onto the Home Office. No joy, though.'

'Absolutely no reason to suspect her, Sir,' said Iain.

'They won't even tell me where she is. And it could be for months... How d'you think she'll cope?'

'That depends,' said Tom. 'But she's tough.'

'So are you,' said the Super, 'but *you* wouldn't like it, not one little bit.'

*

'This business about Aliza has really got to me,' said Tom to Iain once they were settled in the police cafeteria. 'Surprised myself... Let's talk about something different,'

Iain looked around. The place was empty apart from them. 'How about the biggie?' he said at last.

'Ah yes!' Tom laughed. 'The biggie. Why not? The damned Americans can't stop us speculating during our coffee break.'

Iain nodded and unwrapped his Cadbury Flake.

Tom ran one hand over his chin, then slowly

downed half of his coffee. 'Right,' he said at last. 'Al-Qaida knew all about the Brize Norton plan.'

'*And* they knew it had been changed,' said Iain. 'So the big question is, who leaked?'

'The Israelis,' said Tom at once.

'My conclusion, too,' said Ian. He bit into his Flake and wiped his mouth on a paper napkin. 'According to John Smith,' he said, 'it was late May when the Israelis decided to move Sharon out themselves… and the terrorists set up their Plymouth Plan almost as soon as that decision had been taken.'

'And by 28th May Suspect B had turned up to work for Aliza's father.'

'Exactly.   And they bought the motorhome in Marseilles on 6th June.'

'*However,* the Israelis only revealed these plans to us and the Americans at the last minute,' said Tom, smiling.

'Which proves our point,' said Iain. '… While on the other hand…'

Tom grinned again. '… the cell clearly *didn't* know about the US cruiser in the Bristol Channel…'

'… and the Israelis were never told about that part of the plan, so it wasn't there in the Mossad files to be stolen.'

'And the CIA and MI5 also had other reasons to suspect Israel was leaky earlier. We don't know what they were.'

'Do you know anything about how Israeli intelligence is organised?'

Tom smiled. 'No, I don't—I always understood they were rather good… It might be interesting to find out.'

'Nobody's going to tell us that,' said Iain. He drained his coffee. 'Oh, by the way, I meant to say,' he added. 'After those Special Branch heavies took away

Aliza's files I thought it might be a good idea to check her file space on the group server.'

'Sound thinking,' said Tom.

'I took a look this morning. Everything important is there.'

'Well done Aliza!' said Tom.

'*Plus* something she filed just before they came for her.'

'Oh! What?'

'An idea. She'd worked out that Dr Said was in Cairo about the time Suspect D was recruiting members for his cell.'

'That's quite true,' said Tom thoughtfully.

'And she remembered he knew a certain amount about extremists in Cairo. Her notion was, we ought to get SIS to interview Dr Said, to see if between them they could make some shrewd guesses about who those recruits might have been.'

'Not bad,' said Tom.

'On the other hand,' said Iain, 'Dr Said couldn't name A, B or C in our CCTV photos. And he didn't recognise Kali in Bristol.'

'No,' admitted Tom. 'Still, he might be able to suggest names even if he didn't know them by sight. It's worth a try.'

So when coffee was over he rang David Manfield.

'But the new edict, Tom!'

'What edict?'

'From JIC.'

'What's that? Nobody's told us anything.'

'Bloody madhouse! … You're not supposed to be calling me direct. Not any more.'

'Why not?'

'New chains of information. CIA's in the driving seat. We can't forward anything to you direct now.

Everything to go via the Americans—ideas, intelligence, the lot.'

'Which means via Halbrit?'

'Bloody pot-stirrer! Everyone here is fuming.'

'Well, no one's told *us*,' said Tom. 'And I was just calling to run an idea past you… As it happens.'

David said nothing for a moment. 'What idea?' he said at last.

Tom explained.

'That's not a bad suggestion,' said David.

'We thought so too.'

'But it'll have to go via Halbrit. And the CIA think Dr Said's al-Qaida.'

'We never heard why they thought that, and MI5 gave him the all-clear… Can't you go direct to John Smith?'

'Unfortunately, no… He's hopping mad too.'

'This is ridiculous,' said Tom. 'OK, go via Halbrit. He isn't going to like the idea, and you'd better not tell him it was Aliza's.'

'I'm bloody tempted to tell you where she is.'

'Are you?' said Tom hopefully.

But David did not develop this thought.

'There's another thing,' said Tom at last.

'What?'

'Iain and I were having a little chat over coffee. And we came to the conclusion that it must have been the Israelis who leaked.'

'That much is pretty obvious,' said David quickly.

'And John Smith told me that higher authority had their own reasons earlier for thinking the Israelis were leaky… D'you happen to know what those reasons were?'

'Come on, Tom! I couldn't tell you that, even if I knew.'

'We thought al-Qaida must have used either a mole or some sort of digital eavesdropping.'

David hesitated. 'Probably the second,' he said.

'Why?'

Another pause. 'Well,' said David at last. 'It was GCHQ drew the conclusion in the first place, and moles aren't their thing... Also, about six months ago they told us to be on the look-out for a hacker.'

'An al-Qaida hacker?' said Tom, and thought for a moment. 'Did you mention our Suspect B to them, by any chance?'

'Suspect B? What about him?'

'Said to be in love with his computer.'

'Is he, though? Don't think I knew that.'

'You should, it's in our reports... Can you pass *that* on to GCHQ?'

'Hell...' said David. 'Officially, that ought to go via Halbrit, too... '

'I dare say... Are you in touch with anyone there?'

'I know the contact we were encouraged to report to earlier...'

'Good,' said Tom.

*

To Tom's considerable surprise, this conversation bore fruit, and rapidly. The next day he found himself driving up the M5 to Cheltenham, and before lunch was sipping a liqueur and nibbling a Bath Oliver in a tall and airy regency first-floor flat near the city centre with a slight man in his sixties wearing rimless spectacles, whom he found hard to make out.

'Well now,' said Dr Sampson, pottering at large around his reception room, 'here we are.' The room was distinguished. It boasted a large white grand piano, open and covered with sheet music. The piano, however, failed to dominate the room—there were double entrance doors, newly decorated pale blue plaster pillars, and gilt upholstered chairs set below tall mirrors. The sofa and easy chairs were modern and luxurious.

'As I think you might agree, Chief Inspector,' Dr Sampson continued, 'circumstances have recently become decidedly irritating. And the Director felt it might *suit* this new situation,' he added, and twinkled like a boy of twelve exploring a new conjuring set, 'it might suit convenience, in various ways, if the conversation with you that he sought were to… to *eventuate* with a person not currently on his staff. I retired, as it happens, four months ago, so here I am, at your service. Acceptable to you? Good!' He looked as though he would have loved to astonish Tom by producing three or four rabbits and a fluttering of silk handkerchiefs from his corduroy sleeves. 'I understand that you and your colleagues are engaged in tracking down the terrorist cell that worked in Plymouth? And you have discovered that one of them spent a lot of time on his computer?'

'That's it,' said Tom.

'Mm, good… But before we come to that, would you mind telling me a little of how you've gone about your work?' His voice had become a shade less like a clever schoolboy's, and he had paused by the piano to look directly at Tom, with a slight smile.

Tom, wondering how easy it would be to interact with this elf-like person, gave as clear an account as he could of their progress. Dr Sampson nodded quietly.

'And I suspect we both of us have questions in our minds about how the cell may have communicated?' he asked, when Tom had finished.

'Yes,' said Tom.

'Just go over again what you know so far.' He pottered slowly around the room again.

'For their operation itself,' said Tom, 'pay-as-you-go mobile phones bought for cash. Apart from that, nothing. We've watched for mail, checked the phone accounts for places where they stayed, looked for e-mails in likely places, and been over bank accounts. Nothing, except for regular in-payments from a Hamburg business man who's now disappeared.'

Dr Sampson stood still and rubbed his hands. 'Very good!' he said. 'What I'd expect. Changed their tune, you see. Word-of-mouth only, unless operationally essential. There won't *be* any other communications.'

'What about contacts with the al-Qaida hierarchy?'

'None during the operation. Bin Laden and the Mullahs don't bother their heads about detail.'

'But there were two satellite calls intercepted before the operation began, and an e-mail deciphered.'

'Yes, odd, isn't it? Until recently, their top operatives, in their own territory, were sometimes quite slapdash. They left a lot of paper evidence behind in Afghanistan—I expect you know.'

'Am I right,' asked Tom, 'that their top men rather enjoy western technology?'

'They like *using* it.'

Tom nodded, and Dr Sampson smiled delightedly. Tom felt piqued at this seigneurial approval of his general knowledge. Dr Sampson looked quickly at him.

'We heard from Special Branch that you were looking for a hacker,' said Tom.

'Ah, yes!' Dr Sampson looked portentous again. 'Well. As to that, I'm instructed to pass on to you two rather revealing stories.' He bent his brows, and thought for some seconds. 'You must keep the details to yourself, strictly. I shan't draw conclusions—those you'll work out for yourself! Yes, you will!… Ready? Story number one…

'We have here in Cheltenham for many years been watching radio and TV stations and web sites, of all political persuasions, to see whether they are being used to send out *concealed messages to agents*.' He nodded several times. 'Sophisticated game. Our engineers watch everyone and everything.

'Nineteen months ago, they noticed a tiny change in the photograph of Ariel Sharon on the Israeli Government public web site. Got that? You're aware that a digital photo's stored as a sequence of binary numbers? *The least significant bits in these numbers had been modified.* Almost no effect on the picture, you see. It just looks slightly fuzzier. But if you extracted these modified bits and spelled them out as ASCII code, they made a couple of sentences!

'Our engineers were a little taken aback to find that they read, in English, *There is no God but Allah! And Muhammad is his prophet!* After three days, the photo returned to its original state. So, if the Israelis noticed, it took them three days to do so. But *I* think the hacker himself changed it back and our Israeli colleagues never noticed at all. It hasn't changed since.

'Evidently, you see, somewhere on the Islamist side a skilled hacker had been enjoying himself. I say skilled because, as you might imagine, the Israelis take trouble to protect their official sites from interference.

'It occurred to us, however, that this was unlikely to be just a game. More probably a test of Israeli alertness. There are millions of innocent web sites around the world, and many of them are easy to hack. They'd provide a simple way for al-Qaida—or indeed anyone—to send messages. The sender hacks a site—any site with a picture on it will do. He doctors the picture, and tells the intended recipient which site to look at. All the recipient needs is a PC with web access plus a simple programme to strip out the least significant bits of the picture file. If, unlike the *jeu d'esprit* that we detected on the Israeli Government site, such messages were encrypted, the bits involved would look random. And since the least significant bits of a picture usually look random anyway, this would make it hard to detect when a given site was being used in this way.

'Such a signalling system would be difficult to break, and we've made little progress so far in detecting any such messages. Got all that?' During this recital, Dr Sampson's manner had gradually become more straightforward. He looked sharply at Tom, who said:

'What are we looking for? A computer engineer?'

'Not necessarily. All sorts of people make good hackers. Crossword buffs, nerds. Idiots with delusions of grandeur. Anyone sharp, good at logical and numerical puzzles… Al-Qaida does have a few. But the ones we know of are mostly in Pakistan, and we've seen no sign that any of them are interested in the Israelis.'

'Mathematicians?'

Dr Sampson looked thoughtful. 'Not for everyday hacking, no… However! Story number two. Which you know already: *Someone, somehow penetrated Israeli security!* Not much doubt it was Israeli security that leaked.

'Only a few ways it can happen. The Israelis are very careful, tough, and unforgiving: we didn't think it was likely to be loose talk, or a mole penetrating an office. They are also very tight and professional about bugging devices, and making sure that their computers are shielded against leaks of electromagnetic radiation. So how did al-Qaida do it?' Dr Sampson scowled.

'We have professional hackers of our own, and I went to talk to them. They'd worked out some time ago that the Israelis have a dedicated internal network for sending secure messages. Authorised users have a special messaging application on their desktops, which links them to this network. The network only accepts them if they have a log-on card with a built-in chip that makes use of a sophisticated algorithm, plus a passcode, and the passcodes are frequently changed.

'Our experts found a way of hacking into this Israeli system—I shan't go into detail—and once inside, they explored how far it spread. It turned out to cover several departments, including the Prime Minister's Office, Defence, Mossad, and the Foreign Office.

'But last week, after I'd spoken to them, they discovered something new—a Trojan horse, a disguised programme deep inside the Israeli network that was copying all messages between the Foreign Office and Mossad and downloading them to a remote server from time to time, when prompted from outside. Whoever was doing this had arranged that the read destination was not obvious, and the link to it was obliterated within a few milliseconds. Our people haven't been able to follow the trail, so far.'

'Have you told the Israelis?'

Dr Sampson smiled. 'We've made it clear we think they're leaking, but we haven't told them we've hacked into their system, no. But we'll have to soon—once we've found who installed the Trojan horse.'

'So, a good hacker again?'

'Yes, but considerably more skill was needed for this. It would need a clever man to cover his tracks so well that our own experts have trouble tracing him.'

'Could they track him to a particular computer?'

'Eventually, if they are lucky. But it won't be a simple trail. He probably works through a chain of hacked machines that might be anywhere in the world, and logs on at public facilities like internet cafés, or through a laptop hooked up to the internet through a pay-as-you-go mobile phone that can't be traced. But there's something else...'

He frowned deeply, pursed his lips, and stared quizzically at Tom for several seconds with one hand on the open piano.

'In this Israeli system, *all messages are encrypted.* To give you the detail, they're sent using a public-key/private-key protocol. This means that the receiving station automatically sends the transmitting station a public key when a message is to be sent. The transmitting station encrypts the message using the public key, and the receiving station decrypts it using the private key (which never leaves the receiving computer)...

'Now, such systems are generally regarded as impossible to break. Our experts in Cheltenham did eventually crack the Israeli encryption code on a few occasions, but they had the benefit of a key piece of insider information, and even then it took them nearly a week of computation using their entire server farm— and they have the most powerful computers in the world. So it looks as though al-Qaida not only has a pretty good hacker. They seem also to have decrypted somehow messages that they had absolutely no possibility of being able to decrypt, given their resources.'

Dr Sampson gazed again at Tom. His face unwound entirely and he spoke quietly and simply. 'Sounds unbelievable, doesn't it? We're worried, you see. It looks very much as though al-Qaida may be reading all the traffic between the Israeli Foreign Office and Mossad. You understand? *Both* the new developments require a skilled hacker, and the second seems to require decryption that's regarded by all experts as essentially impossible.

'*It is far, far more important to find out how this breach of security is being managed than to find the particular cell of terrorists you are hunting.* I'm telling you all this for the following reason. They must have a man—or a woman—who are doing this magic, and it may be that you, or someone like you, can lead us to them quickly. The story I've just told you is highly confidential, and not to be passed on to your team. But we *do* want you to make sure they understand that if, in their investigations, they come across a real mathematician, or an expert hacker, or come across messages that refer to obscure web sites, it's *essential* to tell us quickly.'

'Yes,' said Tom.

'Of course, there is no reason to suppose that this talented person would necessarily be a member of your cell, but, as we noted when you first arrived, one of your suspects is thought to be a computer addict?'

'Yes,' said Tom. 'That's why I'm here.'

'What else do you know about him?'

'Virtually nothing,' said Tom. He gave the details, and Dr Sampson scribbled them down in very tiny writing on an unruled pad.

'His English sounds educated? And might be Lebanese?'

'Yes.'

'And no idea where he is now?'

'No.'

'And really nothing else?'

'No.'

'You do realise I've just passed on *far* more top-security detail than we would normally give the police?'

Tom nodded.

'In your case our Director seems to value the contact, and has decided he can trust your discretion. I believe he also made a few enquiries.' Dr Sampson paused at this point and looked down grimly at Tom for rather a long time. Then his quixotic manner reasserted itself, and he refused to answer any more questions. 'Work it out, work it out!' he grumbled, and turned suddenly to his piano. '… Like Mendelssohn?' he asked, but without waiting for an answer he leafed through his sheet music, sat down at the piano, and propped something on the music stand: Tom saw it was the *Rondo Capriccioso.* Dr Sampson squared his shoulders and threw out his arms; he played well. Tom, in spite of himself, rather enjoyed the performance.

As he was leaving, Dr Sampson said, 'Just now, I prefer our American friends not to know that I'm active. And they're not unobservant. So, if you do have any information for us, please call this number. It's not mine. Don't refer to me by name on the line, and don't contact me directly. If you *really* must talk to me personally, just drive over and sit on that bench on the green opposite, under the lime tree. I'll see you from here. Be reading some Jeffrey Archer.' He saw Tom's face and chuckled—his cheerful laugh was almost a cackle. 'No, no! Silly of me. Le Carré? No? Jane Austen man? *Northanger Abbey*! Gothic—make it Northanger Abbey! If the coast is clear, I'll open this window, and *then* you can come and ring my door-bell.'

Tom drove thoughtfully back to Plymouth. He felt

oddly reassured by Dr Sampson. How had he managed to light on Jane Austen? Tom felt that his taste in
reading fitted his public persona awkwardly, and he
usually concealed it.

Detention Task

When the body search was over, the prison officer told Aliza to don the issue underclothes and green dungarees. The heavier woman, who had watched the whole process, carried Aliza's police uniform and underclothes back to the lobby and stuffed them into a plastic bag, which she secured in a locker. The officer made a record in a book, and then seemed to lose interest.

The heavier woman jerked her head, and Aliza followed. They traipsed back down the echoing main corridor, past empty classrooms, and across a deserted grassy court, where a white flagpole was set in the grass. It carried another CCTV camera, high up, which was swivelling around, following their movement. They entered another building, and the large woman stopped and inspected Aliza.

'I'm Una, dear,' she announced in a creaky voice.

Aliza inspected Una in return.

Una shook her head, turned and trudged slowly on, up two echoing flights of stairs, and along a corridor to a solid oak door, which she unlocked, and jerked her head inwards.

Aliza entered. It was a student's room, with a divan bed, a table and a chair. There was a crucifix on the wall above the divan, with a reproduction of the *Light of the World* above. On the wall facing the window was a travel poster of a dusky Hawaiian beauty, wearing a *lei.* Aliza smiled. Whoever's study this was, she appreciated complexions other than English rose.

Una had followed. 'Them's what you use,' she said. A stainless steel chamber-pot stood under the hand basin. Next to it was an enamel bucket with a lid, and a new bottle of antiseptic fluid.

'So I don't leave the room?'

'No.'

'What happens about meals?'

Una scowled. 'Bring 'em to you.'

'I don't get to leave here at all?'

'Only for questioning.' Una moved towards the door, the key still in her hand.

'Could you get me some antiseptic cream?' asked Aliza quickly.

'What for?'

'What d'you think? I'm bleeding.'

'Oh! … I dunno.'

'Is there a nurse here?'

'May be.'

'Can't you ask?'

'Have to do the best we can, 'ere, dear…' Una frowned, then seemed to push the issue from her mind. 'Policewoman?' she asked conversationally.

Aliza didn't reply.

'Funny old world.' Una laughed shortly. 'I got teachers, doctors, you name it… Them sort of people I *don't* know. Policewomen I do …'

'So, what are you?' said Aliza. 'Prison staff?'

Una scowled. 'Course not.'

'What then?'

'I'm a *trusty.*'

'Oh… ' Aliza smiled at her encouragingly. 'What sort of trusty? A detainee?'

'Trusty *prisoner*' said Una proudly. 'Exeter Jail.'

'And they moved you here?'

'Short-staffed, they were.'

'What were you in for?'

'Shoplifting,' said Una dismissively, as though that would be obvious... Out in five weeks, I am. Gotta be a good girl! ... Now, I best be off.' She peered around the room once more, backed into the corridor and locked the door with deliberation from the outside. Her heavy steps retreated.

It became very quiet again, apart from the coos of distant pigeons. Aliza dropped onto the bed, gazed at the ceiling and reality at last begin at last to sink in. But after half an hour of misery, she pulled herself together and assessed her surroundings. The room was clean and the bedding good. There were soap and flannel, a towel, toothbrush and toothpaste. She tried to deal with the bleeding, washed, and tidied up.

She tried the door. It was securely locked, and very solid. The window had an attractive view over trees; that must be the River Exe to the east, lost in the heat haze, a line of poplars. But the window wasn't barred—and its catch turned. Very odd: only a trusty as guard, unlocked windows, yet a full body search and an elaborate CCTV system. Outside the window there was ivy and a heavy drainpipe. With her experience on the climbing wall at the police training college, escape would have been very easy. But of course, if she wanted her day-job back she needed to be a model detainee. On the other hand, that drainpipe and its route to liberty, however unusable, provided an odd comfort, an emotional resource, of sorts.

She found no personal items in the room apart from a few books: school science texts, two romances, and a few standard novels in school editions. The title pages showed their owner's name in block capitals: Alice

Pryce-Jones.

She needed to keep her mind occupied. First, something serious and factual. That A-level chemistry book would do—help her forensics. Then, something relaxing. Of the two Mills & Boons, she picked out *The Bedroom Business:* she could identify shamelessly for an hour or two with that 'Emily Taylor, PA to cynical self-made millionaire Jake McBride'—the two of them were pictured on the cover, smiling hungrily, lips a-tremble, nose-to-nose. And thirdly, what really mattered, she could keep on thinking about the case.

But she soon found that she couldn't immediately get to grips with this admirable programme. Instead, she sat and watched the view from the window. Nothing was moving within the school grounds. About half a mile away she could see a combine harvester working, a cloud of dust rising. She imagined the rank scent of freshly cut stubble and opened the window hungrily, but the delightful smell failed to reach her nose at that distance, though she could just hear the mechanical clatter. At last the field was done and the machine moved slowly away; she could follow its bulk above the hedges for a long time. But after a time its faint noise finally departed, and she felt deserted.

The whole place, this dream-school, had suddenly become too soft, too surreal to be coped with. As the light drained slowly from the sky, she felt an urge to scream. But what good would that do? She allowed her eyes to close instead.

*

For her first interrogation two days later Aliza was escorted by Una to a deserted classroom. The questioner was a bland Special Branch officer with no features worthy of description. He seemed to know as little about why she was there as she did. All he did was to ask, in the most plodding and desultory way, about her religious attitudes and her family.

It made her angry. She had, however, managed to recall some of the provisions of the two Terrorism Acts. There was the Act of 2000—she was *sure* that allowed detention only for seven days, and pretty sure it permitted access to a lawyer. Then there was the Anti-Terrorism and something-or-other Act 2001. *That* one allowed the Home Secretary to detain foreign nationals indefinitely, without access to a lawyer. But only foreign nationals. They *shouldn't* be holding her incommunicado, or for more than seven days... Surely it was safe to check on that, if she was polite about it?

So, at the end of the day's questioning, she asked cautiously about the terms of her detention, pointing out that she had British citizenship. The man said he'd check, and the next day, he told her:

'You're held under TACT, the Terrorism Act 2000.'

'But it allows access to a lawyer.'

'Not any more.'

'Why?'

'Emergency legislation. Home Secretary can now approve by warrant indefinite detention for any British subject, without legal access.' He said it like a school lesson. 'Duration of the emergency.'

'So I'm held on a Home Secretary's warrant?'

'You should have been shown it.'

'I think I was. I wasn't sure what it was.'

She bit her lip hard. Indefinite detention... Halbrit could do whatever he wanted with her now.

Two days later, she faced a new interrogator. He was tall and thin, grizzled, with a tired bow tie and a gravelly mid-American accent.

He chain smoked, apparently completely bored. He sat her down at one of the desks in the deserted classroom, and explained in a drone that she would be held until he personally was satisfied that everything he sought had been wrung out of her. She soon discovered that he knew details of her father's business, humiliating facts about their time in Dusseldorf, even police records of black-sheep relatives in Turkey. He quickly laid bare her anxiety about her father, and she saw his slow smile. He rarely looked directly at her, however: his grey eyes mostly studied some distant object outside the window. Sarcastic, he never raised his voice or lowered it. He appeared so totally convinced that the terrorist bomb had been concealed in her father's shipment of lambs, that Aliza flagged in urging that to be impossible.

That night, she wept.

On the second day he went on relentlessly for seven hours. On the third it was a contemptuous ten minutes.

'This Kali,' he said on the fourth day.

Aliza looked at him.

'Talk Arabic to him? Turkish?'

'No, English.'

'Attractive young guy?' He raised a lazy eyebrow.

Aliza said nothing.

He flipped Kali's photo onto the table.

She glanced down at it.

'Like him?'

She shrugged.

'When you're alone together, Aliza... *Kind* to you, was he? Nice manners?'

'He was polite.'

'Which made him just a wee bit *attractive?* To lil' ol' you?'

She looked at him. It had been spoken distinctly, but looking steadily out of the window as usual. 'Not your business,' she said at last.

He laughed. 'Not my business, d'ya say? Wrong, darlin', wrong.' He chuckled again, his voice shot up in pitch. '*Nothing* there? Nothing? *Not a thing to give ya the hots, Aliza?*'

She said nothing.

In truth, Kali's hands *had* been beautiful.

'Healthy young man, Aliza. Familiar skin tone. *Nothing* about him turn you on?' Lazily extended glance in various directions. 'Something wrong with you, girl?'

You creepy shit! Nothing wrong, as it happens,

'Men not *do* it for you?'

Is this idiot *really* visualising Kali and me getting it together? And, moreover, that he can bully me into admitting it?

'He wasn't interested.'

He nodded sagely. 'Feminine charms not up to it, huh?' He suddenly looked directly at her, lips curled slightly, eyes challenging, amused. 'Opened those big dark eyes but no joy?'

Kali liked me well enough, Mister. Just, he couldn't pursue it.

'What's your problem, girlie? Not enough up here, maybe?' Cupped hands to indicate.

Aliza closed her eyes.

'Could get it seen to, you know.'

She opened her eyes again and raised them to the ceiling.

He laughed quietly. 'Lil' olive mouse! …' Then he was back to peering out of the window.

But he changed the subject. He discovered, and set out to amplify, her sense of disloyalty to her parents in not being a committed Muslim. He attacked tiny discrepancies between statements made days apart. He made it seem so fatuously naïve to give any credence to Dr Said that her natural caution swelled into active doubt. Had Tom and Iain been too trusting? What *were* Dr Said's mysterious links with the Cairo extremists? Wasn't her idea of the importance of talking to Dr Said not only wrong but dangerous? … Keep quiet, keep quiet!

Worst of all, he uncovered her anxiety about losing her job, and smiled again to himself. He took care to imply icily that she'd no hope of returning to it, ever.

Hour after hour in the morning. Lunch alone in her room. Hour after hour in the afternoon. Supper alone, sleep alone, breakfast alone. Hour after hour next morning…

Just before lunch on the fifth day, to her surprise, James Coghlan appeared briefly in the interrogation room for a quick word with her tormentor.

'Mr Coghlan… James Coghlan!'

For a moment he focussed on her. But only as though she had been some unsolved clue in a crossword puzzle.

*

At first, she saw no other detainees. Later, she occasionally observed from her window women being escorted to the interrogation room. Most she did not recognise, but one day she caught sight of the Lebanese student, Deborah Ishmail, and on another,

Dr Said's receptionist Farideh. Well, if they were detained, it was inconceivable that her father wasn't. The family business must surely be on the verge of collapse.

Fearing she was now within range of cracking completely, she tried to rally her resources. As an intellectual defence, she sat down in the evenings to tackle the terrorist question on her own account, as an exercise. She could work out later what to do with her thoughts, if they were any good. She decided she must store her developing ideas in her head—it was safer, and anyway the only writing materials Una had managed to find her were three small sheets of paper torn from a reporter's pad, and a stump of pencil.

On the seventh day Aliza saw, in one of the school courts, Colonel Halbrit himself, standing talking to James Coghlan, hands hanging loose at his sides, palms turned slightly forwards. Her stomach turned over. James made her sick, but Halbrit she feared.

He'd recognised her. He said nothing, but stood and, from some distance, smiled a particular smile, a smile of which she could not rid herself. An oddly restful smile, and yet a smile of intrusion; the smile of a man who knew he was free to come to her tomorrow, or the next day, or any day, and *violate* her; the smile of a man with control.

Up to then, she had toyed with the idea of communicating any bright ideas that she had about the terrorists to James Coghlan, for onward transmission to the Plymouth team. But after she'd seen Halbrit, she knew that would never be possible. She had to find some independent way of getting her thoughts to Tom and Iain.

Holiday Camp

On the eighth morning of Aliza's detention no one came to escort her to interrogation. She remembered her questioner's appetite for psychological games, and resignedly started on the second Mills & Boon. At eleven o'clock, however, solid footsteps echoed along the usually silent corridor. Keys rattled, and Una unlocked the door.

'You're wanted,' she said, and stood in the breeze from the open window, looking around with a broad smile.

'By who?'

'Front desk.'

'Oh.'

'Don't you ask me why. She said to bring your stuff.'

Wondering, Aliza stuffed the three unused sheets of paper and stub of pencil into her dungaree pocket, and followed Una to the entrance lobby. The impassive woman prison officer handed her the bag containing her police uniform, made her sign for it, and told her to wait. Una raised a palm in dignified farewell and removed herself.

Aliza found a chair and sat down. The lobby became silent, time passed slowly.

At 12.30 she heard a distant rumble. It grew gradually, then ceased. Through the narrow window, she could see there was a coach outside. The woman officer pointed her towards the entrance door. Aliza stumbled out into the dusty August breeze, carrying her plastic bag.

A male prison officer stood waiting, and waved her aboard. Swinging herself up the steps and along the coach gangway, she found five other detainees already seated, all men, wearing bright green dungarees like her own. None spoke, but she recognised two. Near the front slouched Ibrahim al-Khalif, the Iraqi student. He stared fixedly ahead as she passed. Further back on the other side sat Dr Said, reading a newspaper.

*

As she passed him, he seemed not to notice her. Clutching her plastic bag, she worked her way slowly to the back, and the driver set off towards Exeter. Ahead of her she could see Dr Said's grizzled head occasionally nodding.

She felt an immediate impulse to quiz him about al-Azmeh's recruiting in Cairo. But caution soon prevailed. It was all very well: although she quite liked Dr Said and knew that Tom was inclined to trust him, he was not by any means ruled out as a suspect. He knew extremists. It was not impossible that he was an al-Qaida sympathiser. The CIA had something on him. As James Coghlan had asserted, he might have identified al-Azmeh to Tom as a blind, trying to throw them off the scent by placing him in Bristol: Tom had admitted it was possible. Properly, any questioning of him ought to be done by someone who understood the Cairo situation in depth and knew what the CIA's suspicions were. And anyway so far as the Americans were concerned she herself was as much a suspect as Dr Said. If Halbrit got to hear of any discussion between them it would be sure to prejudice her own position; it wouldn't be safe to attempt it.

Time passed slowly. Her fellow-passengers sat silent. And by the time the coach had joined the M5 and was grinding down the long gradient to the Exe, Aliza's thoughts had moved on. Were some of the terrorists, she'd been wondering for some time, perhaps Palestinians? Hamas? The attack on the ferry, she thought, hadn't been a typical al-Qaida operation: it had obviously been planned to kill Sharon in particular and allow the attacker to escape, not to maximise civilian casualties and turn the attacker into a martyr.

*

The coach, meanwhile, had crossed the Exe, and turned up the A30. Not Exeter Prison, then, nor Bristol. Shepton Mallet was for lifers and Dorchester a local—and anyway they were male-only. Holloway? Aliza's heart sank again. Her fellow passengers remained silent. The August sun beat down.

After Honiton, the driver took the A303. The quiet fields flowed past, there was a steady flick, flick of traffic going the other way, and, from time to time, the buzz of a car overtaking. Aliza became drowsy.

A few miles past Stonehenge she was jerked awake. The coach had swung sharply left. They passed Woodhenge and turned again. A military establishment, family quarters. They swayed onto an approach road and halted for a moment by a guard post. A red and blue signboard with a cannon: The Royal School of Artillery.

They moved on towards a huge expanse of concrete, a row of field guns drawn up along one side. The coach drove slowly onto it, and came to rest in the centre, beside a group of three bristle-haired Military Police sergeants, standing with a Royal Artillery warrant officer. Nothing was said. Dr Said folded his newspaper. Everyone clambered out. After an abortive attempt to form the male detainees up as a squad and get them to march, they were herded off by the three redcaps.

The warrant officer watched them go, smiling. He turned and jerked his head at Aliza. She followed him off the parade ground, through a gate in a wire fence, up a slope to an area of dilapidated low buildings and into a hut overseen by a bored female redcap. From inside came a buzz of female voices.

Aliza pushed through the double door, and found herself facing a long space full of beds, and some thirty women detainees, dressed as she was, except that several of them had contrived head-scarves. They were sitting about, talking, some washing underwear in an attached washroom. There were cornflowers and buttercups in jam jars, and clothes hanging from strings. The windows were wide open, and the gentle warm breeze stirred the drying washing. A TV flickered in one corner. There was a tape recorder belting out a Turkish lyric. Aliza smiled.

The women waved her cheerfully towards an unused bed and locker, and one of them, of about Aliza's age, came over. She wore heavy lipstick and eye shadow. 'Hi!' she said. 'I'm Hulya.'

'Hi!' said Aliza, dropping her plastic bag onto the bed. 'I'm Aliza... Hulya? Are you Turkish?'

Hulya grinned and nodded. She looked down at the bag. 'That's a police hat!' she said and did a double-take.

The corners of Aliza's mouth turned down. 'Yes,' she agreed.

'Hey!' shouted out Hulya delightedly. 'We got *police* here! Come to join the party!'

Many faces turned, and most of them looked doubtful. But an older woman in a headscarf looked up, smiled, and walked over. 'I *thought* it was you,' she said. 'Whatever are you doing here?'

It was Dr Said's receptionist. Aliza looked at her and said in a low voice, 'I got detained.'

'That's crazy!'

Aliza sat down on the bed and looked around uneasily. 'I don't get it, Farideh,' she said at last.

'What?'

'What is this place?'

Farideh laughed. 'Nobody seems to know. Perhaps a holding unit... Oh—and your father's been here. Did you know?'

'Dadda?' It was scarcely a surprise, but Aliza's world staggered nevertheless. She screwed her eyes up. 'But he's left now?'

'They moved him two days ago.'

'Oh! Why did I have to miss him? ... How did he seem?'

'He was OK. Not very happy, though.'

'So where did they take him?'

Farideh shook her head. 'We don't get to hear where the leavers are taken.'

'I suppose not.'

'We all got questioned about him. The Americans thought the bomb was on one of his lorries.'

'I'm sure it wasn't.'

'Of course not. It's a crying shame, Aliza! We all know how strong your dad is about being a good citizen.'

Aliza made a face. 'Poor Dadda.' She sniffed, swallowed, and changed the subject with an effort. 'I saw you at that boarding school, Farideh. Deborah Ishmail too. Is she here?'

'That's her bed. She's gone to get some exercise… All the women here were at that place first. I was interrogated there.'

'Who by?'

'Special Branch, I think. Then once or twice by an American.'

'An older man?'

'Yes.' Farideh scowled. 'Nasty piece of work… He knew a lot about Jordan. But as I hadn't been there for twenty-eight years, I couldn't help him much.'

'Do we get questioned here too?'

'That seems to have stopped.'

'It's all very strange… Are there investigators about the place? Special Branch? Americans?'

'Not so far as we can see. It seems to be just a camp.'

'So what happens?'

'Nothing. The redcaps count us in each mealtime at the canteen, but otherwise we can do what we want. We're free to move around inside the wire fence. They even take us for walks outside.'

'Walks?'

'Yes. With a redcap, along the edge of the range. There are trees.'

'Weird,' said Aliza.

'The men are in a separate enclosure, but we meet them at mealtimes.'

'Which reminds me,' said Aliza. 'If you're wondering about Dr Said, he arrived with me, on the same coach.'

'Oh! Did he look all right?'

'I think so. He was reading a newspaper. I didn't speak to him.'

Farideh looked concerned, then nodded.

'What happens about food?' Aliza went on after a moment.

'Army chefs. It's so-so. Supposed to be halal, but the girls aren't confident. We want to cook our own, but they won't let us.'

'Can we write out or phone?'

'No phone. They allow us one letter out a week, but it's censored.'

'Mm.'

*

When she had done what little she could to settle in, Aliza took a quick wander around the female enclosure. As Farideh had anticipated, she encountered no restrictions.

At half past six, the bored redcap rounded up the whole crew and walked them to the canteen. Aliza was hungry. She collected her tray and sat down to eat with her new companions at one of the trestle tables. The food was eatable. Not long afterwards the men appeared, with a male redcap. Dr Said was with them.

Aliza looked around cautiously. The army cooks serving the food seemed completely preoccupied. The female redcap had collected food of her own and was eating at a table near the entrance. She might have been keeping an eye on the doors, but otherwise appeared to be making no attempt to watch what was going on. The male redcap walked over with his tray to join her, and they began a conversation.

At first, Dr Said seemed not to notice Aliza. But when she had finished her treacle sponge and custard and went to fetch coffee, he rose and walked over to stand behind her in the queue. Uncertain how to react,

170

she paid him no attention, but from the corner of her eye she saw that he was looking around carefully, as she had done.

'Sergeant Akinci,' he murmured over her shoulder, 'I should very much like to speak with you. If you will permit me.'

The queue was moving slowly forward, but their immediate neighbours were in conversation and no one seemed to be listening. The coffee urn ahead of them was self-serve. 'No,' she said firmly, without looking directly at him.

He seemed taken aback. 'No? Why?'

'Too risky.'

'In what way risky?' murmured Dr Said. 'There is no one here trying to watch us or listen.'

'I don't know that yet, not for sure.'

He hesitated. 'I have some information,' he said quietly at last, 'that I need to communicate to you.' They had reached the urn, and filled their cups.

'No,' Aliza said again, firmly. 'I need time to think… And please not *Sergeant*, not here. Call me Aliza.'

Dr Said looked thoughtfully at her. 'Well Aliza,' he said, 'please don't over-prolong your thinking.' He gave her a tiny bow of acquiescence and walked slowly back to his table.

*

As she got used to her new bed that night—harder than the previous one—Aliza planned what she should do. At breakfast next morning she avoided catching Dr Said's eye, and he made no further move. She also took the opportunity to look for signs of surveillance equipment inside the canteen but found none.

The morning was warm and showery, and she cautiously spent the drier spells examining the women's enclosure more thoroughly than the afternoon before and peering through the wire fence to observe what she could of the rest of the site. Apart from the redcaps she could detect no staff inside the enclosure, and there were no buildings within it other than the four barrack huts with their attached washrooms. Beyond the fence army cooks were moving around in the cookhouse area. Beyond that again was the men's enclosure, which seemed to be similar to the women's. The rest of the site was harder to observe, but as far as she could see it was a typical long-established army complex. Khaki-clad soldiers in the distance were moving field artillery around with gun tractors, and a small group was drilling noisily on the concrete parade ground.

She hunted around for CCTV cameras, but found none in the enclosure apart from an obvious pair trained on the main gate in the fence. The wooden structure of the sleeping hut made its electrical circuits easy to see, and she could find nothing more suspicious than lighting cables and a couple of power points. It seemed that Farideh had been right: they were in a large military establishment part of which had been hastily converted to a holding unit, with no special facilities for observation or interrogation.

Dr Said had something he wanted to tell her. How wise would it be simply to listen? Personally, she was not inclined to suspect him. And weren't James Coghlan's suspicions pushing it a bit? The discovery of the bomb-making warehouse in Avonmouth showed, surely, that placing al-Azmeh in Bristol had been no deception. And if Said really was an al-Qaida man, how could he have been certain British intelligence already knew al-Azmeh was a member of the cell? If he hadn't been sure, would he have risked letting it out? Moreover, the CIA's suspicions of Dr Said might well be based on no more than his admitted knowledge of some Cairo extremists; MI5 had found nothing wrong with him… Surely, it was her duty to listen? And as to where and when this could be done, it had to be during mealtimes, there was no other option. After pondering the case for a second time, she made up her mind.

When lunchtime came round summer rain was roaring on the canteen's metal roof. She settled herself at a table partly screened from the two redcaps, some distance away from a mixed group of men and women already seated, and when Dr Said arrived she caught his eye and gave him a tiny nod across the canteen. He collected his tray, and came to sit opposite her.

'Well, Aliza,' he said at once, battling a little with the roar from the roof. 'You are ready to take the risk?'

'Yes, if we don't talk for too long.'

He unloaded his tray. 'Then I must come quickly to the point… Some time ago Inspector Tallis showed me photographs of four people and asked whether I recognised them. I thought it reasonable to assume that they were the cell members.'

Aliza said nothing.

'One of them was certainly Uthman al-Azmeh. And as you know, I saw him later in Bristol. Another of them was the young man who was with Uthman there. At the time I did not recognise him. However, I now think I know who he is.'

'You do?'

'I think he could be a Lebanese whose first name is Farhad, who has Islamist links.' Dr Said picked up his knife and fork and started at last to eat.

Aliza's heart did a little jig. 'What do you know about him?'

'He is an electrical engineer.'

'In Cairo?'

'He used to be. He had a government job. In electricity supply.'

'So it shouldn't be hard to track him down… He's not a member of your family?'

'No. But he is a family acquaintance.'

'Ah… But, Dr Said—you've been questioned, haven't you?'

'Yes.'

'Did you give this information to your interrogators?'

'No.'

'But now you've chosen to give it to me. Why?'

The rattle on the roof was easing. Dr Said hesitated, and his jowls seemed to sag a little. 'I think you yourself must be here because the Americans required it, Aliza,' he murmured at last. 'I do not think Inspector Tallis would have approved…'

Aliza was watching his large eyes.

'And moreover,' he went on, 'I guess that I also am here because of the CIA. If Inspector Tallis had wanted me here, he would have detained me sooner… I was interrogated by an American. His name was James Coghlan.'

Aliza nodded.

'You know him?'

'I know who he is.'

'He was very sharp… He knew much more than I had expected about my contacts in Cairo. I was not very willing to talk about them, you will understand, Aliza. The CIA has a long arm, in Egypt especially. I do not trust the Americans with my family and friends.

'But I was in a dilemma. When you first came to me with your enquiries, I thought, to be honest, it was a fantasy, a chimaera. But now we have suffered these appalling disasters.' Dr Said's face had become even more sombre. 'That ferry, the American plane. I have a duty as a British citizen to help prevent such acts. As a Muslim too, I believe. But I had to consider also my prospects of being released. So I decided I ought to tell Mr Coghlan certain things, but cautiously…

'Then, one day, came that Colonel Halbrit.' He looked up enquiringly, and Aliza nodded again. He inclined his head. 'A dangerous man. I would not willingly let him within a hundred miles of anyone I cared for. With him, I thought it better to cease communication. And I did cease, but again cautiously. I made it seem that I had no more to tell. I think he must have believed me or I should not be here… So do you now understand why I have preferred to give Farhad's name to you? I believe the British police will understand better how to be cautious, given that this is a suspicion, not a certainty, and will be less likely to consider me an enemy.'

'I see.'

'But what I have told you must not get back to the Americans.'

'That puts me in a difficult position.'

'I am willing to trust you.'

That's all very well, thought Aliza. But she didn't wish to provoke and made no comment. 'What about the other two?' she said quickly. 'The tall man and the woman. Do you have any ideas about them?'

He looked hurriedly around the canteen again. 'Perhaps we have talked for long enough?' he said. He picked up his knife and fork again and attacked his

175

food.

'But any ideas?'

Dr Said looked at her. 'No,' he said firmly.

Aliza felt herself frowning. Unsatisfied, but prepared to be patient, she nodded, gathered her plates together, left him at the table and returned her tray to the rack. The rain had stopped; hot afternoon sun was streaming in at the smeary western windows.

*

By supper time Aliza knew that it wouldn't do: she needed to ask Dr Said more. So she adopted the same strategy, and once again he brought his tray over, sat down opposite her and started to eat. He seemed a little more wary this time, she thought.

'Dr Said,' she asked at once, 'what made you believe that the man in the photo was this Farhad?'

He sighed, and hesitated for several seconds. 'It involves my family,' he said at last.

'I know how to be discreet,' said Aliza.

His heavy face and sad eyes turned towards her, and he seemed to be considering. 'When I first saw the photo of the young man,' he said, 'I didn't recognise him, but for some reason, I thought he was Lebanese. After I spoke to Inspector Tallis I began to ask myself why I thought so: why not an Egyptian, for instance? The answer was, I did not know. Something about his clothes, perhaps. Simple but stylish. It had reminded me of a certain type of young intellectual in Beirut. A touch of European sophistication. I was possibly quite wrong...

'But then this reflection reminded me of something Rabia had told me, that Uthman had a young Lebanese friend.'

'Rabia?'

'I am getting ahead of myself... Rabia is Uthman's father. He is also my cousin.'

'Ah!'

'This young friend is the Farhad I described to you. Rabia was afraid that, like Uthman, Farhad had Islamist links. I have been thinking over the circumstances, you see. Uthman was perhaps the leader of this terror cell. Cairo is a dangerous place for him, so he would not have gone there without good reason... And a possible reason at that time was to recruit members for his cell, was it not?'

'It sounds quite likely,' Aliza said cautiously.

'Well, Farhad had left Cairo some years ago. But Rabia happened to mention to me that he had returned to Cairo to visit, during the time I was there. So I put two-and-two together. That was my reasoning.'

'I see.'

'It is no more than plausible reasoning. Farhad may be entirely innocent.'

'You never met this Farhad? You had no idea what he looked like?'

'Never.'

'Do you know his other name?'

'No.'

It wasn't sure-fire logic, but believable nevertheless. At last Aliza said, 'I have a problem, Dr Said, however. Your family seems to have links with certain Islamists. Inevitably that makes you suspect. To the CIA, it seems, you are a very serious suspect. So why should I believe you?'

Dr Said looked mournfully at her. 'Have you ever lived in Egypt, Aliza?' he asked at last.

'No.'

'Then I need to explain to you some history… I studied medicine at Cairo University from '56 to '60. I followed my cousin Rabia there. He is ten years older than I, but his course was delayed by the war and I overlapped with him. He studied economics… It was a time of hope. But it was also a time when militant Islam was raising its head. In 1947, Maududi was forced to move from India to Pakistan, and the Cairo students all started to read his writings.'

'Maududi?'

'An exceptionally charismatic man. He brought back to us all those Muslim Brotherhood ideas from the 1930s. My family, we are Sunni, we have always been moderate—my cousin Rabia was shocked; like many of us he saw these ideas as dangerous, not a true path for Islam… Then the Brotherhood in Egypt started to kill. They assassinated Prime Minister Pasha in '48, and they tried to get Nasser in '54.'

'But all this was long before I was even born,' said Aliza. 'How do you expect it to help me believe you now?'

'That is my point,' said Dr Said. 'I need to show you how very long the history of Islamism in Egypt is.'

'Does that matter?'

'Of course it matters. It affected our families very much.'

'How?'

He gave her an anxious smile of encouragement. 'Many students were seething, determined to make the state more Islamic; there was much secret support for the Brotherhood. I knew many who were active. But I and my immediate family do not support an Islamic state, we think democracy is safer. We wanted Egypt to be democratic.

'Soon Rabia married and his sons were born. Uth-

178

man went first to University in 1980, when he was nineteen. Because he wanted to train as a surgeon, Rabia asked me to advise him and I got to know him quite well. He should never have taken up doctoring! He had the scientific mind, always wanting everything clear-cut and precise… By the time he began his studies, there were Islamists everywhere. In Iran, Khomeini had come to power in '79. The Cairo students were all reading Qutb. There were thousands of arrests. The Brotherhood assassinated Sadat in '81.

'Uthman was young, he was drawn in. He wasn't the only one. No others from my close family, but many friends and more distant cousins. Rabia and I tried to dissuade him. He just laughed. He patronised us, gave us tracts to read, hints of what he was up to.

'Then, suddenly, he became respectable. He got his degree, Bachelor of Medicine, and went to America to train as a surgeon. We hoped he had seen sense… But it did not seem very likely.

'But by the time they massacred the sixty tourists at Luxor in '97 he was back in Egypt. Coming and going. Nominally he was working as a surgeon, but I saw his operating list in the hospital and it seemed to me very slight. That was when al Qaida was coming into high profile, and we started to hear rumours he was involved. Oh dear!'

'Surely, at that point you should have told the police.'

'You do not understand, Aliza. In Cairo many, perhaps most, families are divided. We may disagree violently. But we do not betray family members to the police, however much we may disagree politically. Never. Egypt is not like England. In Egypt those who disappear into police cells and prisons do not reappear, or if they do, it is in pieces on the river bank. So, you see, our family traditions are necessarily different from yours… In Britain it was very hard for me to accept that I had a substantial moral duty to inform the authorities about Uthman.'

*

Aliza was not convinced, and for two days, she had no further contact with Dr Said. But she nevertheless did start to wonder how it might be possible to get the new name to Tom without alerting the Americans. She was forbidden outside contact except the censored weekly letter home, and detainees' mobile phones had all been confiscated. There were presumably public phones and post-boxes somewhere in the camp, but not in the part she had access to. For a moment she even considered dropping a letter somewhere public in the hope it got found and posted. But that was far too risky: if any message from her was intercepted, the names in her message would surely go straight back to Col Halbrit, exactly what Dr Said was trying to avoid.

He's quite right, too, she thought.

On the third day however, Dr Said caught her in the breakfast queue again; they were both trying to make up in orange juice what they were missing in bacon.

'I have no further suggestions for you,' he said. 'But now I am very anxious! Perhaps I should not ask what you intend to do. But will you be passing the name I told you to Inspector Tallis? Perhaps even to British intelligence agents in Egypt? I should like to know.'

'I'm no more in contact with Inspector Tallis than you are.'

'No, no! Of course, I understand. But perhaps you will be finding some way to contact him.'

'If I ask officially, it will alert the Americans,' Aliza said. 'All I can think of is to keep my eyes open, to see if there is some way to get discreet access to a phone or post box. Or perhaps, if someone is being released, I could ask them to carry a message by word of mouth.'

'You should have to be very sure they would be discreet.'

'Of course. It would depend entirely on who it was.'

*

A day later he caught her again in the breakfast coffee queue as numbers in the canteen were already thinning. Aliza felt irritated.

'I fear I have misled you,' he confessed when they were seated.

'Misled me?'

'I have risked with you one who may be innocent...'

'You're afraid you've given me the wrong name?'

'No, no, not that.'

'What then?'

'There are perhaps others that I ought to have risked also...'

'Others suspects you *should* have mentioned?'

Dr Said sighed. 'I have been doing some more thinking, Aliza.'

'About?'

'About the other photographs.'

'The tall young man and the woman?'

He nodded, uncertainly. 'I told you two days ago I had no idea at all who they might be. But I misled you. It was not strictly true.'

'Mm.'

'I *did* have some ideas idea. About the young man...

Long ago, you see, when Uthman was at university, he used to meet a young friend of his family, who was then only ten or eleven, but very tall for his age. His name was Ali Zubaida. He and Uthman were interested in football; they used to watch Liverpool on the television. They also played for the same football club, though the boy played in a youth team… In early July, I heard that Ali, too, had been in Cairo after a long period of absence.'

'How did you hear?'

'In another phone call from Rabia.'

'Do you think this Ali was there to meet up with Uthman?'

'I was not able to discover that. But he must have been in Cairo during my visit, though I never saw him. I have thought it over. I now think it is possible—not more—that the tall man in Inspector Tallis' photographs might be Ali.'

'Just because he was tall?'

'Not only that… You see, I heard later from an acquaintance that Ali had links, not with the Brotherhood, but with the Islamic Salvation Front in Algeria.'

She thought at once of the Marseilles connection. 'Any idea where he might be now?'

'No. He was not based in Cairo.'

'Mm.'

'But there is absolutely no certainty about it. He may be perfectly innocent.'

'Of course.' Aliza thought it over. 'What about the woman?' she asked at last. 'Did you think any more about her?'

'Yes, I did… But she was more of a problem. Traditionalist Islamists do not approve of women as fighters, and I have never heard of a woman playing any active role in al Qaida. Hamas is different—several women there are actively involved, and some have been suicide bombers. But I could not think of any woman in Cairo who could be recruited for such a role.

'But yesterday afternoon it occurred to me that, of course, she might be someone not a native Egyptian. And I was able to think of two that I knew of but had never met. There is a young academic, Professor Khan, Riffat Khan, who used to lecture in the American University. She was originally from Karachi, but grew up in America. She was so vigorously Islamist that no one was surprised when she went underground eighteen months ago. A very bold woman.'

'She sounds a serious possibility. But did Uthman know her?'

'I have no idea.'

'Mm... Do you know anything else about her?'

'No.'

'And the second woman?'

'The other is quieter, a Lebanese electronics engineer. Her first name is Alifa. She has not been in Cairo recently—she disappeared three years ago, maybe into a police dungeon, though rumour says she went to England.'

'What's her other name?' asked Aliza.

'I don't know. But when she disappeared, I remember that Rabia worried, because he thought Uthman knew her—she worked at one time as a technician in his hospital. And he heard later that the police suspected she was involved in making bomb timers.'

'So in her case, a more definite link, but not a recent one?'

'Yes. But again, these are only ideas, Aliza. I beg you to remember that these people may be entirely innocent.'

The canteen was now almost deserted, but no one had paid them any attention. Perhaps by now people were used to seeing them together.

*

She now had not one but four new names to investigate: for A, the tall footballer Ali Zubaida who had links with Algeria; for B (alias Kali), Farhad the Lebanese electrical engineer; and for the woman C, either Prof Riffat Khan from Karachi and the US, or Alifa the Lebanese electronics engineer. It all sounded desperately tentative, and Aliza felt uneasy. But she had to admit that—in spite of all proper professional caution, and with some irritation over his cautious hesitations—she found herself distinctly inclined to trust Dr Said.

There, however, the matter had to rest because she could think of no safe way of communicating with Tom. The summer heat and cloudbursts continued and her nights were becoming more and more fractured by depression; she had lost weight, and the barracks food wasn't helping. But at least during the day she could take regular walks: they made up to some extent for the nights, and provided an opportunity to reconnoitre phone boxes.

Air Traffic

The Monday 16th September, David Manfield rang and told Tom where Aliza was.

He raised his head sharply. 'Say that again,' he said.

'The School of Artillery, Larkhill.'

He scribbled hastily. 'On Salisbury Plain?'

'Yes.'

'Any news of her?'

'Interrogation's over. No decision yet on release.'

'Why not, if the questioning's finished?'

'The Commandant wouldn't say. Got the feeling he didn't know.'

'That nut Halbrit again, isn't it?'

'Probably.'

'Did you speak to her?'

'No, not permitted. And you can't either... But he did say she was OK.'

'Nicer to have heard direct... But thanks very much, David, for letting us know. Much appreciated... Was this off your own bat?'

'Not entirely, no.'

'Ah.'

'Nobody here likes Halbrit any more than you do, Tom. And that's having certain effects. For instance, our mutual friend Mr Smith would quite like a bit more direct collaboration with you. Unofficially, of course.'

'In the hunt for suspect C, for instance?'

'Why her?'

Tom explained about the phone call, the AF1 call sign, and the importance of understanding better the information flows of Air Traffic Control.

'Got you,' said Manfield when Tom had finished, and was silent for a moment. 'Good thinking... There's a report covering some of that... I'll see whether he thinks you could see it.'

*

Next day a sealed packet arrived by courier, and Tom and Iain sat down in Tom's office to digest it.

SECRET
Serial 132/26
Air Force One Flight Information

1   Air Force One landed at Filton from
Fairford at 1856 hrs 31/8, using call sign
SAM29000. The aircraft was scheduled to
take-off at 1930. It was cleared for take-
off by the Filton control tower at 1925,
started its run at 1927, and left the ground
at approximately 1928, under call sign AF1.
This call sign was used even though the
President was not on board.

2   At 1932 two Stinger missiles exploded
in the vicinity of the aircraft. At that
point it was still under Filton control.
There was a garbled communication with the
control tower after the missiles struck the
aircraft.

3   As is normal, the flight plan had been
filed with Southern England ATC in advance.
Although at the time of the attack the aircraft had not been handed over to Swanwick

control, electronic information that it had been cleared for take-off was forwarded automatically to the Swanwick computer system at 1925, as was the fact that it was airborne, at 1928.

4   The data logs show that the aircraft's identifying transponder registered both on the local Filton airfield radar and on the West of England traffic radar system, with the AF1 call sign. Because control had not yet been transferred to Swanwick, only an abbreviated 'taking-off tag' would have shown on the Swanwick controllers' screens. However, the call sign would have been visible to them from 1925, and every traffic controller would have known its normal significance.

5   For this reason, MI5 has made a thorough investigation of the backgrounds of the two Filton controllers, and of every controller on duty at Swanwick at the relevant time. No leads of any sort emerged. Security at Swanwick was substantially tightened after 9/11. All ordinary telephone calls from the control room are monitored and staff are not permitted to use cell phones. No cell phone calls were made from Swanwick at the relevant time. Other staff at Filton and Swanwick have also been screened. MI5 consider it unlikely that any leak occurred from inside either organisation. However, it is judged possible that information was obtained by a visual observer inside or outside the Filton perimeter. It is also conceivable that the data feeds between the radar stations and Swanwick were tapped electronically at some point, though this would require an opponent with unusual access and expertise.

6   Flight information also passes directly
from Air Force One into various US radar
systems and communications networks. CIA
have made investigations equivalent to ours
of the US Air Force staff and others involved and have found no sign of any leak.

'Those times are pretty damn important,' said Iain when they'd finished.

'Yes, indeed,' said Tom, and extracted the mobile call folder from his filing cabinet.

'That second call came in at 1926?' said Iain.

Tom consulted the timing sheet. 'Yes,' he agreed. 'Immediately after the taking-off tag appeared on the screens. And it lasted forty seconds, which means it ended slightly before the plane was definitely air-borne.'

'Those timings just about prove our theory.'

'They do,' said Tom. 'And that's a very clear report,' he added, wondering who had written it.

'They've been thorough,' said Iain. 'I'm thinking there's nothing we can usefully do now at Filton or Swanwick.'

'Agreed,' said Tom, a little unwillingly—he disliked seeing avenues closed off too quickly.

'However,' said Iain, 'although this tells us that the electronic data reached Swanwick, it says nothing whatever about where *else* it may have gone. That phone call came from Harmondsworth, possibly Heathrow.'

'Exactly,' said Tom. 'Which means we've work to do out of area. But is the hierarchy going to let us do it?'

*

The Super was in shirt sleeves, sipping water from his cooler, and offered beakers to Tom and Iain as they settled into his steel-frame chairs. Tom reported the news about Aliza, and the Super harrumphed; then he argued the issue of air traffic control.

'So!' said the Super. 'You reckon there's a ninety per cent chance that young woman got access to the electronic take-off data, somehow. But probably not in Swanwick—you reckon other establishments will have received the same data, including RAF air traffic control and the US air force?'

'Yes.'

'So now you want permission to investigate the RAF? And because the phone call came from near Heathrow, you also want to see what can be discovered there?'

'That's about it.'

'Surely, the security agencies will have covered these angles long ago?'

'Our information is they haven't.'

'Mm… You're asking a heck of a lot, requesting to work so far out of area.'

'Manfield hinted the authorities might be happy for us to take a first look.'

The Super looked sceptical. 'I doubt it,' he said. 'You'd require liaison, of course?'

'Yes.'

The Super sighed. 'All right, I'll see what they say… What about the US Air Force, Tom? Don't you want to investigate them too?'

Iain raised his eyebrows.

'Time for Halbrit to give you some help?' the Super suggested evenly, eyeing Tom, who didn't reply.

*

Col Halbrit responded briskly to Tom's cautious request and said he would be in Plymouth the following afternoon. He appeared in uniform as before, refused an offer of coffee and settled impassively onto the office chair that Tom pushed forward.

Putting Aliza firmly out of his mind, Tom explained yet again the issues surrounding the mystery phone call.

'Got you, Tom, I understand.' Halbrit placed his fingertips together judicially. 'Several points you're making here. First off: Communications. Can't give you details on Air Force One, naturally. But I can confirm to you the status of every aircraft of the President's flight is collected and recorded by Air Mobility Command. Automatically.'

'Whether the President is on board or not?'

'Affirmative... Second: leaks from US staff. All personnel involved with the President's safety are fully screened, and were re-screened after the attack. Not your concern.'

'OK.'

'Moreover, none of our communications transit via West London. *And* all the staff involved knew the President wasn't on board, in any case.'

'Could Air Force One's radio transmissions have been intercepted?'

'Negative.' Halbrit looked dismissive.

'Why?'

'Highest level of double encryption.'

Dr Sampson hadn't explained whether the Americans used the same method of encryption as the Israelis, and Tom chose to say nothing.

'Your third issue: air traffic control. Your security over here's fucking lax—you know that? You aware?

... But you want to investigate, we've no objection. Copy me in to your conclusions.'

Tom frowned. 'You say UK traffic control security is lax. Do you have information about its leakiness that we need to know?'

'We made some checks.'

'On what? The air traffic controllers?'

'Sure.'

'Where?'

'Filton airfield and ATC Southern UK.'

'Any suspicions?'

'No,' admitted Halbrit. 'Not them.'

'Who then?'

Halbrit slowly shook his head.

Tom allowed himself a tight smile. 'What about your own controllers?' he persisted.

Halbrit stared at Tom for a moment. 'US aircraft are subject to civil regulation if they enter commercial air lanes,' he said, 'Otherwise tactical control over Britain is handled by the RAF.'

'And that would include Air Force One?'

'Affirmative.'

'So flight plans and routing data would be copied to the RAF?'

'Sure would.'

Remembering his web searches, Tom said: 'We were wondering about the way the plane was brought down. Was it armed with anti-missile devices?'

Halbrit looked sharply at him and frowned.

'Did its defences fail against the Stingers? Is there a security issue there?'

'*Way* outside your terms of reference.'

'In general terms,' continued Tom, 'can you see *any* means by which a terrorist in Harmondsworth, in West London, could have obtained access to intelligence that Air Force One was taking off from Filton?'

Halbrit pursed his lips. 'No specific scenario, Tom, no. But I figure it could have happened a hundred ways.' He smiled. 'Better go track it down.'

*

Once again the Super's representations eventually turned up trumps, so Iain and Tom set off for London on 20th September. Afterwards they met at Paddington.

'How was the RAF?' asked Tom, once they were settled in the Plymouth train. The carriage was nearly empty and there was no one within hearing distance.

'Very good,' said Iain, slurping at a carry-on coffee.

'Cooperative?'

'They even nominated a Flight Sergeant to run around with me.'

'And had national security checked them all out?'

'Yes and no,' said Iain. 'Special Branch checked out the staff early on. But once they realised the RAF never got as far as controlling Air Force One, they lost interest.'

'Ah.'

'But, Tom!' said Iain. 'Do you realise where the RAF control centre is? It's in London: West Drayton, just north of Harmondsworth.'

'So the mystery phone call could've come from there?'

'Looks very like it.'

'Have to check with the phone engineers,' said Tom.

'Of course. Promising, though?'

'Certainly.'

'Their system works like this. As far as maybe, the military keep their planes away from the civil flight corridors and most of their control work is done from West Drayton. But in case there's a conflict, they keep a few of their own people at Swanwick, too. West Drayton gets all the same radar information as Swanwick. So all the info about Air Force One was definitely displayed on the big screens right under their noses.'

Tom nodded.

'And, get this!' Iain said. 'They were using it, too. There were four US fighters and a helicopter gunship deployed to protect the President's helicopter and Air Force One, and *they* were all managed from West Drayton.'

'By RAF controllers?'

'No, they have American controllers there too. But it wasn't just the Americans knew about it.' Iain, usually so deliberate, was talking fast, and his voice bobbed up and down.

'Was the helicopter on the screens too?'

'Yes. Using its normal call sign. The RAF staff I spoke to were right mad. They got told of the plan to fly the President out by helicopter only an hour in advance. The US Air Force knew a day ahead and had laid on the escort, but they kept it secret till very late in the day, so all the flight plans had to be integrated safely at very short notice.'

'But does that mean everyone at West Drayton knew the President wasn't actually aboard Air Force One?'

'I tried to discover that. The top people knew, and so did the controllers in charge of the West Country airspace. But I talked to two who were working on the Midlands sector. They didn't hear all the details until after the plane went down—so *they* had the AF1 tag showing up on their screens without knowing till later. And there's a gang of lower grade staff who carry information slips around. They wouldn't have known, and they had more opportunity than the duty controllers to make a surreptitious mobile call.'

'But they were all included in the security check?'

'Oh yes,' admitted Iain. 'And,' he added gloomily, 'no one at West Drayton recognised Suspect C. I kept passing her photo around and getting blank looks.'

'Same at Heathrow.'

'But then I discovered something else, Tom. There's *another* control organisation at West Drayton, the London Terminal Control Centre.'

Tom laughed hollowly. 'How ever many more?'

Iain grinned. 'This one handles take-off and landing for civil flights using Heathrow, Gatwick, Stansted, and the smaller London airfields. The screen coverage for its controllers extends some way west, but it doesn't show low-level flights near Bristol, so Air Force One *wouldn't* have shown on their screens, and they wouldn't have seen its flight plan. They coordinate with the military, but they don't hear about the planning for military flights outside their airspace. So the controllers there *wouldn't* have seen the key information.

'But on the other hand the raw radar information is piped to that part of the site too, so a knowledgeable engineer working there might have been able to get at it. It's a big organisation, and the security services have only just got round to checking out the staff.'

'Slow of MI5,' said Tom. He mulled over what Iain had said.

Iain slowly finished off his coffee. 'So…' he enquired at last. 'What about Heathrow?'

'Sorry, yes… The airport police couldn't help much. They'd no idea how electronic information about flights is routed around, so I had to do a lot of leg work... The information in the control tower only covers Heathrow flights, so the controllers there wouldn't have known anything about Air Force One... And the public information service gets its stuff from the control tower.'

'What about the airlines?' asked Iain.

Tom shrugged. 'There are dozens, and they gave pretty confusing answers. But the nub of it is, they never get to see the radar information itself. They all have some system for checking the progress of their own flights, but it's usually by direct radio contact with the flight crew, or via a satellite voice channel, or sometimes by an automated data link. In most cases they don't know about flights operated by other airlines. All in all, as far as I can see, no airline staff would have known that Air Force One had taken off.'

'What about Suspect C?'

'No-one I spoke to at Heathrow recognised her, but they mostly just laughed: the place is huge, so far too many faces around for a particular one to have much chance of registering.'

'Sounds like Heathrow is out?'

'Not quite. It turns out that Filton is the technical centre for Airbus. So any Heathrow airline that flies Airbus planes has a permanent link there. So information about Air Force One's take off could easily have travelled from Filton to someone at Heathrow.'

Iain frowned. 'Where does all this leave us?'

'Well,' said Tom slowly. 'For Heathrow, probably nowhere. Your military centre at West Drayton's an interesting possibility. But on the other hand you said the security checks there have thrown up nothing. And nobody there recognised C.'

Iain frowned. 'What about the Terminal Control Centre?'

'We'd better make sure Special Branch get the security checks finished, and we can flash C's photo around... And we need to talk to the engineers who route these radar signals round the country and make sure we understand everywhere they go.'

'Re-interview staff at both establishments?'

Tom shrugged. 'Maybe... And we've still had no luck in identifying the originator of our mystery phone call... Must check again with network Orange.'

*

Next day the cell phone engineers, contrary to what Tom had been led to understand earlier, decided that the call might indeed have come from the West Drayton complex, but definitely *not* from anywhere inside the Heathrow perimeter. So Iain's investigation now seemed to have been in the right direction, whereas Tom's two days at the airport had probably been wasted. He and Iain were left racking their brains over what more could usefully be done next.

'How about the hacking community?' suggested Iain.

'What about them?' The early autumn heat had passed and Tom's desk fan was idle.

'Aren't they buddies, always yacking on the web? Shouldn't we be locating these shadowy gentlemen and asking what suspicions *they* have?'

Tom smiled. 'According to Manfield, Scotland Yard's already doing that... But maybe I should ask him what's emerged.'

'And then there's our CCTV pictures, I suppose.'

'Yes.' Tom nodded thoughtfully. 'Maybe it's time we went public.'

'*Crimewatch*?'

'Why not? We know al-Azmeh and Kali lived in England for some months, and there are signs that C lived in England too. She may still be here… There's a good chance someone'll recognise one or other of them.'

'Put it to the higher powers?'

'Don't see why not,' said Tom.

Cairo

At about the same time as Iain and Tom reached this conclusion a slender but sinewy young Englishman was sitting, knees spread, in a club chair in the Napoleon Bar of Shepheard's Hotel in Cairo's Garden City, sipping a Turkish coffee, and smiling as he turned the leaves of a dog-eared copy of *The Restaurant at the End of the Universe*. His sleek black hair was centre-parted, unruffled by the slowly revolving ceiling fans, and his suit grey and impeccable. His particular occupation tended to alternate between frantic endeavour and extended inactivity, and at the moment he had nothing to do. The bar was his usual retreat at such times because its attempt to replicate Boodle's so far from St James's tickled his taste in tat, and also because he was enamoured of the espionage ghosts of the place. He looked up occasionally and allowed his eyes to rest on the Nile shimmering beyond the plate glass.

*

Tom called Special Branch, and once again the contact proved productive. Manfield explained that the authorities had already been pursuing the *Crimewatch* idea for some time and were planning to include an item in the programme scheduled for 26th September—in four days' time. He also put Tom into contact with the computer fraud team at Scotland Yard who had been trying to glean information from the hacker community.

The *Crimewatch* screening generated a reasonable response. The photo of Mr Al-Azmeh produced a number of Yorkshire sightings, and a new witness came forward in Plymouth who remembered selling him Ordnance Survey maps of the Bristol area. Other Plymouth witnesses remembered Kali from the time when he worked at Akinci Halal Ltd. But, strangely, no one had recognised the lanky male suspect A, or the woman suspect C. In the CCTV picture she'd been wearing a straw hat that partly shaded her face, but the lack of recognition of A was disappointing.

When Tom went up to London to consult the computer fraud team they gave him a long description of how they had been injecting obscure electronic messages into the web, intending that they would percolate through to esoteric chat rooms, flutter down onto obscure black web sites, and so find their way through to the disembodied members of the hacking community. To Tom's surprise, some of these shadowy figures had proved public-spirited, and a list of suspect hashtags had been generated. But the hackers had in most cases no idea of their brother miscreants' real-life identities, and it was taking time and effort to discover them. This also meant that their suspicions of sympathy with al-Qaida were often proving to be ill-founded. For the moment, this had led nowhere, but information was still emerging. Tom returned to Plymouth in a more positive mood.

Then on 1st October a report arrived from the Marseilles *Police Judiciare*. Of the three suspects in the apartment block, they'd ruled out two. The other was away from home—an Egyptian who called himself Ali

Farag, aged about 30, who'd lived in Marseilles for more than ten years, was single and lived alone. A local firm producing turbo-pumps had at one time employed him as a design engineer, but he had no known current employment. Other residents in the block reported that he had in June bought a large motorhome, apparently identical with the one blown up on the ferry, though the registration number on its plate in the apartment car park disagreed with the ferry booking, and also with the sale document. Investigations were continuing, and they would send his fingerprints.

*

Nothing then happened for several days, but on 7th October, the Super rang Tom.

'Something for you,' he said cheerfully. 'News... *Better* news.'

'Aliza?'

'They're releasing her this morning.'

'At last! Thank God for that.'

'I've sent a squad car.'

'They've bloody well taken their time... Any comment on the change of heart?'

'Nothing, just a formal fax from Special Branch.'

At eleven Tom and Iain hurried down to the headquarters car park to greet her.

She was back in uniform, and grinning broadly. Iain grinned back and Tom put his arm round her shoulders. 'Thank God the CIA have come to their senses!' he said. 'The whole thing's been appalling. The Super's done his best to make contact, but we've all been frantic.'

'I guessed.'

'Now: be honest, how are you feeling?'

'I'm OK,' she said.

She did seem remarkably cheerful, but Tom saw how pinched her face was. 'Bloody Halbrit,' he remarked, and they all went inside to his office.

'That man deserves to be shot,' he added. 'Now, Sergeant, we want you to go straight home and take three days leave,'

'No, Sir!' she said.

'Why not?'

'I need to report to you first.'

'Something important?'

'I think so.'

'I'll find some coffee,' said Iain.

*

Iain, his eyes widening a little as he did so, carefully wrote down all Dr Said's suggested identifications.

Tom immediately called David Manfield to pass them on, having first checked that it would be possible to keep them from the Americans, as Aliza had insisted. David in turn reported that 'John Smith' would be in Exeter the following day, and invited Tom to drive up with Aliza to talk to him.

John Smith quizzed Aliza at some length, and to Tom's relief immediately took up her proposal that MI6 should be invited to investigate Dr Said's suggestions. He also agreed that nothing should be said to Halbrit. He said he would get back to them within two or three days, and seemed more pleased than otherwise that there was a compelling reason to keep Halbrit in the dark. He also went out of his way to comment on how unjustly Aliza had been treated and shook her hand when they left.

*

Next day there was more from Marseilles. The residents of the apartments and the motorhome salesman had both made reasonably confident identifications of Ali Farag as Suspect A from the CCTV picture. He had friends in the Marseilles Algerian community, some of them known to be opponents of the Algerian government. Visitors from Egypt had stopped over in his apartment, but none identifiable on any suspect list.

Tom, who knew the city only by way of *The French Connection*, pictured to himself a steamy Algerian quarter, apartments perched somewhere above the exotic waterfront, with overweight Egyptian visitors panting up some steep and eerily-lit passageway to reach Ali's sombre eyrie.

The police reported that he'd departed with his motorhome on 10th June and not been seen since. They were keeping watch in case he returned. Their report included his fingerprints, and later that day Sgt Howe matched them to a set found in the Avonmouth warehouse.

'Very good!' was Iain's reaction. 'Progress. At last a suspect with a believable backstory.' Thanks to Aliza, Ali Farag had of course now been provisionally identified as Ali Zubeida, and at this point she went off to take three days of well-deserved leave.

*

Two days later John Smith appeared unannounced in Tom's office. He had a hesitant air about him, but gave Tom a slight smile. 'Got a response for you,' he said and produced a printout from his briefcase. 'It comes, as it happens, from an old friend.'

Tom glanced down at it, inched his chair forward and read:

```
P203565 TO SJ 593
SERIAL 159.26
CAIRO TERMINAL 1737 26.09.02
TOP SECRET
MESSAGE BEGINS:
```

Forward the House and all Johnian cohorts!

Tom's eyebrows inched up a fraction.

From the restaurant at the end of Ahmed Ragheb Street—here's the best we can do *pro tem*. (And boy, should it de-light your jaded palate: rump of Perfectly Normal Beast, skilfully augmented with strictly local Turkish delight, belly-trimmings—do you, Mr Dent?)

The ghost of a smile crossed Tom's face. '*Perfectly Normal Beast,*' he mused. 'That would be referring to Mr *Arthur* Dent?'

John Smith nodded a little sheepishly.

'And the restaurant?'

'That's a real place.'

'Aren't your communications logged and officially recorded?'

'He was using ORP.'

'Which is?'

'Off-the-Record Protocol. Double encryption. No record kept as default.'

'I see…'

To descend:
1 **Dr Raja Said**. Zilch on extended family—and boy, is it extended. Far as second cousins we went,

all clean, if well-heeled and over-weight. Daughter plump and fragrant Cairo lady, wraps herself up like a mummy. Luscious younger beauties proved a wee bit hard to access. But your **Uthman al-Azmeh**'s the only rotten pippin, and pretty rotten at that, getting to be a big wheel. When in town keeps to a safe house in the Casbah—unrelated family with long-standing Brotherhood ties. But no signs of him hereabouts recently.

'That's very clear,' said Tom cautiously.
'Yes,' said John Smith.

2 Re al-Azmeh's Lebanese pal Farhad in electricity supply. Must be **Farhad Faroukh**, we opine, born Beiruit, aged 36. Cairo University, heavy electrical engineering. Disappeared 19/5, not seen since. Your pic Suspect B a maybe. Definite Islamist links—bit of a rumble on the waterfront when we nosed around yesterday, I fear. No known links with major plotting groups. The lodestone havers, Watson.

3 Your lanky **Ali Zubaida**. Confirmed mechanical engineer. Confirmed links with Algerian Salvation Front. Definitely Cairo 29/4 to 7/5, first time for many years, they say. Attacking left back, they say—and rather good, they say. Your pic Suspect A CONFIRMED, so this baby watertight. Fingerprints, however, no can find. Best guess: back in Algeria now.

'That's rather more useful,' said Tom.
John Smith nodded.

4 The two lovely ladies. You pic Suspect C went down a bomb for both, so you can take your pick:

Riffat Khan: Certainly used to shoot her mouth off, George Tenet's likely lads hunting her. George T. thinks maybe in Canada, not around here since early last year. Maths in Karachi, Economics at Vassar. Family money, father in chemicals in Paki. Lesbi, contacts problematic. Al-Azmeh kept up his university links, so they could've met.

'George Tenet is head of the CIA?'
'Right.'

Your Alifa person: **Alifa Elabd**, ex Tripoli, age 26, mousey. Trained in electronics, definitely a plotter, makes bombs, knows al-Azmeh, smells the likelier to me. Little bird says in England for three years. But it was a very little bird.

5 And our very, very own vaguely tentatives? Quite a few, little real evidence. Mr al-Azmeh contacted lots. Several conceivable cell-members, no reason to plump. List later if you want. Links upward into al Qaida circles clearer, but they won't help you.

So there you have it, O Deep Thought. One firm, two wobblies, almost nothing on whereabouts. Velly, velly solly.
Passionate devotion, yours truliest,
Ford Prefect.

MESSAGE ENDS

'There are nuggets of clarity buried in all this,' admitted Tom.

John Smith nodded.

'But what does it amount to? Names clarified, yes. Just one new firm identification: Suspect A is definitely Ali Zubaida. For B, Farhad Faroukh is doubtful, and for C, bear in mind Riffat Khan and Alifa Elabd… Nothing firm on any whereabouts.'

'No,' said John Smith. He smiled at Tom.

'And nothing useful at all on which of them if any might be the hacker: the mathematician *and* the hospital technician *and* both engineers might or might not know about computers and code-breaking.' Tom paused for thought.

'I'll take the printout back with me,' said John Smith at last. 'Got it clear in your head? I'll forward a digest later.'

Tom read through the message again. 'OK,' he said, and handed the paper back.

John Smith got silently to his feet, found his coat and waved goodbye from the door.

Come to think of it, thought Tom after he'd left, the *Guide* always was annoyingly short on detail whenever Ford Prefect or Arthur Dent really needed it. But on the other hand John Smith's new-found friendliness had proved rather extraordinary—there had been, after all, no need for him to reveal his friend's remarkable style. It seemed to imply, in fact, a rather encouraging level of increased trust. Or at least a closing of the ranks against Halbrit.

Identification

It was now 11th October; the early autumn heat had passed and Iain's desk fan was idle.

'So far,' said Tom with a frown, 'we have two firm identifications: Suspect D is Uthman al-Azmeh from Egypt and A is Ali Zubeida, also originally from Egypt but via Algeria and Marseilles.'

'And we also know their roles,' said Ian.

'Yes: Al-Azmeh was the leader, and Zubeida dealt with the bomb.'

'But the other two are a lot hazier.'

'Agreed,' said Tom. 'The shorter man B helped al-Azmeh fire the Stingers, and we also know he loved his computer, so he might be the hacker—though Zubeida and the woman C also might be knowledgeable about computers. B may or may not be the Lebanese Farhad Faroukh, but we definitely know he is the same as Kali.

'Which leaves C,' said Iain. 'Who *may* be Riffat Khan or Alifa Elabd.'

'The SIS guy thought Elabd was the more likely,' said Tom firmly. 'And he said she might have moved to England… But as to her role in the plot, it seems to be a complete mystery.'

'And where they are now?'

Tom furrowed his brow. 'Seems clear that A, B and D have all left the country,' he said and leaned back in his chair. 'There's not a lot we can do to catch them.

SIS will presumably be watching for al-Azmeh in Cairo.'

'And his contacts there.'

'Yes. And the SIS man put Ali Zubaida in Algeria. The French police are beavering away in Marseilles, but there can't be much more to come from those apartments, or the motorhome hire. So unless Zubeida returns to France… Anything new for us there?'

Iain hesitated. 'No.'

'It looks as though B left the country through Heathrow, but we checked all those passenger lists and found nothing. If he's Farhad from Lebanon, the SIS have no idea where he is now.'

'If the suspects have any sense,' said Iain, 'they'll all be lying low, well away from home ground.'

'True,' said Tom gloomily, and ran the fingers of one hand up through his hair. 'As to the woman C, all we have is she left Plymouth heading for London on 20th August and *may* have been in West Drayton at the time of the attacks.'

'We haven't heard the results of the checks at the Terminals Control Centre yet.'

'Maybe we should concentrate on Suspect C, Iain. It occurs to me that if she was living in London, then she must have *left* England by some route or other just before 10th August, when she left Roscoff with Zubeida on the ferry.'

'Mm… More passenger-list checks?'

'I think we should.'

*

But later that day, just before leaving work, Tom received a telephone call.

'Inspector Tallis?'

'Yup.'

'On *Crimewatch* two weeks ago?'

'Yes.'

'Bill Silverman here… Professor of Mathematics, Imperial College.'

'Imperial College, London?'

'That's it. I've just been watching that programme—one of my students records them, and he suggested I should take a look.'

Tom drew a pad towards himself and scribbled his biro on it to make sure it was working.

'Point is, Pierre thought he recognised one of your suspects.'

'Ah! Which one?'

'Suspect B. The shorter of the two in the small Peugeot.'

'Ah!' said Tom. 'And who do you think he is?'

'We were extremely surprised—but we believe he's someone who used to work with us here in my research group.'

'Really?'

'Yes.'

'Name?'

'Saddiq. Dr Hasan Saddiq.'

Tom scribbled. 'And did you agree with Pierre's identification?'

'Yes.'

'And when did Dr Saddiq leave?'

'Eighteen months ago.'

'This is important,' said Tom. 'I'd better meet you, and if possible other members of your group, too. Tomorrow? Can you manage that?'

'Any time—we'll make time.'

'Where?'

'Department of Pure Mathematics.'

'At Imperial College. Good. Tomorrow about 3 pm?'

*

Tomorrow was a Saturday. Tom hurried up to London again, and, having a little leisure on the train, found his mind turning to Miranda's complaint that he had no feelings about the terrorists. He had in fact, purely for professional reasons, tried to get himself inside the mind of a terrorist planning an outrage—a dedicated West Bank Palestinian, say. But in one sense Miranda had been quite right: his imagination had failed.

He found his way to Exhibition Road. It was 12th October; chilly, with wet plane leaves covering the pavement. Bill Silverman was waiting at the entrance to let him in, in shirtsleeves with a green waistcoat. He had curly greying hair. They took the lift to the fifth floor, where the research group members were assembling in a reading room, making instant coffee in individual mugs; the professor's carried a Union Jack. One of them handed Tom a hot plastic cup, with a crumbling digestive biscuit.

'Where's Mike?' asked Bill.

A saturnine figure ambled from a side office.

'Oh, here he is... Welcome to the Modern Algebra Group, Chief Inspector. You know who I am. This is Pierre... Annie...'

'You all know the reason for my visit?' asked Tom.

Indistinct nods all round.

'And you all of knew Hasan?'

More nods.

Tom smiled. 'I'd like to keep this informal,' he said. 'And I feel very ignorant about your work. What is it you all do?'

210

Bill raised his eyebrows and looked around. 'Topology, mostly,' he said. 'But Annie here does analytical geometry.' Annie was freckled, with red hair.

'And Dr Saddiq did the same?'

'Topology, yes.'

'Which is a sort of maths?'

'Pure maths,' said the professor. 'The maths of shapes, you might say, and how they connect. Nothing applied, we're not theoretical physicists.'

Tom nodded. He began by handing round the computer-enhanced CCTV picture of Kali. Professor Silverman picked up a folder from the table at which he was sitting and extracted from it an eighteen-month-old group photo that included Hasan. Everyone compared them and agreed that the two images looked very much alike. And indeed, there was something very characteristic about the slight figure with the quiet smile and long hands.

'And where was he before he joined you?'

'Al-Quds University,' said Bill Silverman. 'In East Jerusalem. He did his Ph D there.' He opened the folder again. 'Here we are...'

'And before that?'

'Maths at the University of Jordan.'

'So he came to you after his Ph D?'

'Yes, in 1999.'

'Three years ago... I suppose some of you must have been friends with him, to some extent at least?'

There was a general exchange of glances.

'All of us, I think,' said Pierre, who was wearing a well-cut grey suit.

'Really?'

There was a general murmur of agreement. 'He was a very friendly man, you understand,' said Pierre. 'He liked to laugh, he made us laugh. He liked to drink and to cook. And he was a good mathematician.'

'Mm,' said Tom. 'Did he talk politics?'

'Yes and no,' said Mike. 'About UK politics, yes. And he was concerned about the Palestinians, critical of the Americans and Israelis. But I never heard him say anything that a liberal British academic couldn't have said.'

'Do you all agree about that?'

'Yes,' said Annie, speaking for the first time. Her voice was light but incisive. 'He never sounded extreme. He didn't talk about Islam, and I don't think he was religious. He didn't talk about Jordanian politics at all.'

'But he is Jordanian?'

'Yes. He grew up in Amman.'

'What was he like as a person?'

'Very wide-ranging,' said Mike. 'And it's like Pierre says, you couldn't help liking him. He was interested in all sorts of things. Always off to exhibitions. Read the Economist and the New Yorker. Knew about London University politics… And he must have gone in for ballet at some time—he showed us the ballet steps.'

'Really?'

'Yes,' said Pierre. 'He moved very gracefully.'

Annie nodded.

'And if I'd been in trouble,' Mike went on, 'I wouldn't have minded telling Hasan. He was that sort of guy… Those *Crimewatch* pictures came as a real shock.'

'And how did you react when you saw them?' asked Tom.

Mike didn't hesitate. 'I thought—well, if Hasan is a terrorist, it must be for some damn good reason.'

Bill Silverman opened his eyes wide but didn't comment; Annie frowned and looked down at her hands.

Tom's eyes narrowed. 'You know how many people died on that ferry?'

'I know,' said Mike, scratching his head. 'I know what I just said sounds dreadful. But I couldn't help it. All I can think is—if it was Hasan, he *must* have had a very good reason. He wasn't a sloppy thinker.'

'Did he have *personal* reasons?'

'He never spelled out anything like that. But I suppose he might have been careful not to. He talked a lot about friends in Amman, but I don't think he ever said much about his family... I know he had a sister, but he never talked about her.'

'Did you ask?'

'Yes, I did once, but he just changed the subject.'

'You know,' said Pierre hesitantly, 'sometimes he wouldn't explain what had become of a person he'd talked about. Sometimes, I thought: *mon ami*, this friend of yours, he came to a sticky end, yes? And you are preferring not to tell me.'

Annie was still frowning.

'You had the same experience?' Tom asked her.

'Yes. Twice, I think.'

'We're all in a difficult position, Chief Inspector,' said Bill Silverman. 'We all feel that Hasan's been a real friend. And by speaking to you about him, we're probably getting him into deep trouble.'

'But you've chosen nevertheless to do so.'

'Well, yes,' said Bill firmly. 'In a situation of this seriousness, and after so many people have died, given that we've recognised someone, we're surely bound to speak up.' He spoke firmly and without glancing around the group for confirmation: they must have

213

agreed their stance before he phoned Plymouth.

'I understand,' Tom said. 'But from what you're saying, nobody here felt there was anything bad about Hasan at all?'

'That's right,' said Bill.

'There's one thing you might say was bad,' said Annie.

'What?'

'He was a hacker.'

There was a moment's pause. But Tom detected more surprise than shock.

'Really, Annie?' said Bill. 'Are you sure?'

'Yes… It was soon after he got here. I came into his office once, late one night, and I happened to see what he had up on his laptop. It was a bank account screen. HSBC, same as me. When he saw me he logged out quickly. I said sorry, and left.'

'So what?' said Mike.

'I caught sight of the account name.'

'And?

'It was *Neil Hamilton, MP.*'

This time, there was a much longer pause.

'The brown envelope man?' asked Mike at last.

'That's the one… And Hasan was grinning to himself.'

Mike laughed. 'One might well grin,' he said.

'Didn't you ask him about it?' said Pierre.

'Well, no,' said Annie. 'But in the tearoom later that day, the conversation happened to get round to hacking. He was there, so I remarked acidly that it must be quite exciting, especially something as difficult as breaking banking security…'

'Did he respond?'

'He just looked quickly at me. Then he glanced down at those long hands of his and slowly shook his head.'

'And that was it?'

'Yes. He never said anything to me about it.'

'And you never told anyone?'

Annie hesitated. 'No,' she said.

Tom wondered: did Hasan have some particular reason to feel safe with Annie? And said, 'I guess all of you know a lot about computers. How difficult is hacking?'

'It depends on the hacking,' said Pierre. 'From what one hears, at a low level it is quite easy.'

'But breaking into a bank account would be very hard,' said Mike.

'Has anyone else got any evidence of hacking by Hasan? Or interest in code-breaking?'

'Not hacking,' said Mike. 'But he was interested in Alan Turing.'

'Yes he was,' said Annie, and looked sharply at Tom as if to be sure he knew who Turing was.

Tom nodded. 'Yes,' he said. 'That's important... Tell me, is there anything in Hasan's maths background relevant to code-breaking?'

Bill Silverman screwed up his face. 'It's number theory you need,' he said. 'So, not in this group... He did his doctorate with Mustafa Haniff.'

'Did Haniff do number theory?'

'No, no; he's a topologist, like us. In fact, Hasan was following up some of Mustafa's ideas when he was here.'

'And topology could never help with code-breaking?'

'Well,' said Bill doubtfully. 'I wouldn't go as far as that. All maths is linked together—and there *are* links between topology and number theory, so probably with code breaking too, if you look into it far enough.'

'Ah,' said Tom. He waited, but nobody added any-thing to Bill's reflection. 'And where did Hasan go when he left?' he asked at last.

'Back to work at in his old university, in Amman.'

'Did he leave a forwarding address?'

'His home address, I think. Yes, here it is… It's where he grew up.'

'Have any of you been in contact since?'

Bill considered. 'Only very shortly after he left,' he said. 'I've had no reason to since.'

'I got a card last Christmas,' said Annie.

'Anyone else?'

But there'd been no other contacts. Tom continued the conversation for some time, and then talked to each member of the group individually, spending longer with Annie, and with Professor Silverman who photocopied the details in the file and handed over his copy of the group photo. Nothing further of im-portance emerged. Annie had clearly admired Hasan and liked him, but no more than that, so far as Tom could tell. Bill Silverman thought Hasan's thesis adviser might be currently in the US, attending a conference that finished in about a week's time. 'Very nice man,' he said. 'I know him quite well, we worked together at Stanford. Terribly concerned about the future of the Palestinians. Idealist, probably a pacifist.'

Official signed statements would have to come later.

'All very friendly and informal' said Tom to himself as he settled into the Plymouth express. As the train gathered speed through West London he set himself to consider the practicalities of catching his suspect, but found it hard to concentrate. He found himself instead picturing Hasan using those expressive hands to gesture about the iniquities of London University politics, or demonstrating a pirouette to Pierre, or whisking Annie into a *pas de deux*.

*

On the 14th October Dr Said was released. Tom drove with Aliza to collect him and took him to Exeter to be interviewed by John Smith, who reassured him that his suggested identifications had all been thoroughly investigated, that useful information had emerged—and that this activity had all been carefully concealed from the Americans.

'A self-assured young man,' Dr Said commented as Tom drove them home down the A38. After that he exchanged an occasional smile with Aliza, but remained silent, and sighed heavily once or twice.

They dropped him off at his surgery. As the car drew up Farideh Osman rushed out to welcome him with a tearful embrace: she had been released the previous day.

'Ah, Farideh,' said Dr Said, beaming. 'So we meet again, in happier circumstances! Now, can we manage some coffee for Inspector Tallis and Sergeant Akinci, after our long drive? And whatever has become of all my patients?'

*

On 17th October Tom called Aliza into his office for a further conference; she marched in with a big smile.

Tom grinned too. 'Sit down,' he said. 'I'll just give Iain a buzz… But first, there's something I want to ask. I was wondering whether you'd care to come round for supper sometime?'

Aliza looked somewhat shocked.

'As a celebration of your release. Purely socially, just

with me and my daughter. But only if you'd like to…
It's not against regulations, you know,' he added with
a smile. 'In fact, I told the Super what I had in mind
and he approved. I'd been telling him how hard you'd
beavered away at Larkhill.'

She seemed to be thinking rapidly. 'Thanks very
much, Sir,' she said at last.

'Would Saturday week be all right? That's the
2nd November.'

'I'm sure I can make that.'

'Good,' said Tom.

'If your daughter didn't cook pork?' she added cautiously.

'Of course,' said Tom. 'Miranda had something
vegetarian in mind.'

Aliza smiled and nodded.

'About eight?'

She nodded again.

'Right,' said Tom, and picked up his phone.

*

Tom's report on the Imperial College link made its
way in due course to Dr Sampson, who found it
disturbing, for various reasons.   He held several
discussions with his old boss in Cheltenham; and then,
after extensive debate at the highest levels, the
Americans were told for the first time what GCHQ
knew about the Israeli computer system and the Trojan
horse within it. This provoked an eruption: why had
intelligence of such importance not been more
promptly transmitted to close allies? The Israelis must
be informed forthwith; and shortly thereafter a team of
CIA computer experts was dispatched to Tel Aviv.

Arrest

The topology meeting was in full swing, and Mustafa Haniff rushed down to breakfast. He loved Chicago. The night he arrived, he'd revelled in the Symphony Orchestra under Barenboim. Now, he collected his usual V8 juice and bagel from the student hostel self-service counter, found himself at a table with no-one he knew, and swung into animated conversation nevertheless, pausing only to air his usual complaint of too many elderly delegates and too few mature papers. Then onto the conference bus. Neighbourhoods rolled past—spacious downtown, impoverished Hispanic, flashy Italian—trains squeaked on the corners of the el. The lakeside skyscrapers were cleaner and more vivid than New York's, the sky behind them blue after rain. They drew up outside the University Math Department.

In the conference lobby, he was at once the centre of a group of Middle East postdocs and graduate students, all in the same out-of-school mood. He got pumped about a new preprint posted on the results board. In the middle of this discussion, an ex-colleague from Stanford came up and shook his hand.

'By the way, Mustafa,' he said, 'air-letter for you on the message board. English postmark.'

Mustafa felt suddenly uneasy. With the need for coffee as his excuse, he made his way to Conference Administration. When he saw the handwriting, he was reassured. But the envelope felt thick, this wasn't the place. He slid it into an inner pocket and joined the crowd jostling into the first plenary session of the day.

*

Two days earlier in Amman, Hasan had found his regular backdoor to the Mossad computer blocked.

Moving fast he struggled to obliterate all traces of his activity. Then, remembering he'd retained a user account on the Imperial College network, he hastily hacked into its management system. There he discovered a new tracer, set to siphon off his e-mails.

Uthman, as it happened, was also in Amman, and they met briefly. Uthman would warn Ali, now somewhere safe in the Algerian desert. But contacting C was more tedious: Hasan needed to post a warning for her, concealed within a photofile on the Hounslow Council web site.

But the third time he used his cell phone Jordan Telephone were ready for him. They located the handset, and security police caught him with baseball bats as he emerged blinking from the back of a windowless van in the university car park. His first interrogation and torture, in a concrete basement at security headquarters, was as foul as he'd been warned to expect. But he managed to give little away and Uthman escaped.

The CIA team, when they reached Amman, found his laptop frustrating. The only application they found on it was one whose sole task was to obliterate all working files at the end of each session. They concluded he must have used innocent third-party sites to store his programmes and send his e-mails, which might be anywhere around the globe.

*

At six in the evening, back in the graduate hostel, Mustafa opened his letter. It was in Arabic:

> *To my honoured father,*
>
> *You must be wondering, papa, why I am writing to you at your conference in America.*
>
> *I have been very, very happy working in England. But unfortunately, I have to leave and return home. I am writing this letter to you now to say good-bye, for the time being. When you return home I shall not be there, you will not see me. But it will not be for ever, if Allah is willing.*
>
> *Honoured father, I am afraid that you will not approve of what I have been doing, you are a man of peace. At the moment, you know none of it, but you will know later. Papa, I tried to be a daughter of non-violence. But I could not. I keep a list of my friends, like this:*
>
> *My closest friend, the other Fatima, was killed by a rocket when she was only 15.*
>
> *Her brother tried to avenge her by joining Fatah; but he died defending the refugee camp.*
>
> *The twins became scholars of the Qu'ran. The Israelis interned them.*
>
> *Aisha, she died when the tanks came to Bethlehem.*
>
> *Farhad was shot dead when he threw stones.*
>
> *These are the ones I liked the best, but the others are hundreds. The Israelis prevent our education. They took our land when they came first, and they have continued to take it ever*

221

since. There is no end to their murders of us. They enlist all the infidels of the World to do their dirty work. Papa, I cannot believe that the Prophet—peace be upon him—would not cry out that we must fight, and fight with vigour. Anyway, I have done it, even as a woman. So it is. Honoured father, I ask humbly for your forgiveness if you do not agree with me.

The people my partners are good men. The first of them is like you, it is hard for him to kill infidels. He is a good Muslim, he says his prayers more than I do. He is kind, and it is hard work for him to be brave. I do not need to tell you what a good man the second is, you know already. The third, our leader, is hard like adamant, I am a little afraid of him. He is certain of his principles and he knows how to fight.

He has asked me to hand you a letter—when I am at home next time, he said. But because I shall not be seeing you there, I shall place it now beside this my letter. I was not able to disappear without sending you a message. I fear it is a danger to write to you, but it is sufficiently unlikely that anyone will yet be intercepting your mail in Chicago. However, I must urge you, I must insist, please, that you destroy these letters when you have read them.

I must not be sounding too serious. We shall meet again, and I shall wish to bring you sweetmeats and to play for you on my violin as though I were a little girl again.

From your respectful daughter,
Fatima Haniff

This letter so appalled Mustafa that at first he failed to understand it beyond the first few sentences. He'd known she had some sympathy for the intifada—but this sounded like terrorism, and it sounded as though she was being hunted. Those attacks on Bush and Sharon? Was Mossad after her? The CIA? He searched in his mind for anything he could do to protect her, and knew there was nothing.

The enclosure was a sealed but unaddressed letter written on thin paper, also in Arabic:

> *Honoured Sir,*
>
> *It is a deep sadness to me that my path through life has never intertwined with your own. I wish to acknowledge that I and my brothers and sister have been blessed through you, and write now that we know how great a thing we have received.*
>
> *'This is nothing but a revealment taught to him by one terrible in power.'*
>
> *The time is a difficult one for all peoples of our faith, and*
>
> *'Right-minded men shall save the people together'.*
>
> *Now that your support has come to us once, we shall be happy to look to you again when the time is ripe.*
>
> *'Blessings be upon him who comes in the name of Allah.'*

There was no signature. The quotations from the Qu'ran infuriated Mustafa. He shouted aloud in his empty hostel room, scrunched up the paper, and threw it violently into the trash box. Then he paused, fished it out, and read it through again. Someone had left a complimentary book of matches on his bedside table. He took the letter to the en-suite, burnt it, and flushed away the ashes and the match.

Then he re-read Fatima's letter. He folded it small and placed it in his wallet inside his Palestinian driving licence.

He must ring his wife. But perhaps their phone was already tapped? To discuss the letter with her—or even to make some guarded reference to danger impending—would surely be unsafe. To return home was the only option. Now, at once! And better not to use the conference facilities. He hurried out onto the humid street to search for a travel agent.

*

The earliest flight Mustafa could arrange landed in Amman at 7 pm; the sky was clear, the air cold, the stars were coming out.

Jordanian immigration accepted him without any sign of interest. But if Fatima was being hunted, didn't that mean he must come under suspicion too? Could they know already that he'd rearranged his return? He decided to hire a taxi to drive all the way home, crossing into the West Bank at the Allenby Bridge. He called Leila to let her know when to expect him. She didn't answer. Which was unexpected: it was unwise to be out in the evening in Al 'Ayzariyah. He left a message on the answerphone, and went to find a taxi.

What with the border and check-point delays it was nearly ten before he drew up in the dark street and paid off the taxi driver. He listened as the noise of the taxi faded. The street was silent, the air colder still. The lift had not worked for years, and he clambered slowly up the stairs with his one suitcase.

There was no light under the front door of the flat. He fumbled with his key, got the door open, and called. There was no response. He hauled his case into the vestibule, closed the door, turned on the light, and saw there were two messages on the answer-phone. The first was from Leila herself, timed two days earlier: 'Mustafa, listen. I have had to leave the flat. Do not stay here yourself, it is important. I shall find you when I can. Allah be with us.' The second was his own message to her.

He quickly switched off the light again, and stood in the darkness wondering who might have seen him arrive. All was silent. He opened the door into the sitting room. Heavy curtains covered the windows; he felt his way to his usual easy chair and sat down, still breathing hard from the stairs.

He heard a slight noise. Then, blindingly, his own reading light burst on.

There was a man sitting at his desk, a heavy man in his fifties with a bald head. In the shadows at the back of the room were three young Israeli soldiers in uniform, light glinting from their Uzi sub-machine guns.

Mustafa stared around him. 'What are you doing in my flat?' he asked quietly.

'What do you think?' replied the man, in Arabic with a strong Hebrew accent. 'Where have you come from?'

'That is not your business.'

'Of course it is my business,' said the man. 'Think, Professor Haniff. We are not going to go away and leave you. You would be wise to answer.'

Mustafa considered. 'I have come from Chicago, from a mathematics conference.'

'Where is your wife?'

'I have no idea. You heard her message.'

'Where is your daughter Fatima?'

So they knew. 'In England, so far as I know. She works there.'

'What is her address?'

'Surely you know that already?'

'I like to check my data.'

Mustafa told him.

'Where is your ex-student Hasan Saddiq?'

They know *everything* thought Mustafa, despairing. 'In Amman, as far as I know. I have not spoken to him for about a year.'

The bald man scowled. 'That is not correct. You spoke to him by phone in January. Why did you call him?'

Mustafa struggled to get his bearings. 'Perhaps I did,' he said slowly. 'Yes… It was the day a small girl was killed by a tank near our Police Station. I knew the girl's mother; the girl's father died earlier. One of your rockets—he was my student.'

'Is that relevant?'

'Hasan knew the mother and father. I thought I should tell him what had happened.'

The man stared at him. 'I am sorry about the small girl,' he said.

Mustafa returned the stare, and raised his eyebrows expressively. 'May I ask your name?' he said.

'I am Major Amos Stein… Did you discuss the RSA algorithm with Hasan?'

'The RSA algorithm? Not by that name… What is it?'

'Then you did discuss mathematics?'

'We probably discussed topology. I can't remember.'

'Did you discuss number theory?'

'No.'

'We think you did. Had Hasan proved a new theorem?'

'Not in number theory. We didn't discuss number theory.' Mustafa knew he was sweating freely.

'Had he proved *any* new theorem?'

'I can't remember,' said Mustafa wearily. 'His job is to prove new theorems. He may have told me about something new in topology, I can't remember.'

'Is Hasan good enough to do important work in number theory?'

'If he put his mind to it, yes.'

'Ah! Had *you* proved any new theorems?'

'My job too is to prove new theorems!'

'But not in number theory?'

'No.'

Major Stein looked at Mustafa closely. Mustafa was afraid that his sweat was too obvious. The Major took out a mobile phone, called a number, and waited.

'Ready,' he said, and rang off.

After five minutes, a tracked vehicle pulled up in the street below with a clatter. Metal studs sounded on the stone stairs. An Israeli Army Lieutenant with an American Air Force Colonel, both in uniform, entered the room.

The American looked at Mustafa.

'Enjoy the Windy City, Haniff?' he said after a while, in English, and paused quizzically. 'Where's your wife?'

'Who the hell are you?' said Mustafa.

'And *I* said, where's your fucking wife?'

'I wish to know who you are and why you're here.'

The American smiled slowly. 'We're not in Chicago now,' he said, 'or in Stanford, or in godalmighty

Cambridge, England… My name's Halbrit. We'll be getting to know each other… You'll learn to answer soon enough.'

Mustafa said no more.

'Plenty of time,' said Halbrit easily. 'But we better get going.'

'Tel Aviv by one am,' said Major Stein. The soldiers handcuffed Mustafa.

*

Within hours, Fatima's letter had been found and faxed to Washington, Paris, and London. Five days later a translation reached Tom. He and Iain took in its implications, and Tom made a photocopy. Later he re-read it several times, and that evening he rang Jane and, wondering more than a little at himself, asked whether she would be free to call round on the Saturday morning; she said she would.

The RSA Algorithm

When Saturday came round the weather was warm and the dahlias still in bloom, so when Jane appeared, before settling down to talk, she and Tom took a quick tour around the garden with Miranda. As they were doing so Tom noticed an ancient Citroen creeping slowly along the road in front of the house. It stopped, and the driver leant over and peered at them through the passenger window. After a moment he got out, locked the car door and turned towards Tom with an apologetic smile.

It was Dr Sampson.

Taken aback, Tom stood silent. Dr Sampson opened the garden gate and walked slowly over the grass towards them, much more sombre than Tom remembered; the elfin style had vanished entirely. Tom introduced Miranda and Jane, and Dr Sampson nodded and shook hands, with a little bow to each, but remained silent; he seemed preoccupied. Miranda looked questioningly at Tom, who hadn't named the new arrival but simply turned to him and asked, 'Talk indoors?'

A slow nod.

Tom looked quickly at Miranda.

'Make you some coffee?' she responded.

Tom smiled gratefully and led the way inside. Dr Sampson followed and Jane disappeared with Miranda to the kitchen.

Once in the sitting room, Dr Sampson settled into an easy chair. He still seemed lost in thought and nothing further was said until Miranda appeared with a tray and cafetière. She poured out two cups and was about to withdraw when Dr Sampson said,

'No, stay please.'

Tom looked sharply at him.

'Dr Allison too, if she's willing.'

Miranda glanced uncertainly at Tom, who hesitated for a second or two, then gave a tiny shrug and nodded. Miranda went off to find Jane.

'I'm sorry to press,' said Tom firmly as soon as she'd gone. 'But what *is* this? This is my home. Why are you here?'

Dr Sampson smiled uneasily. 'You may well ask, Tom,' he said, but lapsed again into silence. However, when Miranda had reappeared with Jane he said at once, 'I'd better explain… I'm a retired official from the government code and signals establishment.'

Tom's eyes opened very wide.

Jane blinked. 'GCHQ?'

'Yes. But it may be better if you two don't know my name.'

Jane and Miranda exchanged mystified glances and found themselves chairs. When they were settled, Dr Sampson said:

'I'm here, Tom, for an extremely irregular reason, as I'm sure you've already deduced.' He smiled cautiously. Then he coughed and said, 'I need some advice.'

'*Advice*?' said Jane.

'Yes.'

'But what for?'

'Yes,' said Tom. 'Whatever for?'

'I'm coming to that.' Dr Sampson turned to Miranda. 'I imagine Tom doesn't discuss police matters with you?'

She glanced at Tom. 'No,' she said.

'But you've realised, I'm sure, that he's hunting the terrorists?'

'That's been fairly obvious.'

'*Hold on...*' said Tom.

Dr Sampson smiled wanly. 'Though I'm sure Tom is about to object,' he said, 'if you're to understand my difficulty I need to tell you something about that investigation.'

Tom's head jerked up. 'I can't accept that.'

'You're perfectly right to object, Tom... But I promise you that I have a very good reason for what I'm doing... and I'm senior to you. Could you, perhaps, just allow the responsibility to rest on my head?' He gave Tom an appealing look.

Tom thought for several seconds, continuing to frown, and Jane looked quickly at him.

Dr Sampson seemed to take his silence as assent and turned to Jane and Miranda. 'The essence of the matter is this,' he said, and took a large breath. 'It concerns code-breaking...'

'*Code*-breaking?' said Miranda.

'Hold on,' said Tom again.

'Yes?' said Dr Sampson.

'You told me that was *ultra* secret.'

Dr Sampson nodded. 'Indeed it is,' he said. '*Please* hold your fire, Tom, until you understand exactly what I'm here for.' He turned again to Miranda. 'The security services have concluded that the terrorists have broken the code used by the Israeli Government. Recently the Israeli security service Mossad have detained in that connection a certain Palestinian mathematician... Let's call him X.' He glanced up quickly, as if to be sure they were following. 'This man has an international reputation.'

Tom was still frowning.

'Thus far,' said Dr Sampson, 'X has insisted to Mossad that he knows nothing about decryption.' He paused, and looked a little uncertainly at all three of them.

'Now,' he went on, 'it so happens that *I* know something about decryption, and for that reason the authorities have asked me to go to Tel Aviv to interrogate X. But I have a difficulty about that on which I'd very much value your opinions.' He paused and looked carefully at each of them.

Tom, extremely disturbed, decided he needed to wait before objecting further.

'But first, before we can get to that,' went on Dr Sampson, 'I need to explain a particular feature of the decryption problem… There's nothing secret about it.'

Miranda looked at Jane. 'Will we be able to follow?' she asked.

'I won't make it hard, I promise…

[Readers who dislike arithmetic may prefer at this point to jump forward to page 237.]

… I told you earlier, Tom, about the public and private keys.'

'Yes, you did,' said Tom uneasily. 'Though I didn't understand properly.'

Dr Sampson frowned. 'How so? Tell me.'

'Why do we have to go into this?'

'Let me be the judge of that.'

'Well… You said that both the public key and the way in which it's used to encipher the message are public knowledge?'

'Correct.'

'Well, I'd imagined that the first step in encryption is for the sender to turn the letters of his message into a string of numbers in some way.'

'Quite right.'

'He might write 01 for A, 02 for B and so on?'

'Something like that, yes.'

'And that he then goes on to do some complicated arithmetic on this number string to encrypt it?'

'Yes.'

'Well, what I couldn't understand was, if the hacker knows both the public key and the encryption procedure, why can't he just reverse the encryption, step by step? You know, adding wherever the encrypter had subtracted and multiplying where the encrypter had divided, or whatever? ... That was it, really,' Tom added, with a doubtful look at Jane and Miranda.

Dr Sampson paused. 'That's a perfectly sensible question,' he said at last. 'But one of the clever things about this method of encryption is that it *can't* be reversed in that simple way... Maybe it's quickest if I just show you all. We might need a calculator.'

'There's one in the desk,' said Miranda, and fetched it.

'They call it the RSA algorithm,' said Dr Sampson. 'It actually uses *two* numbers that are public knowledge, a special number N and the number called the public key K. In real life both these numbers are made extremely large, but to illustrate I'll use small ones. Let's take N to be... say 15, and K to be 7. As you correctly guessed Tom, the sender first converts the letters of his message into a single very long number. Then he breaks this long number up into blocks, in such a way that the digits in each block spell out a number smaller than the special number N. Suppose he wants to encrypt such a block number, which happens to be, say, 8. His first step is to raise the message block number to the *power* of the public key K. Can you do that Miranda? What's 8 to power 7?'

Miranda nodded and punched some keys on the calculator. '2,097,152,' she said after a short pause.

'Now the second step. He divides his answer by the special number N and finds the remainder.'

'So I divide 2,097,152 by 15?'

'That's right.'

'That's 139,810 remainder 2,' said Miranda after some fiddling.

'That's it—we're done,' said Dr Sampson. 'The encrypted version of the message block number 8 is just the remainder, in this case 2. The sender is only interested in the remainder, he just discards the 139,810... Now Tom, can you see now why this process can't be reversed step-by-step?'

Tom thought for a bit. 'Well,' he said, and hesitated. 'I suppose the hacker will never see the 139,810 because it's been discarded, which means he has no way of getting back from the 2 to the 2,097,152?'

'That's it, you've got it... That didn't take too long.'

The three listeners thought for a while. 'But,' said Jane doubtfully at last, 'if he's discarded the 139,810, doesn't that mean he's thrown away almost all the content of the message block too? How can the receiver recover the original block from the remainder alone?'

'That's the second clever thing,' said Dr Sampson. 'In fact, the logical content *hasn't* been thrown away. It's still there, hidden in the remainder, and the receiver can get it back by using the private key. In this case the private key corresponding to public key 7 happens to be 3. To decrypt the message block, the receiver does a calculation very much like what the sender did to encrypt it. He takes the encrypted block, which was 2, and raises it to the power of the *private* key. What's 2 raised to power 3?'

'Eight,' said Jane quickly before Miranda could do anything with the calculator, and Dr Sampson smiled.

'Right, he said. 'And what do you get if you divide 8 by 15?'

'Zero remainder 8,' said Miranda.

'Right. As with the encryption, the answer is just the remainder—and, as you can see, we've successfully got back to 8, the original block number—in spite of the discards.'

Tom did a double-take. 'But how the hell did that happen?' he asked. 'I can't see why all this power-taking stuff should lead back to the original block number.'

Dr Sampson smiled broadly. 'I'm not surprised,' he said. 'To explain why it works would require some heavy maths, which we don't have time for... All of which brings me back to the point I'm trying to reach.

'There's a very important feature of this scheme. For it to work the special number N can't be just any large number. It has to be the product of two prime numbers. For instance, I chose 15, which is the product of the prime numbers 3 and 5. The process for working out the public and private keys is quite simple, but to use it *you need to know the two prime numbers*.

'Now the process for working out the keys is public knowledge, so you might think that the hacker could first work out the prime numbers by factorising N for himself, and then go on to deduce the private key—and indeed, for the small numbers we've been using, that's true, he could. But in real life there's a catch—this is the third way in which this scheme is very

235

clever. It was invented by mathematicians who knew that, according to current ideas, it is *virtually impossible to find in a finite time the prime factors of a number that's sufficiently big.* In real encryption, the numbers used are always huge. Thus although the hacker knows the number N, he has no way of finding its two prime factors, even if he uses a very powerful computer, and so he can't apply the procedure to find the private key.

'The private key will be very well protected, probably in a dedicated chip, and I think we can assume that the terrorist hacker will not be able to get at it. So the only other possibility is that *he has discovered some way of factorising very large numbers reasonably quickly.* For some years now, the security of Government and bank encryption has depended on the assumption that nobody will be clever enough to do this.'

'Got you!' said Tom. 'And the Israelis think that X may have done the clever maths required?'

Coffee and Morality

'Got you!' said Tom. 'And the Israelis think that X may have done the clever maths required?'

Dr Sampson nodded. 'Can we all have another cup, Miranda?' he said. He seemed to Jane, suddenly, to have drawn seriousness about him like a sodden raincoat, and she shivered momentarily. Miranda made more coffee and poured out silently.

'Now,' said Dr Sampson. 'Why have I decided to tell you all this? I'm about to trust you three a heck of a lot.' He peered anxiously at them and paused.

'First,' he said, 'there *is* a way of factorising large numbers quickly.'

Tom jerked upright.

'We discovered it ourselves at GCHQ about four years ago. Or rather... the fact is, *I* discovered it. Huge shock to the community. We decided we must keep it secret initially—the commercial consequences for the banks if it became known were horrendous.'

'And you stopped using that encryption method yourselves?' said Tom.

'Of course. It wasn't difficult, because the British authorities have always had doubts about relying on it, and other methods were already in use for the most sensitive communications.'

'Did you tell anyone else?'

Dr Sampson hesitated. 'After some debate at GCHQ, we decided to tell the Americans,' he said at last. 'But for various reasons we didn't tell anyone else, which meant, of course, that we and the US could read the traffic of any government that continued to use the RSA algorithm.

'Two years ago, the Russians stopped using it—whether they'd heard something, or noticed that we'd given it up, or simply worked it out for themselves, we don't know.

'My method of factorising large numbers was not quite as innovative as you might have supposed, but it's some distance away in principle from the usual approaches to number theory, which is why it wasn't discovered earlier. But it *is* closely related to certain ideas that X has worked on, which makes me suspect that Mossad may be right—he may have discovered independently how to break their code. Obviously, western intelligence sees it as essential to find out whether it was indeed X who did it, because if it wasn't him, they need urgently to find out who it was. So you can see why they've asked me to talk to him…

'And now we come to my question… I have a difficulty about X, you see. *I know him.* Or rather, I did know him a long time ago when he was a research student; I knew him rather well in those days. And I remember him as a very pleasant man—a good man, who wanted to make the world a better place… And if I interview him and discover that he has indeed done what I think he's done, and I proceed to tell the authorities, I'm concerned about what will happen to him.'

'Meaning what?' said Miranda.

Dr Sampson gently cleared his throat. 'There are, I'm afraid Miranda, a number of powerful people in high places who would consider X's knowledge too dangerous to be allowed to spread.'

'And?'

'They'll want to prevent him telling anyone what

he's done, ever.'

'*Bump him off*?' murmured Miranda. 'Really?'

Dr Sampson nodded.

'As bad as that?' said Jane sharply.

'Espionage is a very nasty business, at times.' Dr Sampson's voice had risen a little in pitch. 'And they'll want it done quickly… So there you have it. He is, as I see it, a decent man, whom I knew quite well, and liked, whose only crime is to have invented a good piece of mathematics, and told his own research student. If he guessed what use the student would make of it, does that make him very guilty? And indeed, if you look at what the Israelis have been doing to the Palestinians, from the moral point of view *should* we criticise a Palestinian so very much for using a non-lethal weapon if it comes to hand?'

Jane looked quickly at Tom, but his face remained impassive.

'So, you three,' pressed Dr Sampson. 'Where does the morality lie? Should I agree to talk to him?'

'But hold on!' said Tom sharply. 'You've come here *simply to discuss the morality*?'

'Yes.'

'That's crazy! And all so bloody irregular! *Surely* you should be discussing it with someone senior in Cheltenham?'

'Of course not, Tom! Think! My old work colleagues, however close, are *obliged* to report to higher authority if they think I'm getting out of line in the slightest. That's the GCHQ ethic… And even if I could persuade one of them to talk it through and keep his mouth shut, I'd be involving him in a conspiracy that would certainly cost him his job if it was discovered. That's why I'm here, that's why you're my chosen jury.'

'But I have obligations too,' objected Tom. 'What

about the risk to *my* job?'

Dr Sampson nodded. 'Fair point,' he said. 'But I was stuck in this crazy situation, and had very little choice. I'm gambling that the three of you are good people and true who will agree to keep this conversation… within the jury room, so to speak. The point is, no one will ever suspect *you* of having encouraged me. And I've been careful to reveal to Jane and Miranda only the minimum necessary. I haven't named X. What I've told you about how the coding works is all in the public domain.'

'But why d'you need to talk to *anyone*?' asked Tom.

'Because, Tom, I'm a fallible human being, and don't trust my own judgement. And nor should I—if prime ministers and presidents aren't supposed to take momentous decisions without consulting, surely the same should apply to me.'

'But you're trusting us far more than makes any sense! And why include Miranda and Jane?'

Dr Sampson smiled. 'Because I don't wholly trust *your* judgement either Tom,' he said. 'And I wasn't quite as ignorant as you might suppose about you three and your reliability as jurors… Before you came to see me in Cheltenham I was shown the details of your personal security clearance, which, as it happened, told me rather a lot about all of you. The investigators made it clear that you'd all been judged sensible and reliable—in spite of Jane's problems with the Atlantic shooting. In fact, when I thought about whether to trust you, Jane, it occurred to me that you must have had to face a few issues of your own about life and death, which might have given you an insight into mine a bit sharper than Tom's.'

Jane said nothing.

'It wasn't essential to include you and Miranda, but

I preferred to. I first made a silent phone call here, to confirm that Tom was at home, and then I called your number, Jane, and got your answering machine, which made me think you might well be here, given the relationship, and it being a Saturday. So I drove past, and there you all three were.' He gave her a wan smile. Then he pulled out his handkerchief, mopped his forehead, and put it away again.

'Wow,' said Miranda. Jane turned to look amazedly at Tom, and there was a very considerable pause.

'Well,' said Tom at last. 'This is all *totally* irregular and extraordinarily quixotic, but you've taken the risk, and it can't be undone.' There was another pause.

'So we must try to give him an answer?' said Jane at last.

Tom took a deep breath.

'Do we?' she persisted.

'I suppose we'd damn well better, yes… And there's one rather obvious response, isn't there?'

She looked at him.

'Well,' said Tom. '*Not* to interview X would be wrong, wouldn't it? … It's possible he had nothing to do with it, so morally you *must* see him because there's a chance you can prove he's right out of it… Innocent until proved guilty.'

'I know,' said Dr Sampson. 'But if I interview him, and find that he *did* discover it, then what should I do?'

Miranda opened her eyes very wide, and everyone thought for a while.

'If you were to tell only the Americans, what would happen?' asked Tom.

Dr Sampson shrugged. 'They would never conceal X's knowledge from the Israelis, and Mossad has a pretty ruthless record when their national security's on the line. Moreover, there are several in the CIA itself who might conclude that X was too dangerous to be left untouched. When their top executives conclude that something illegal or immoral needs to be done, their usual response is to farm it out to client states… Jordanian security, perhaps. So, all in all, much the same would happen, I think.'

'And if you limited the information to British intelligence, is there any chance the UK could find a way to save him?'

'Not likely, with Blair in blood-brother transatlantic mode.'

'Couldn't you just pretend that X *hadn't* solved it?'

'I could try. But Mossad would draw a blank when they looked elsewhere for the expertise, and come back to him in the end.'

'But,' said Tom, 'does that leave *any* possible way you could save him?'

Dr Sampson screwed up his mouth. 'Look,' he said. 'It's the *morality* I want to talk about, I don't want to go into operational detail… But the point is, what I have in mind would almost certainly involve the method of breaking the code becoming public knowledge.'

'Which would cause chaos for the world's banks?' said Tom.

'For a time, yes.' Dr Sampson laughed shortly. 'But not too dreadful in the long term, perhaps.'

'But it could do *enormous* short-term harm,' said Jane. 'It could trigger a worldwide crisis.'

'*Huge*,' muttered Tom.

Dr Sampson nodded. 'You need to remember, however,' he said, 'that this secret is sure to be revealed sometime in the next few years. And I happen to know that quite a few of the banks have been preparing contingency plans. It would be bad, but I think it would sort itself out.'

'If it became clear it was *you* who were responsible, you'd be for the high-jump?' said Jane.

'Of course. But I think I'd have a reasonable chance of covering my tracks. And if it *did* all come out, it could be argued in court that it's no crime to publish mathematics.'

'But so far as GCHQ is concerned, you'd have broken the Official Secrets Act?'

'Yes... But I'm retired. And there's a reasonable chance the authorities would choose not to take me to court. They might prefer the tabloids not to know what had happened.'

There was another long pause, and the three listeners all looked doubtfully at each other.

'I think you *should* try to save his life,' said Miranda suddenly. 'If you can find a way. Of course you should.'

Dr Sampson nodded slowly.

Jane looked enquiringly at Tom, but Tom could not bring himself to say anything.

Dr Sampson looked carefully at him. 'Choice between evils?' he said. 'Condemning an innocent man to death *versus* a bit of world-wide chaos—which would have arrived anyway eventually—plus losing a happy retirement, and only maybe?'

'*I* can't advise you,' said Tom at last. 'How could I?'

'Why not, Tom?' said Dr Sampson. 'You're a moral man, and this is a matter of life and death.'

Jane looked very hard at Tom.

Tom at last gave a shrug and a tiny nod.

'And Jane?'

She made a face and nodded too.

Dr Sampson stood up.

'*But*,' said Tom urgently and feeling considerably

annoyed. 'This has all been so *appallingly* irregular.

'Of course,' said Dr Sampson.

'And you'll never be able to get away with it, what-ever it is you're planning! Which means that, by agreeing with you on the moral issue, we've assented in the same breath to ruining the rest of your life, haven't we?'

Dr Sampson looked down at him. 'I'm quite capable, Tom,' he said, 'of taking my own decisions about personal risks. It was the *morals* I wanted your judge-ments over... Thank you very much. All three. And thank you for the coffee, Miranda.' He asked for his coat, and they all walked silently out to the car, Tom feeling shaken, but unable to see what else he could have done.

'I'm well aware,' Dr Sampson added as he settled behind the wheel, 'that I've chosen to trust you three far more than most people in my situation would have, simply to meet a need for moral confirmation in a rather isolated position.' He drew on his driving gloves. 'Many sensible people would say I'd done it for no sound reason whatever—quixotic, really... But on the other hand, given what I have in mind, I ha-ven't really added a great deal to my risks, have I?'

He wriggled the *traction-avant* dashboard lever into gear and the Citroen slid smoothly away.

Suspect C

After the Citroen had turned the corner and disappeared, Miranda said 'Wow!' again, and they all stood silent on the pavement.

'How long have you known him?' asked Jane at last.

'I've only met him once—about a month ago.'

'He must have liked you a lot.'

'Don't know about that,' said Tom, 'I liked *him*.' He led the way inside but halted in the hall, lost in thought.

Miranda settled conspiratorially onto the bottom step of the stairs. 'Is he right about the banks?' she asked. 'Not being too bad?'

'Not sure,' said Tom.

Jane nodded. 'As we said, he could easily trigger a crisis.'

'Which would affect millions,' said Miranda. 'Businesses collapsing.'

'And probably other deaths,' said Tom.

'Exactly,' said Jane. 'It's complex. But I don't think that alters his moral problem.'

'Why not?' asked Miranda.

'Because the death of X would have been a direct consequence of his own actions, whereas the primary responsibility for sorting out a financial crisis wouldn't be his at all. And, as he pointed out, the bank problem is going to emerge sometime anyway... He didn't seem to have much difficulty concluding that morality trumped national security.'

'He was still crazy to trust us so much,' said Miranda.

'Was he?' said Tom thoughtfully. 'Are we going to give him away?'

Jane smiled and shook her head slowly.

Miranda looked curiously at her. 'What d'you think he's planning to do?' she asked.

Tom grunted. 'No idea,' he said. 'He's a clever man… Brave, too.'

'Whatever it is, we all want it to work,' said Jane.

At this point the phone rang. Miranda answered it, murmured, 'Hold on please.' She mouthed, 'Head of Department—take it in my room,' and rushed upstairs. From the landing she shouted down, 'Carry on after lunch?' but didn't wait for an answer.

Tom smiled in her direction, waited, and replaced the receiver on its base when he heard voices from it.

Jane smiled too and then became serious again. 'All the same,' she said, 'I still don't understand why he trusted us so much. Do you? Is there more to this than meets the eye?'

'Not that I know of,' said Tom.

She thought for a while. At last she said, 'This has rather blown other things out of my mind. But wasn't there something else you wanted to talk about today?'

Tom nodded. 'Yes,' he said. He frowned, and then suggested the garden, with still lemonade as a change from coffee. A few moments later they wandered outside, each carrying a cool tumbler, and settled quietly on a seat. He seemed to be hesitating still, and she gave him an encouraging smile.

At last he said, 'That woman terrorist. I think maybe she's come to mean something special, to you.'

Jane looked up.

'Something to show you.' He produced from his hip pocket the translation of Fatima's letter, tightly folded, and handed it to her.

Jane opened it out, started to read, and raised her eyebrows. 'Are you allowed to let me see this?'

'No.'

She took a deep breath, started again and read it through. 'Wow!' She turned to look at him.

'So *not* an incomprehensible fanatic,' said Tom.

'No.' Jane read the letter a second time. 'What's happened to her?' she asked at last.

'We don't know,' said Tom. 'These things are all connected: her father is the mathematician X we were hearing about.'

'Who, judging by this letter, isn't a terrorist at all?'

'Just so.'

'Nevertheless he's been detained by Mossad, and his life may be in danger?'

'That's right.

'His daughter wasn't innocent,' said Jane. 'She was involved in killing dozens of innocent people. In fact she became a killer… For understandable reasons… Just like me.'

Tom stared at the grass for a while. 'What I thought, too,' he said at last.

*

Aliza had been pressing for a review of Suspect C, and on 31st October Tom and Iain got down to it at last.

'Sure you're up to date?' asked Iain.

'I know she was Professor Hannif's daughter Fatima. And that she probably knew Kali—Hasan— because he'd been her father's student. Her letter says

247

she isn't as religious as Hasan…'

Iain nodded.

'… but I was wondering how religious her parents are?'

'According to Mossad,' said Tom, 'they're intellectuals, but they take Islam seriously. Professor Silverman was impressed by her father's peaceableness. That comes out from her letter, too.'

'And it shows she's close to him. But what I really don't understand is, what was her function, what was her job in the plot?'

'Nor do we.'

'At the start,' said Aliza, 'she seemed to have just this WAG role, first playing Ali's wife and then Omar's, but then they drop her off at the railway station, and we don't know what becomes of her, except for that mobile call.'

'And she's the only member of the cell who could have made it,' said Tom.

'It must have been connected with the take-off in some way.'

Tom nodded. 'But you need to remember they already knew quite a lot by that time. From cracking the Israeli codes they would have known that Bush was due to fly out from Filton sometime after noon, but in addition they seem to have got hold of his exact take-off time and fixed their movements accordingly— Omar's cell phone was still in Plymouth at 1.47, and he and Hasan can't have reached Bristol much before four. So they must have found the departure time from somewhere else, long before the phone call.'

Iain nodded.

'But how?' asked Aliza.

'Most likely from the flight plan. We know it was filed with Air Traffic Control for the south of England at Swanwick, and also sent to RAF control at West Drayton.'

'So perhaps she was somewhere where she could see the plan in advance?'

'Or some other helper was.'

'How far in advance would it have been filed?' asked Aliza.

Tom frowned and placed his finger tips together. 'We never looked into that,' he admitted. He thought for a moment. 'Keep talking, Iain, I'll use the phone in your office.' And off he went.

Aliza turned to Iain. 'So we need to look at all the staff at Swanwick and West Drayton?'

'That's been done,' said Iain. 'They've been thoroughly checked, and no one in either place recognised the photo of Suspect C.'

Aliza looked disappointed. 'Did the flight plan go anywhere else?'

'Filton must have known the details. Otherwise, nowhere that we know of. But there's another possible source. Someone at Swanwick puts the flight plan data into a computer, and then it's fed to various places electronically. So in principle the information could also have been picked up by anyone smart enough the break into the data feeds, which could be done at many different places.'

Aliza looked thoughtful.

After something of a pause Tom returned and settled back into his seat.

'Progress?' said Iain.

Tom was shaking his head ruefully. 'Well,' he said, 'flight plans are supposed to be filed at least a day in advance, normally more. But there's something else. He told me flights with Heads of State on board get surrounded by something called 'Purple Airspace', extra air separation. The RAF make the arrangements, and all pilots are informed by a NOTAM, a *Notice to Airmen*. He logged on to his PC to check. There *was* a Purple Airspace NOTAM for the flight of Air Force One out of Filton. It was issued three days ahead, and it gave the take-off time as 7.30 pm. It said it was for a US Air Force plane and gave the call sign as AF1.'

Aliza laughed. 'So any ordinary private pilot could have looked all that up in advance?'

'Anyone could! They put these NOTAMs out on the web.'

'So,' said Iain, eyebrows raised and leaning back in his chair, 'none of our high-powered security experts thought of concealing the routine protection for Heads of State!'

'Bureaucracy's a funny thing,' said Tom. 'But no, hold on! By the time that NOTAM was issued, the Americans had already decided Bush wouldn't be on board. They must've issued the NOTAM deliberately, as part of the deception.'

Iain nodded. 'So from the terrorists' point of view,' he said, 'if suspect C had read the NOTAM, they knew already that Bush was flying from Filton at 7.30 pm that day, or thought they did. So, it was easy for them.'

'But in that case, what was the point of the phone call?' asked Aliza. 'If they knew already from the NOTAM when the plane would be taking off... To *confirm* the actual take-off?'

'We don't think so,' said Tom. 'They could have done that more simply by having Suspect C watch the airfield through binoculars, or by listening in to the Filton controllers' radio link with the flight deck. But there is another possible reason. The president's plane normally uses the call sign AF1 only when he's actual-

ly on board. And the terrorists might well have wanted to be sure that he was.'

'So who would have been in a position to confirm
it?'

'Any of the controllers watching the relevant airspace,' said Tom. 'Once a plane is airborne, a little tag
with its sign pops up on their screens.'

'Or anyone else who could watch the screen?'

'Yes.'

'But they'd only be able to see it once the plane had
taken off?'

'That's right.'

'So maybe Suspect C was somewhere where she
could watch the display, and put in that call as soon as
she'd seen it?'

'Yes… And we know the call came from somewhere
near the RAF control room in West Drayton,' said
Tom.

'But the people there have all been checked?'

'Yes.'

'Perhaps she was able to break into the data link
somehow,' said Aliza. 'We know from her letter she's
been working for an electronics company.'

'That's perfectly true,' said Tom. He looked thoughtfully at her and then at Iain.

'The trouble is, we don't have a clue where the data
links run,' said Iain. 'It could have been done anywhere.'

*

That afternoon, David Manfield called Tom.

'Oh by the way,' he said. 'Your suspect B.'

'Hasan Saddiq?'

'That's the one. You knew they nabbed him in
Amman? On 2nd October?'

'Yes.'

'He's dead.'

'Dead?'

'John Smith told me this morning. The CIA left him in a basement at Jordan Security HQ to be softened up, and someone went too far.'

'Bloody hell.'

'It wasn't a very bright move, either: he still hadn't told them anything useful.'

Tom felt sick, and didn't ask for details.

'Halbrit was in Amman,' David went on, 'and he went berserk. He'd wanted Saddiq kept alive till they'd sweated the gravy out of him.'

Breakthrough

For the celebration at Tom's of her release Aliza arrived in a green headscarf and black trouser suit. She shook hands with Miranda and sat upright on a low stool while Tom passed around savouries and a few sweet things; she selected a crystallised fig. Miranda asked how she was feeling.

Aliza nodded with a little grimace. 'Now I'm home again, pretty good, thank you,' she said.

'Bursting with energy in fact,' said Tom with a grin.

Aliza raised her eyes to his, returned his grin, and turned back to Miranda. 'You mustn't think I'm a crazy workaholic,' she said. 'It's just—thank goodness for being able to get on with my job again.'

'I can imagine.'

'You're an art teacher, your dad said?'

'At the Community College.'

'Which is where *you* did your A-levels, isn't it?' said Tom.

'Yes.' Aliza smiled. 'I started there in 1989.'

Miranda nodded. 'It must have seemed very strange, coming straight from Turkey.'

Aliza glanced quickly at Tom. 'Germany actually,' she said. 'I grew up in Dusseldorf... I'd just started at the *gymnasium* there when we moved. I was thankful for the change, I'd been finding it tough.'

'In what way?'

'The lessons were tough... And the German kids

didn't like Turks.' Aliza seemed to be thinking. 'The weird thing is,' she went on after a moment, with a slightly skewed smile, 'this detention I've had has been a sort of school experience too.'

'Really? How d'you mean?'

'They held me in a girl's boarding school.'

'Oh—where?'

'The other side of Dawlish.'

'Holy Sepulchre School for Girls?'

'You know it?'

'Catholic, rather up-market.'

'Yes… They kept me in solitary there… It took some getting used to.' Aliza's face was a little twisted, and she paused. 'Sorry—I haven't quite come to terms with it all.'

'Oh!' said Miranda. 'I shouldn't…'

'No, no,' said Aliza quickly, 'Please don't apologise, you were being sympathetic. I must learn to deal with it.' She squeezed her eyes shut for a moment. 'But it was very humiliating.' A glance towards Tom, leaning back on his sofa. 'I felt *outraged*. My father's a moral man, he says people must obey the law.'

'Of course.'

Aliza blinked again. 'And the questioning—crude, demanding questioning. Day after day. It didn't get anywhere. How could it? I'd no information to give them.'

'You've lost weight,' said Tom quietly. 'It must have been quite a bit more stressful than you're letting on.'

She looked sharply at him. 'What I've described *is* stressful,' she said simply, and Miranda nodded. 'And Halbrit was there… You've heard of this Halbrit?' she asked Miranda.

'Dad told me.'

'He's scary.'

'I can imagine.'

At this point, however, the front door bell rang, and Tom went to answer it.

'Oh! ...' he said. It was Jane. 'We've got Aliza here.'

'*Aliza*? Oh damn, I forgot!'

'But come in anyway... You'll like her.'

'Won't I be intruding on her special occasion?'

'You can add to the feminine camaraderie. Three girls together.'

'Are you sure?'

'Of course. Come on.' They joined the others.

Tom introduced Jane to Aliza, and they shook hands. Jane found herself a chair and Miranda passed the nuts around again.

'Tom told me about your detention,' said Jane. 'It sounded awful.'

'She's just been describing it,' said Miranda.

'Hm,' said Jane. 'With my doctor's hat on, I'm wondering whether Tom's given you enough of a break.'

'No,' said Aliza with a smile. 'It's better to be working.'

'They were holding her in this girls' boarding school,' said Miranda. '... How long did this appalling questioning go on for?'

'Seven days.' Aliza pushed stray hair out of her eyes and tucked it under her headscarf. 'But it felt like much more.'

Jane was watching her closely. 'You were away a lot longer than seven days,' she said.

Aliza looked at her and nodded. 'When the questioning was over I was in an army camp, for another three weeks.'

'How did you find that?'

'OK during the day, but I did get depressed at night.'

'How much time off has Tom given you since you were released?'

'Three days,' he said. 'It was all she would take.'

'Perhaps you needed more.'

Aliza smiled and clasped her arms to herself. '*Please* don't be worried about me,' she said. 'I'm OK, really I am... Are these pictures on the walls yours, Miranda?'

'No, these are Mum's.'

'Your mother was an artist too? Can I have a closer look?'

'Of course,' said Tom, and walked her around the sitting room, while Miranda went off to divide her meal into four and to finish her cooking. Jane joined the art tour.

Soon the meal was ready, and they started to relax. Tom persuaded Aliza to reminisce about her Turkish grandparents, and about growing up in Dusseldorf. Towards the end of the meal Jane said to Aliza thoughtfully, 'Being in the police must make life difficult at home. I suppose you can never talk to your parents about what you do?'

Aliza smiled. 'There are times when Tom encourages me to,' she said.

'Really?'

'Yes, really,' said Tom. 'When Aliza was investigating the Islamic community, we agreed she should tell her parents.'

'And he was right: useful facts emerged,' said Aliza.

'But,' said Jane, 'there must be lots of things you can't talk about.'

'Well, yes, sometimes. But at other times we take the public into our confidence. For instance, Tom went on Crimewatch.'

Jane nodded. 'I watched it.'

'But,' said Miranda pointedly, 'you *didn't* take the

public into your confidence about the reason for that phone call.'

Tom sighed, then looked quickly at Jane.

'We can't *help* being interested, Dad,' appealed Miranda. 'Everybody in the country is.'

'Well,' he said resignedly after a moment, 'we decided for various reasons *not* to raise that particular point on Crimewatch. But I agree we could have done. And you're right, somebody who knew how the flight was controlled *might* have made a useful suggestion about the reason for the call.'

'How *was* it controlled?' asked Jane. 'I suppose that's public knowledge so you can tell us.'

Tom looked doubtfully at her. 'By the RAF,' he said at last. 'But it was also tracked by the Swanwick Air Traffic Control Centre, just like any other flight.'

'*Swanwick Air Traffic Control*?' said Miranda.

Tom raised his eyebrows. 'That's the name of the place, yes.'

'It's ringing a bell... Wasn't there something in the news about it?'

He looked puzzled.

'Recently?' asked Aliza. 'I don't remember anything.'

'A few months ago.'

Jane was frowning, but nobody responded and speculative silence descended again. Miranda served second helpings of apple charlotte and cream. Aliza at first refused, but changed her mind with a smile once everyone else had piled in. After a while, Jane said, 'Swanwick knew about the flight, and they would have received the same information about it as the RAF?'

Miranda looked up, and after a reluctant pause Tom nodded.

Jane looked enquiringly at him but didn't press and continued eating. But when she had almost finished her sweet she stopped and put her spoon down.

'What?' said Tom.

'You said it had been in the news, Miranda?'

'Yes.'

'It's come back to me... The place was newly commissioned, wasn't it? And there was a scandal. The computer system didn't work properly.'

'You're right,' said Miranda. 'That was it,'

'So they had to go back to using the old centre for a while.'

'The *old* one?' Tom said.

Jane nodded.

'Where was that?'

'I don't remember.'

'Maybe they kept the old one operational, as a back-up?' suggested Miranda.

Tom gave her a long and penetrating look. Then, without a word, he jumped up and ran upstairs. Aliza seemed ready to run after him.

Miranda laughed. 'Go on, if you want to,' she said, 'he'll be in his study-bedroom. Top of the stairs.' Aliza smiled gratefully and disappeared too.

Miranda gave Jane a quizzical look and moved to serve coffee in the sitting room. Five minutes later Aliza reappeared and joined them. 'He's dictating orders into the phone,' she said. 'Nothing for me to do.'

It was a full thirty minutes before Tom came slowly downstairs again. He stood behind Aliza's chair. 'You were quite right,' he said to Jane. 'They *did* go back to using the old place for a while, and they *did* keep it ready for use.'

Aliza twisted around to see his face. 'And *where is*

it?'

Tom paused for a moment and allowed himself a broad grin. At last he turned and mouthed conspiratorially to her: '*Exactly* where we need it to be!'

Her intense look increased in urgency.

He put one hand on her shoulder. 'Relax, Sergeant!' he said. 'Done and dusted. I've been talking to the Met… And Iain's on his way.'

Cotehele

On the Sunday there was for the moment nothing further that Tom could do about Suspect C so he remained at home. In the afternoon Jane rang and, though the forecast was very wet, proposed a walk, and suggested Cotehele.

So, wondering a little, Tom collected her from her flat and they parked by the quay, choosing the upstream path beside the Tamar. It had started to rain. The tide was falling and redshanks were probing the mud. After a quarter of a mile she announced, 'Something I need to say.'

'OK,' he said.

She took his arm. 'Time I faced up to it.'

'Faced what?'

'What I've been doing. Holding you at arm's length for two whole years.'

He looked sideways at her. 'That isn't the whole truth,' he said.

'And the reason for it has been... It was my wanting *sex*, when I was young, that started off that whole appalling business.'

He glanced quickly at her.

'It was *sex* that led—in the end—to my blowing Carl's head off. Sex got itself contaminated.'

Again he said nothing.

'The trouble is, Tom, there are too many destructive things inside me. I've nothing good or affectionate to give to you or to anyone.'

They plodded on, and the rain strengthened.

'Well,' said Tom after a while. 'I know what I think. I have as much right as you to judge whether you have anything worth giving. And I *know* you have.'

She looked down. 'But you want sex. I know you do.'

'Yes. But I want *you* more.' The hood of Tom's cagoule was starting to leak, but for the moment the slow trickle down his neck was oddly electrifying. He laughed. 'Perhaps the sex thing will sort itself out in the end.'

'That's far too dangerous. We could be terribly unhappy.'

'Maybe… I'm not unhappy now, though.'

They trudged on for a long time, silently. At one point she pulled his arm tighter, and Tom wondered whether she was ready to say more, but she didn't. The rain got stronger.

'Something *I* need to say, too,' he said at last, and looked at her.

'Is there?'

'You know we put our suspects out on Crimewatch?'

'Yes, I watched it.'

'One of them was recognised. The smallest man.'

She nodded.

'He turned out to have been a maths researcher at Imperial College. So last week I went up to London and talked to the research group he worked with. They all said he was a delightful and very thoughtful man.'

'Mm.'

'And sensitive… He'd done ballet dancing, of all things. One of the women students told me he moved beautifully… His name was Hasan Saddiq.'

'Did you discover why he became a terrorist?'

'No.'

She looked cautiously at Tom's face.

'They did tell me, however,' he added, 'that he came from a particular university in Jordan… And because I was able to trace him there he got detained by the security police in Amman.'

'Is that bad?'

'They're not exactly gentle. They told me at first that he'd given nothing away when questioned. But now, they must have tried something a lot worse, because I heard on Thursday that Hasan was dead.'

'*Dead?*'

'Yes.'

'Dead because of torture?'

'Yes.'

'What sort of torture?'

'I was too cowardly to find out,' said Tom angrily. 'But I know the sort of thing they do.'

'And you feel responsible?'

'Of *course* I feel responsible. I traced him. And now Dr Sampson is afraid the same may happen to Professor Haniff. You know you used to tell me I had a horrible job. In this case, I *thought* I was trying to protect Plymouth from something very bad. But I've finished up hounding one, and now maybe two, men to extremely nasty deaths, when in fact, as it happens, Plymouth was in no danger at all. I'm not used to sending people to have their genitals electrocuted or their eyes gouged out. That Colonel Halbrit makes me retch.'

'But they were terrorists. They killed all those people on the ferry.'

'I know. And it's my job to catch them. But I keep reading the newspapers, those West Bank reports,' he appealed to her. 'Professor Haniff wanted peace, but his students and their families were getting killed. He saw that little girl blown away...'

'It's *you* telling *me* this, Tom?'

'Yes, it is... What do we *expect* them to do? What would we have done if it had been happening to us? The UN passes resolutions and tries to hold the ring, but the Israelis just ignore them... And civilians get killed in wars—we bombed German cities... I'll buy locking these people up. I can't buy extra-judicial torture and death. But what can I do? I can't stop trying to catch them.'

'We have a right to catch them and stop them.'

'And the Israelis have a right, too. I know. But the fact is, *I've* become a bringer of death, too.'

'To this Hasan?'

'Yes.'

Jane looked steadily at him, her head slightly on one side, but said nothing. Tom said nothing either, and they trudged on silently for the best part of a mile.

'This bloody rain,' said Tom at last. 'Better turn back?'

Reunion

Aliza travelled to London on the Monday to join Iain, and that evening she called Tom from Harmondsworth Police Station.

'Jackpot!'

'You got her?'

'Not exactly... But on the night of the attack a young woman engineer was servicing the displays of the mothballed centre, working a late shift. I showed her manager our CCTV pictures, and he identified her straight away.'

'And she would have had access to the traffic information?'

'Definitely, it gets copied there electronically. She was the only person there that night, and it would have been easy for her to use her mobile.'

'Where is she now?'

'She rang in sick on 18th October, and hasn't been seen since.'

'Meaning we're too late?'

'Can't be sure yet,' said Aliza defensively.

'Mm,' said Tom. '18th of October?'

'Yes. They weren't all that surprised. She'd warned them earlier she was planning to get married.'

Smart, thought Tom. 'Had she been security checked?'

'Not personally. The firm was, originally, and security is supposed to be tight, but the centre isn't normally manned, and they didn't seem to be taking it very seriously.'

'Who was she working for?'

'A local outfit called Uxbridge Radar Systems. The mothballed place is on the same site as the RAF Control Centre, but the Uxbridge personnel never go there, so it's not surprising her photo wasn't recognised.'

'Can the firm help with tracing?'

'Not really. According to their records she was British—she called herself Sarah Nelson. She'd been with them just under a year. Her job references were all false, Iain's checked them.'

'Mm... The manager never had any suspicions?'

'No. He said how competent and friendly she was; sorry to lose her.'

'You checked out her home address?'

'Ordinary bed-sit. Paid up and left. No forwarding address.'

'Any other leads?'

'No.'

'Mm,' said Tom again. 'Anyway... Well done, both of you.'

*

It was decided, in the hope of gathering more information from the public, to explain the new development in a Crimewatch follow-up, and Jane watched it with Tom.

'Her letter said she was working in electronics,' she said.

He nodded. 'These people are clever,' he said. 'She didn't disappear immediately after the attack. They meant to keep her on there, till they realised we were

265

on her track. Think of the scope they had for air sabotage… I wonder when they first thought of it? Come to think of it, she was still in place when Iain was sniffing around RAF Centre. Close! Not quite close enough. We're not going to catch her now.'

He wasn't greatly disappointed.

'Her father won't be seeing her, either,' said Jane. 'I wonder where she is?'

*

'Good afternoon. My name is Sampson.'

The ventilation system three floors underground hissed gently and Mustafa Haniff stood in silhouette with soft lighting behind him. He didn't look happy; but neither did he look like a man who'd been tortured.

'Who?'

'Sampson!'

'I suppose I must show you in.' Mustafa pointed his visitor towards a sitting area in what appeared to be a self-contained flat, closed the door behind him, and dropped down listlessly onto a leather sofa. He drew up his heels, spread his knees, leant back, frowning. 'I don't know you,' he said at last.

Dr Sampson was still standing. 'I am a mathematician,' he said cautiously. 'I used to work for the British Government. But now I'm retired.'

Mustafa looked up at him. 'Another code breaker!' he said with irritation. 'I've had enough of code breakers. I'm a topologist! I have nothing to say about code breaking.'

'That's OK. I know what they've been asking you. And I know about your topology, too. Professor Silverman told me.'

'Silverman?'

'At Imperial College, where your student Hasan went. You remember?'

Mustafa looked up sharply, under hooded eyelids.

'And then I talked to Professor Stonham at UCLA.'

'Stonham too? … I enjoyed Los Angeles.'

'Yes, it's a good department… May I sit down?' Dr Sampson settled into an easy chair, his delicate hands clasped over his knees. 'The Israelis have tried to make you comfortable?'

'Physically, yes. They even brought some of my own books and ornaments. I can't think why they bothered.'

'Before we talk, there is something particular I should like to explain to you.'

'We are to talk, are we?'

Dr Sampson smiled gently. 'That's the general idea.'

Mustafa frowned.

'I wish to explain that I've been getting to know a certain British policeman. Who happens to be investigating the terror cell that your daughter Fatima joined.'

Mustafa winced.

'His name is Tom and, like you, he has a daughter. He also has an assistant who's a young Muslim woman. He is not a ruthless man and he works independently of Colonel Halbrit and Major Stein. I believe he comprehends Fatima's motives. He also knows you saw the child killed by the tank and I think he understands quite well why you sympathised with Hasan.'

'And what is *that* supposed to mean?' asked Mustafa, drawing his hand over his moustache. 'If I listened to Hasan, so what? Does this exceptionally pleasant policeman understand what it is like to have one's wife snatched away and not likely to return?'

'In a certain sense, he does. *His* wife died suddenly of a heart attack, when the two of them were out walking with their children.'

'That is not the same.'

'Perhaps not. But he feels he's to blame for not having saved her. Perhaps *you* feel responsible for the dispersal of your family?'

'How can I be responsible?' asked Mustafa. 'I did nothing… However, I should be interested to meet this kind-hearted English policeman and his daughter, and especially his Muslim assistant. Why should he have a Muslim woman assistant?'

'It just happened…' Dr Sampson looked carefully at Mustafa and smiled. 'Let's talk about something different. Can you cast your mind back to when you were a research student? In Cambridge. To the group topology colloquium? You gave a seminar there once. In the discussion after your talk, someone asked you a question. About a particular homomorphism. And you didn't know the answer… I think you might remember that.'

Mustafa looked sharply at him. 'Why, yes!' he said. 'It is not the sort of thing a young and anxious student would forget…' He peered more closely. He frowned, but then his eyebrows shot up. 'It was you? … Dr Michael? You're Dr Michael!'

Michael Sampson smiled. 'A very long time ago,' he said.

'It was. Another world, I think… And after my seminar, I talked to you more?'

'You did.'

'And you explained how my research was related to your own? You were a senior person in the department!'

'Not so very senior, then.'

'And later…' Mustafa looked down doubtfully and then up again. '… we talked politics?'

'We did indeed.'

Mustafa smiled sadly.

'I knew already, you see, all those years ago,' said Dr Sampson, 'that you were a good person… Do you have a little time to spare?'

Mustafa laughed with gentle irony.

Dr Sampson laughed too. 'I should like to show you something. I don't imagine you have a blackboard?'

Mustafa looked at him.

'But perhaps something I can write on?'

'I have a pad of paper.'

Dr Sampson quietly took a deep breath, and looked with some care around the apartment. There was a dining table, and they sat down at it together. He took the pad and, after a moment's consideration, began to write mathematics on it, in small, precise handwriting.

'This is topology,' he said, without looking up, 'your sort of topology.' Every one or two lines, he stopped and handed the pad over. Each time, Mustafa took it into his large hands to study. Usually he nodded, occasionally he asked a question.

At first, he seemed puzzled and impatient. They covered one page. It took about forty minutes. Mustafa became quieter, watchful, but he followed the argument as before.

'Now, this is related, but isn't topology.' Dr Sampson spent a few minutes explaining notation, and shifted position so that he could watch Mustafa's face. Mustafa had become very still. There was steady progress for a couple of lines. At that point, Dr Sampson saw Mustafa's eyebrows rise a fraction and his eyes widen. After three more lines, their eyes met briefly.

Dr Sampson had his answer.

He took another deep breath and continued. At the end of the third page Mustafa's questions restarted, sharply, with a hard edge, then subsided. At the end of the fifth, Dr Sampson stopped, with a slight smile. It had taken nearly three hours.

Without comment, Mustafa paced slowly out to his kitchen and made a small pot of bitter Turkish coffee. Carrying two small cups, he returned, and they drank together. He sat, plunged in thought, the coffee smell lingering. Eventually, with a sigh, he returned to the table, caught Dr Sampson's eyes and wrinkled his mouth expressively. Then he took the pad, drew an arrow from the end of the third page onto a fresh sheet of paper, and wrote for about a page and a half. He looked up.

'But that's much neater,' said Dr Sampson, annoyed in spite of himself. 'In fact, brilliant.'

'Where did you find that derivation?' asked Mustafa, anxiously. 'When did you first see it?'

'I discovered it myself.' Dr Sampson smiled quizzically. 'Eight years ago. It wasn't published, of course.'

'Oh dear,' remarked Mustafa, 'and I thought I was a new Mohammed ben Musa al Kworesmi!'

'But, if you found it independently, and better, then perhaps you are?'

'Perhaps I am.'

'Would you like to shake hands?' And they did.

They sat down again at the table. 'In a moment,' added Dr Sampson, after thinking for a while, 'there are a few further aspects of this derivation I'd like you to comment on. But before that we ought to discuss some more practical matters. Did Hasan tell you in any detail what he was going to do with your result?'

Mustafa again looked hunted, and said nothing.

'Ah,' said Dr Sampson, gently, and nodded. 'I think perhaps they haven't told you about Hasan?'

'No, what?' said Mustafa. 'They tell me nothing. Not about my wife, nor about Fatima, nor about Hasan.'

Dr Sampson paused. 'They have not located your wife, nor Fatima,' he said slowly. 'But they did find Hasan in Amman, and interrogated him there… You know the Jordanian Secret Police?'

Mustafa's head jerked up, his eyes searching.

'I am afraid that Hasan is dead.'

Mustafa flinched but his expression did not change.

'He gave nothing away, and his laptop had nothing of importance on it. He must have kept his working programmes somewhere else.'

Mustafa dropped his gaze. 'You would not deceive me?' looking up again fiercely. He screwed up his eyes briefly. A tear was running down one cheek.

'No, I would not.'

'Very well.' He seemed distraught but resigned. 'So, there is no protecting Hasan now… Well. He warned me not to leave evidence around. I gave him my notebooks, and together we securely wiped the disc on my laptop. We also cleared my files on the UCLA computer, though we were not able to be sure that all evidence had been removed from their back-up system or their hard drives.'

Dr Sampson nodded quickly. 'I understand,' he said. 'Now, if it's not too unreasonable, I'd like to press on a little further… As I mentioned, there's some more maths I'd like your comments on.'

Mustafa sighed, but leant forward.

Dr Sampson took up the pad again. But he held it on his knee so that any hidden camera would be unlikely to get a good view, and, with a slightly shaking hand, wrote:

> *Don't tell me aloud—write. Who knew about your discovery besides Hasan?*

He handed the pad to Mustafa, who bent over it, studying it for some time. Eventually he wrote in his turn:

> *Nobody, probably. But I cannot be certain.*

'No, it goes like this,' said Dr Sampson. But wrote:

> *That puts you in a particularly dangerous situation, personally. You'd be much safer if you'd published. Think carefully, and don't speak till you're ready. Then, if you agree, tell me aloud that you've already sent off a paper to JNT. Say you handed it to Prof. Stonham on a disc, at the Chicago conference.*

Mustafa spent some time collecting his thoughts. He was sweating. He wrote:

> *Are you sure he will collaborate?*

and returned the pad.

Dr Sampson nodded, and wrote:

> *Quite sure. And I have prepared a suitable draft paper.*

Mustafa put his head in his hands. Then he collected together the sheets of paper and read them slowly again. At last he looked up and said, a little unsteadily:

'That's most interesting. Thank you for showing me.'

Dr Sampson smiled and nodded. He took the used

sheets of paper and began to stow them in his brief-case.

'But there's something else I ought to explain to you,' said Mustafa.

'Yes?'

'After Hasan left, you see, I heard of the failed attacks on Sharon and Bush. I began to be afraid about what Hasan might have done with my result.'

'Afraid?'

'Yes. And I decided that he and I would be safer if my theorem were published.'

'Published?' said Dr Sampson sharply.

'Yes. So I wrote a paper.'

'You did? Where is this paper now?'

'I left it with Prof. Stonham at the Chicago meeting. As you know, he's on the editorial board of the Journal of Number Theory. It was on a CD. I asked him to forward it to the journal if he thought it was acceptable.'

'In which case it's probably been refereed by now.'

'And they'll be putting out a pre-print on the web.' Mustafa looked up anxiously. 'I realise it's bound to cause a great deal of trouble,' he added apologetically.

'It surely is,' said Dr Sampson, 'and no mistake.' His face was grim, but he was gently rubbing his hands under the table. 'Do you think Stonham will have had the sense to warn the security authorities and the banks?'

'I believe he will have done. He raised that issue when I told him what I'd proved, and I said I had no objection.'

Dr Sampson allowed himself a little smile. He closed his brief case and put his hand on Mustafa's for a moment. 'Thank you for telling me all this,' he said. 'We'll have to look into what the Israelis intend to do with you now.' He stood up. Something of his elfin style had reasserted itself. 'Now, what happens about food down here? Can we call for some supper?'

'I can cook you some myself. It would be a great pleasure.'

*

Dr Sampson left Maj. Stein a written report, hoping fervently that it agreed sufficiently closely with what the hidden microphones and cameras would have picked up. It confirmed that Mustafa had indeed worked out how to factorise the large product of two primes. It also explained that Mustafa had decided to publish, had submitted a paper to Stonham, and that it was almost certainly now too late to halt the publication. He proposed that he should contact Dr Stonham, who was an old friend, at once and see what could be done.

Fingers crossed, he hurried to the British Embassy, found a secure satellite link, and put through a phone call to California. Prof. Stonham was just starting his day. 'So,' he said when he had understood the situation, 'you're willing to publish in Mustafa's name epoch-making work in which you have priority!'

'Certainly.'

'Remarkably generous! Irregular, too, of course.'

But he was willing to play ball. He agreed to alert the banks and the security services to what was happening, but in such a way that they would be too late to block the appearance of the submitted paper on the web.

Thank God, thought Dr Sampson, that quick-witted and liberal-minded Americans continued to exist. He had first to alter the draft paper he had prepared to include Mustafa's more efficient proof.   He then arranged for the Cheltenham hacking experts to insert it into Stonham's in-box, with a header doctored to make it seem to have been sent by Stonham, from himself at the topology conference, to his own inbox at UCLA, on an appropriate date.   When he finally returned to Cheltenham, he had a long and only partly amicable conversation with his old boss.

*

Maj. Stein went to find Col Halbrit, who was wearing uniform as usual.

'Sampson's done the interview,' he said. 'And it *was* Haniff. But it seems he's published the maths!'

'*Published?*'

'In a well-known journal.'

'The hell he has!'

'You know what that means?'

'Sure I know... Shit for the banks. Big trouble for the French—the Securité aren't ready.'

'That's not what I meant. What this man has done is huge in the world of mathematics, is it not? He is going to be a hero. To the whole Arab world. And they will be asking where he is.'

'So?'

'He can't tell us any more now—he doesn't *know* any more. He's no further danger to us... Politically, Colonel, we should be wise to send him home. We shall learn more when his wife or daughter try to contact him.'

Halbrit was silent, but his mouth tightened. 'Maybe that lousy slob knows nothing,' he spat out at last. But the CIA is *gagging* for guts. These guys *come fucking near killing our President—you remember that?* Your

Prime Minister, too. They blast Air Force One out of the sky and burn the crew to death in the sea, and all you can think is, *fucking send him home?* To a shitty hero's welcome? Jesus, man!'

'This is your response to my suggestion?'

'Sure as hell is! What that softarse earned himself is a week, maybe two, three weeks, with that goddam Amman sweat crew. Let *them* screw him. And by Christ I'm gonna get it for the motherfucker!'

'Not so, my friend! I am going over your head.'

'Like hell you are! Whatever sort of a fucking bleeding-heart Jew d'you think you are?'

But Amos Stein had shut up shop.

Loose Ends

Major Stein did go over Colonel Halbrit's head, and was successful. On 15th November, Mustafa was released, and found his way back to his flat in Al Eizariya. The experts who had searched and bugged it were well trained, and the place seemed to him surprisingly little disturbed. Few of his university colleagues realised where he had been—his head of department had discovered somehow, but gave out that he was taking sabbatical leave. Some friends realised that Leila was no longer with him, but refrained from asking why.

Mustafa was not so foolish as to suppose himself unwatched. He established a monkish existence, careful not to display friendships. When not lecturing, he remained quietly at home. He visited no restaurants and avoided travel by car or taxi. No word arrived from Leila. At first, this did not worry him: it probably meant that she and Fatima were in safe hands. But he missed her—he wanted particularly the ability to put out his hand in the night and find the soft spot inside her elbow. And he disliked cooking for himself in the silent kitchen.

But then his paper appeared in the *Journal of Number Theory*—and his world erupted. Major Stein had been right that Mustafa would be fêted: it became an Indian summer for him. In al-Quds University, dinner parties multiplied. Within days, he had been rushed from

Jerusalem to Cairo and to Damascus to deliver hastily prepared seminars to packed audiences. Invitations arrived to visit Cambridge, Imperial College, UCLA, and even Moscow, but he declined everything outside the Arab world: he wanted to stay where news of his family could reach him.

And he suffered from a recurring dream. It appeared first while he was overnighting in Damascus: in a roaring street, Leila and Fatima stood erect, facing him, their arms hanging down, their palms turned towards him, their feet lifted slightly from the ground. Each face was like a soup plate, a blank O, silent and slightly transparent, fading. For some reason, it provoked him to think again of the English policeman of whom Dr Sampson had spoken. That man had lost his wife, too. He, also, had a daughter. Like ships passing in the night, he and that man were miles apart, moving in opposite directions. Sampson was right: each had influenced the other's course. Each could detect the other's lights, moving... but that was all.

Soon Al-Jazeera heard of Mustafa's mathematical prowess and dramatised it in a dedicated TV programme. Western film crews turned up unannounced at the university. His discovery's huge disruptive effect on the western security services and banks became heady news, too: in Cairo cafés and Islamabad street markets it became the stuff of wry comedy, and pundits pontificated on the imminent prospect of financial crisis. Mustafa sensed he was running into danger and refused all interview requests.

Then western newsmen unearthed Mustafa's links with the Plymouth cell members, and on 27th November Al-Jazeera learned of his detention in Tel Aviv. It was Mustafa's new theorem, they trumpeted, that Hasan had used to break the Israeli codes! All hell was let loose. Hasan was glorified as a martyr. American terrorism gurus thundered against the risks in leaving Mustafa at large. The Israeli press clamoured for his re-arrest. Enthusiastic crowds collected on campus. His status in the West Bank and Gaza became mythic.

Although he was still receiving no visible attention from Mossad, he decided he must get into hiding now, before it was too late. Yet how to achieve this he did not know, and was hesitant to ask for fear of observation.

But his head of department had wide contacts. Mustafa plunged, and decided to consult him during the next dinner party. As usual, he walked from his flat. It was now 18th December, and the Jerusalem nights were cold. He wore a heavy sweater and camel-hair overcoat, and watched the sparkle of the stars above the few remaining street lamps. After the meal, with its adulatory chatter, he drew his host aside, and explained what he wanted and his anxieties about asking. The professor smiled gently, promised nothing, but said he would see what he could do.

Mustafa walked home, quietly desperate, the crisp frost crunching beneath his feet.

For two days, nothing happened.

*

About the same time Jane again suggested a Sunday walk to Tom. She left the route to him, and he chose the Moor, driving up the A38 to South Brent, and then along country roads above the pretty Avon valley, its woods sombre under a heavy sky, to the Shipley Bridge car park. Here he was tempted by a small patch of blue sky in the west, and they left the car and set off up the track beside the river, below Black Tor.

There was no one else about. They were silent, and on the narrow path Tom walked ahead of her for the first half mile, and she watched him.

At last he stopped to let her catch up. 'Hamish is here,' he said. 'Miranda got him down for a serious talk. I think she's decided it's time they shacked up together.'

'What do you think?'

'Hamish is all right,' said Tom. 'It's not too early.'

'He's not as thoughtful as she is,' said Jane, a little mischievously.

He looked seriously at her. 'You have doubts, then?'

She gave him a quick grin. 'Of course not… I was just wondering how they'll make out. Do they take the big decisions together?'

'Pretty much. But she's the one who thinks most clearly. She's reckoning on finding a job in Scotland.'

'When?'

'For the next school year. Probably July.'

Jane considered the implications. A few snowflakes had appeared, drifting slowly downwards, but not enough to disturb them and they trudged on.

'Tom!' she said some time later. 'You remember when we walked at Cotehele?'

'Yes,' said Tom.

'You said that day you thought your terrorists weren't terribly different from airmen who bomb enemy civilians.'

'Yes, I did.'

'But the whole point about terrorism is that you go out of your way to kill innocent people.'

'And we British deliberately burnt to death ten thousand innocents in Hamburg, during the war.'

'But that wasn't right either.'

'No. It would be treated as a war crime now; my

parents used to talk about it. And Churchill made a point of bombing Berlin, just like al-Qaida attacking the Twin Towers.'

Jane frowned.

'It *is* the same,' he insisted. 'The fact is, once people are convinced of the rightness of their cause, they become ready to do *anything*. Hitler retaliated by blitzing British cities. By the end of the war, civilians had become just targets. We tried to hit theirs harder than they hit ours.'

'Weren't they just trying to get the war over with?'

'Of course. All I mean is, people do awful things in war. The longer it is, the more awful the things they do.'

'And the war in Palestine's been going on for sixty years?'

Tom nodded.

'But when I saw those people sliding down the deck of that ferry into the water, I was sick. It contaminated *me*. Shouldn't it have made me hate the four who did it?'

'Maybe. There's the crew of Air Force One, too. Burnt alive in the aviation fuel. I detest Halbrit, but he's right to be angry.'

A black crow wheeled slowly over the wood below them.

'Is what you're trying to say is that demonising people doesn't help?'

'Well, it's true,' said Tom. 'And I have to admit it: I *can't* just demonise those four when I remember what the Israelis have done to the Palestinians. But I'm not saying what they did was morally justified.'

'And what about the Israelis?'

'I can't demonise them either. They're haunted by the Holocaust. They're paranoid about being pushed

281

into the sea.'

'And what about us?'

'Us?'

'Demonising us.'

He looked at her.

'Because it isn't just me any more, is it? Like you said, each of us now carries responsibility for a pretty appalling death.'

'That's true,' said Tom. The crow disappeared amongst the dark trees. 'There have been some other odd things about this case,' he went on after a while. 'Usually, I'm in charge. Get to know the criminal element. They may be cunning, usually pretty stupid as well. And normally I feel that, on the whole, I've wound up my investigation nicely, controlled the outcome, and I'm content with the justice, the punishments...

'In this case, it's been different. Yes, at least we've managed to identify the miscreants, understand their roles in the plot. So far at least, three of them have got away scot-free and there's not a lot more I can do about catching them. But on the other hand an absolutely appalling death has been meted out to the one I personally identified. That death was vindictive and immoral—and I set it in train.'

'Mustafa has suffered too.'

'Of course. *He* never set out to be a terrorist, and the effect of the whole sad story has been to bust up his family.'

'His daughter on the run while yours is setting up with her man?'

'Exactly.'

'Hasn't injured his reputation, though.'

'No. I lie awake at night sometimes wondering what's going through his mind. I guess he deserves a lot for what he did as a mathematician. And not just that. He deserves something because he's a man of peace.'

They could see the dam of the Avon Reservoir ahead of them now, and the snow had stopped. They climbed slowly up the track to the side of the dam and followed the stream up to the right.

'You know,' said Tom, taking a deep breath, 'There's another reason why I feel tainted by guilt, more longstanding.'

'Your wife's death?'

'Yes.'

'Didn't it happen somewhere near here? Is that why you chose this path today?'

Tom looked stricken. 'It may have been,' he said. 'Yes, it was near here. I wanted to show you...'

They had passed beyond the reservoir now, and the clapper bridge came into sight as they rounded Huntingdon Warren. The small flat bridge seemed desolate and isolated, and yet there was a patch of sun on it, and the greys and browns were clean.

'This is where it happened?' said Jane.

'Yes.'

'Show me... You don't mind my asking?'

'No,' said Tom, and, in spite of himself, a few warm tears joined the rain on his cheeks. He walked on, came up to the bridge, and sat down on the bank beside it. 'This is where I tried to give her the mouth-to-mouth,' he said. 'I'd sent Jack and Miranda to get help. I just went on and on. In the end, I knew she was gone. I just laid her out on the hot grass, here, and covered her up and waited for the help to come.' He wept again.

'But it wasn't your fault you hadn't learnt cardiac massage. Just as it wasn't my fault Carl came to kill me.'

After a while they set off home again. It remained very still and a good deal of time passed.

'Tom,' said Jane eventually, 'can we stop for a bit?' They found a rock beside the track.

'We've just been saying that something has changed,' she said slowly. 'I'm not the only one who's tainted.'

He looked at her. 'I always was tainted,' he said. 'Nothing new there.'

'But something *has* changed. I can feel it, I can share it... Listen. I'm ready to give it another try, if you are.'

'Jane! Are you sure?'

'Yes. But it's terribly important that you don't expect too much. Expect anything, really.'

'I'd made up my mind about that already.'

'Had you?' They sat quietly. After a few minutes, Jane very tentatively slid a warm hand around his waist under the anorak and rucksack. She found that she did not cringe, or want to withdraw it. Tom tilted his cheek very gently onto her head. She still had her hood up.

Then he sat upright again. 'I'd better ask what you really meant,' he said. 'I *think* you meant just seeing each other and... trying again from time to time? Nothing drastic about living arrangements?'

Jane put on a wicked grin that Tom was not used to. 'No, nothing drastic,' she said and laughed.

As they came down through the wood, she added: 'Definitely not shacking up. There is *one* change of arrangements I was thinking of, though. I've lost confidence in sailing *Ariel*, and I want to give time to us, you see. I think I should sell her.'

Tom stopped. He was horrified. 'What's the real reason for saying that? Because it was on *Ariel* you shot Carl?'

'No, it isn't. Giving up *Ariel* because of him would be a defeat, and I don't want that. I want to concentrate on you.'

'But that's all wrong,' said Tom. '*Ariel* is an old friend. You can't abandon friends just because you've got a new romantic attachment!'

Jane thought for a while, and smiled. 'Well,' she said seriously, 'for the moment let's agree to differ. Give it time… We've plenty of time ahead of us.'

*

Two days after the dinner party, at dusk, Mustafa was easing himself between the beat-up cars in the faculty car park when two dark figures jumped on him from behind a small van, bundled him into the back, and drove quickly away.

The driver looked back over his shoulder. 'We will help you to disappear,' he said.

The man in the passenger seat was a Hamas activist that Mustafa knew but disliked. 'We could not come near your flat, it is very closely watched,' he said. A well-oiled Kalashnikov lay across his knees. 'We shall also show you where to find your wife.'

Mustafa felt a welling of repressed emotion at this, but the yearning struggled against a deep anxiety. 'Perhaps it is better for me not to know,' he said.

The man laughed. 'You are a great man! We can keep you safe from the Israelis. What man does not wish to be with a good wife?'

'What man indeed?' thought Mustafa to himself. The van was driving north, and the cold dark had descended on them sharply, like a prickly blanket.

*

Exactly one hour later they entered the outskirts of Nablus.

As they did so, suddenly the ground around them was illuminated intensely from above. The Hamas man snatched up his gun. The driver frantically speeded up and made a violent left turn, but simultaneously there was an ear-shattering detonation. A sheet of flame erupted from the van, it leapt into the air, blew apart, and fell back—a helicopter overhead had been tracking it for some time, and had fired a missile.

The explosion killed the Hamas man and his driver outright.

Whether the assassination team had been aware that Mustafa would be with them in the van, who can be sure? He had been thrown out of its back doors. Part of his scalp had been scraped off, both his legs were broken and blood was spurting violently from his left femoral artery. Adrenaline racing, he clamped both hands onto his thigh in a desperate attempt to stop the flow, an image dancing before him, not, to his hazy dismay, of his wife or of Fatima, but of Hasan pounding his laptop in a frenzy.

The flames from the van rose higher. Waiting Israeli soldiers with automatic weapons appeared from side streets. Palestinian civilians poured out of nearby buildings, but were held back, shouting. No-one approached Mustafa, who had struggled to rise and fallen back; perhaps the Israelis were afraid he was armed. Blood was now pouring from his head, too. The rush of adrenaline passed. Hot gases had seared his lungs; he began to shake, excruciating pain welled up. Perceptions swaying, he could feel the flames of the van scorching his cheeks and a rising cold deep inside his body. His image of the scene darkened rapidly.

He could still see dimly the flashing light of a Palestinian ambulance, and hear its siren. The soldiers would not let it approach the wreckage. There was a fierce argument with the local people.

During this argument, Mustafa's wracked shivers came to a stuttering end. His final thoughts did not cohere but flitted from scene to scene, fading meaninglessly, and he died where he lay, in a warm spreading pool of his own blood.

As time passed, the blood at the edge of the pool cooled, and finally froze, leaving a halo of crusty congealment encircling his body on the sandy ground.

Printed in Great Britain
by Amazon